8/9/93

LAWMAN AGAINST LAWMAN!

Longarm was moving even before Sam could realize he was shot. The sheriff's mouth had fallen open at the sound of the gunfire, but now recognition was setting in. He was three paces from Longarm and starting for his revolver. He had it half drawn when Longarm hit him with a looping, driving right hand. It was as if the sheriff had been hit in the face with a sledgehammer. He went straight backwards, falling so hard as Longarm followed through with the punch that he almost seemed to bounce as he hit the ground. . . .

D0724254

*   *   *

SPECIAL PREVIEW

Turn to the back of this book for a special excerpt from the next exciting Western by Giles Tippette . . . .

CHEROKEE

. . . A stunning novel of family pride and frontier justice, by America's new star of the classic Western.

Available now from Jove Books!

TABOR EVANS

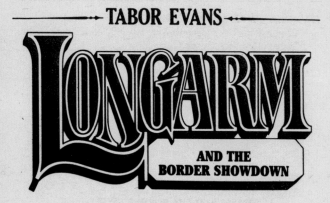

LONGARM

AND THE
BORDER SHOWDOWN

JOVE BOOKS, NEW YORK

LONGARM AND THE BORDER SHOWDOWN

A Jove Book / published by arrangement with
the author

PRINTING HISTORY
Jove edition / June 1993

ISBN: 0-515-11119-8

Jove Books are published by The Berkley Publishing Group,
200 Madison Avenue, New York, New York 10016.
The name "JOVE" and the "J" logo
are trademarks belonging to Jove Publications, Inc.

PRINTED IN THE UNITED STATES OF AMERICA

10 9 8 7 6 5 4 3 2 1

AND THE
BORDER SHOWDOWN

Chapter 1

She was sitting on the edge of the bed, innocently naked, the small of her back just touching his side. He had a good view of her in profile. She wasn't especially pretty, but she wasn't homely either. She had light brown hair that was brushed clean and shining, and her body was slim and shapely and warm to the touch. He idly put out a finger and ran it slowly down the mound of her firm young breast. He knew she was twenty years old because she'd told him so without guile or reason to lie. Under his finger her skin was smooth, not smooth-silky like the skin of rich women who could afford oils and creams to rub themselves with, but smooth like the skin of a country girl who kept herself clean and did what she could to be proud of her body. He traced the tip of his finger over the top of her breast and reached the rosette, and her nipple came instantly erect as his finger went over its grainy top.

He thought that if this wasn't the strangest encounter he'd ever had with a woman, it was damn close to it. He was lying full length just behind her, still naked, but now content and satisfied from her body. He lay there now reflecting on just how he'd come to meet her. He'd arrived in San Antonio the night before by train from Denver, figuring on giving himself a few days in the old Mexican capital to get the feel of Texas again, and maybe polish up what little Spanish he had before heading on down to the border at Laredo. That afternoon he'd been wandering around town, just having a look-see, when he'd spotted her sitting on a bench in the middle of the Military Plaza, the huge, brick-paved parade grounds where Mexican cavalry had once gone through maneuvers. Of course, once Texas had

1

won its independence, the plaza had been turned into a sort of park with water fountains, trees, and benches. He'd studied the girl from a distance for a good long while before approaching her. With a long-practiced eye for gauging people, he'd known at first glance that something was troubling her. He could see it in the bunched way she was sitting, her hands clenched in her lap, her body kind of huddled together. She'd been wearing a blue frock, open at the neck, and high-button shoes, but he'd been able to tell she was a country girl by the country-girl hat she was wearing in imitation of city women. He'd known that her hands would be a little roughened by work, and that her speech would reflect her education, or the lack of it.

But knowing all that still hadn't told him what was bothering the girl. She didn't turn her head back and forth like she was looking for someone who was running late, and she sure as hell wasn't relaxing in the late spring sunshine. Something was bothering the young woman.

He started sauntering toward the girl, taking his time, not at all sure if it was any of his business to be going up to her and inquiring after her troubles. But after all his years as a United States deputy marshal, he'd been pulled into other folks' troubles so often that it didn't seem as if one more time would matter. So he went straight up to her on the bench and stood right in front of her. He said, "Anything the matter, miss?"

She'd been aware of him and she'd seen him coming. At first, judging from his boots and jeans and pearl-gray wide-brimmed Western hat, she'd figured he was just another cowboy. But as he'd gotten closer she'd seen his kindly, handsome face with the drooping mustache hanging down toward the corners of his mouth. Most importantly, she'd seen the certainty with which he carried himself, the quiet authority, and she'd known he wasn't just some cowboy. He'd asked her the question about anything being wrong, and now she looked up into his face and suddenly burst into tears. He said, "Here now! Hold on here!"

He sat down on the bench by her, put his arm around her, and patted her on the back. "Here now, little lady, we can't have this cryin'. Ain't nothing can be bad enough for you to go and mess up a face as pretty as the one you are hiding behind them hands."

Little by little he got her calmed down, and the small sobs stopped. Finally she wiped her eyes with a handkerchief she had clutched in her hands and said, "I just don't know if I kin do it. I come here to do it, but I ain't sure I kin."

What he finally got out of her was that she'd come to San Antonio from a little town outside of Fort Worth to go to work in "one of them kind of places." She blushed when she said it. She said she hadn't wanted to try that "line of work" nowhere near her home, and she'd heard that San Antonio was the wickedest city there was, so she'd figured it would be the place.

She said, nodding her head across the busy street at a place called the Red Rooster, which he'd pretty well figured was a saloon on the bottom and a whorehouse up above, "I been settin' here since ten o'clock this morning trying to get my grit up to go in there and take the job. I seen the woman what runs the place—they call 'em madams, you know—and she said I ought to do just fine." She turned to him and said, "Do you know she just up and asked me, like it was any of her business, if I was a virgin. Now how you reckon that?"

He wanted to laugh, but he kept a straight face and told the girl the woman had certainly had her nerve. And yes, she had every right to be scared and nervous and to sit there on the bench to think it through. But, he said, what he couldn't figure out was why a nice girl like she obviously was would want to consider doing such a a thing in the first place.

Of course he'd known the answer. Things were bad back home, the crops were poor, the young men were moving away, and there was never enough left over after food and a roof for even the smallest thing that could thrill a girl's heart. So she'd made up her mind to get herself a few of the things she'd seen the fine ladies wearing in magazines and newspapers—and even once when the whole family had gone into Dallas and she'd seen the women right there on the street. And she said that everybody said she was the prettiest girl back home, so she'd just made up her mind to sell her body, and did he think a girl could sell her body without selling her soul in the bargain?

He started in to talk her out of the fool idea, but she immediately set her jaw and started shaking her head from side to side. She said she'd spent every penny she had to get to San Antonio, and she didn't have no way to get home, and so she was just going to have to get up her nerve or think of something else.

That didn't surprise him much. In fact he'd kind of been expecting it from the first. But what the hell, it was a nice afternoon and she was a pretty girl and he had a particularly ugly piece of work ahead of him, so he reckoned it wouldn't

3

hurt him overmuch to get suckered this one time. He reached into his pocket and pulled out a five-dollar bill and offered it to her.

Then she really surprised him. She shook her head even more violently than before, and said she wasn't looking for charity and didn't want no money. He tried to argue with her, pointing out that five dollars was more than enough to get her home, and with even a couple of dollars left over for some trinkets. But she had her mind fixed. She wasn't taking any money from him. He was a kind gentleman, but she'd got herself into this mess and she'd get herself out.

He gave up then. It was after noon, or he'd offer to buy her a meal. He contented himself with telling her which hotel he was staying at, and that he'd be there a couple of more nights if he could help her. Then he got up and started to walk away. From behind him he heard her say, kind of timidly, "Mister?"

He stopped and looked around.

She said, blushing, "I wonder could I ask you a real big favor." She blushed even deeper. "I don't even rightly know how to put this, but . . ."

"What?" he asked.

"Well . . . see, I ain't really never been with very many men. If you know what I mean. I mean there was just that one time when I was just fifteen, and he wasn't but a year older'n me, and I don't even know if we knew what we was doing." She stopped, looking very nervous. "I ain't making myself real plain, am I?"

"You are if you're talking about what I think you're talking about."

"I been sittin' here all day thinkin' all kinds of things. I ain't real sure I'd know what a girl is supposed to do in one of them places. I mean . . ." She looked at him in mute appeal.

He stared at her, surprised again. "And you want to practice on me? Is that it? Try your hand on me, so to speak?"

"If it wouldn't be askin' too much. I mean, I know we just met." She looked down, embarrassed. "I reckon you think I'm crazy or something, but it was just that one time when I was fifteen. I don't even know if we done it right. I've thought of askin' some of my older girlfriends, married ones, you know, but I just never could seem to get up the nerve. I mean, you're a mighty nice-looking man, gentle and kind-looking."

4

That made him want to half smile. He knew a good many men on the wrong side of the law who would have gotten a hell of a laugh out of that description. He said, trying to make a little joke out of it, trying to put her at ease, "What makes you think I know? How to do it, I mean? All the particulars?"

That made her blush again. "Pshaw! Man like you? I bet you been near everywhere. I bet you know all there is to know about girls and . . ." She stopped and blushed again.

He wasn't quite sure what he was feeling. He reckoned himself near old enough to be the girl's uncle. Not that that mattered, but what he couldn't figure out was who was being taken advantage of. It would be outside of his code to take a naive young country girl to bed just to satisfy her curiosity, but he was also aware of an uncomfortable swelling in the crotch of his jeans as he contemplated the proposition. And was he taking advantage of her or was she taking advantage of him? For all she knew, he was a happily married man and she'd be asking him to cheat on his wife.

But he kept staring at the swelling bodice of her frock as all those thoughts ran through his mind, envisioning what was beneath the cheap blue gingham material of her dress, seeing those white breasts that would be there with their rosy tips. And what that kind of thinking did was make his jeans all that much tighter.

In the end he took her by the hand and walked her over to his hotel and up to his room on the second floor. He didn't try to figure it out or wonder about it, any more than he'd have tried to figure out why he'd been chosen to draw four aces. You either got the good hand or you didn't; wasn't any point in dwelling on it.

He had been exceptionally tender and careful with her, leading her step by step through the kissing and the caressing and all the other ways there were to get the excitement and the good feeling started, and then to get it to building and building until you never wanted it to stop. Only once, after she'd been shy about him helping her off with her clothes, had she faltered, and that had been when he'd been slowly kissing his way down her belly. She'd put a hand down to stop him, but then he'd assured her it was a good thing to do, and then she'd relaxed and let the feeling come over her. By the time he'd entered her, her breath had been coming in short, hard gasps. Using every bit of skill he'd picked up with many women in many beds, he'd

5

brought her to climax. It had frightened her, the intensity of it, but then, when it was over, she'd sighed and just relaxed into the mattress.

For a long time she didn't say anything, just lay there with a fine mist of spray on her upper lip and between her breasts. Then she said, "That wasn't nothing like the time when I was fifteen. I don't know what we did back then, but it wasn't nothing like what we just done."

Then she sat up, and he lay there, watching her. She said, "You said your name was Longarm. Is that what you said?"

He laughed softly. "Yeah, out of habit."

"That ain't a real regular name. Least I never heard it before."

"It's sort of a nickname I got. My real name is Long, Custis Long. But I used to be a deputy federal marshal," he lied, "so folks got to calling me Longarm. Get it? The long arm of the law? Just because my last name was Long."

She suddenly turned around and gave him a look, her eyes getting big. She said, "You mean I been in bed with the *law*? Heaven have mercy on my soul! You gonna arrest me?"

She made him smile. "I told you I wasn't a lawman no more. And even if I was I wouldn't arrest you. You haven't broken any laws."

His clothes were piled on a cane-bottom chair that he'd pulled up close to the bed. On top of his clothes, with the butt handy, was his .44-40 Colt double-action revolver. The sidegun had a six-inch barrel with the front sight filed off, just as it was filed off by all men who had any use for such a gun. It wasn't accurate much over ten or twelve paces, and all the front sight was good for was to snag on the holster when you were in a hurry to get the gun out and put it to work. He seldom used the double-action because the pulling of the trigger to bring the hammer back caused barrel deviation and poor accuracy even at short range. His normal habit was to have the hammer thumbed back by the time he'd drawn, and if that first shot didn't get the job done, he could thumb off another shot almost as quick as he could use the trigger. It had been in his mind for a good many years to disconnect the double-action mechanism, but he'd just never gotten around to it.

Over in the corner was his saddle and his Model 73 Winchester lever-action repeating rifle. He had two saddles, an army McClellan saddle that he used in rough country to save his horse, and a Western riding saddle with a deep-dish seat and a big saddlehorn in case he had to put the saddle on a horse that wanted to get cute and cut up and act the fool. He'd brought the Western saddle because he didn't want anything to identify him as ever having had anything to do with the law and there was a big U.S. stamped on one of the McClellan saddle's small skirts.

She turned her head around and looked curiously at his long, lean, hard body lying on top of the bedspread. She said, "You're kind of big, ain't you?"

"No, not really. Little better than average size, I'd reckon. Inch over six feet, about one hundred ninety pounds before breakfast."

She looked at his face, studying it. It was not an easy face to read. He was a little handsomer than she'd first thought, but she had no idea how old he was. It was a face aged by work and weather, and yet charged with youth by vigor and health. She thought he must be somewhere in his mid-thirties, but she didn't want to ask. Instead she reached out a finger and gently touched the scars on his left shoulder and his side and the big one almost in the middle of his right thigh. She couldn't see the one in his back that had almost ended his life. She said, "Where'd you get those? Are those from bullets?"

He smiled and cupped her breast with his hand. It was warm and seemed to almost pulsate. "Fell on a picket fence when I was a kid."

She gave him a little slap on the belly and said, "Big liar."

She turned and looked at the chair where his clothes and gunbelt were. She reached out a hand, and for a second he thought she was going to touch his gun. Instead she put her hand on his shirt. She said, "That's such a nice shirt, all soft and easy-feeling. Is it silk?"

"No!" he said, laughing. "It's linen. Men don't walk around in silk shirts, not unless they want to get shot."

"Oh." She gave the shirt a little pull, and his six-pointed-star badge fell out of the pocket he'd hidden it in. It fell to the floor. He rolled quickly to the edge of the bed and scooped it up off of the floor. He hadn't wanted the girl to see it. As deftly as he could he slipped it beneath his pillow.

Her eyes got big again. "That's a badge! You are too law!"

"Was," he said. "Not anymore."

"Then what you got with that badge?"

"A keepsake," he said. "Something to remember."

7

But the sight of the badge had had a strange effect on the girl. She seemed to huddle herself together. "My lord, here I sit nekid in front of the law!"

She suddenly jumped up and ran across the room to where her clothes were folded on a chest. She bent over, her rounded buttocks facing him. It was as if she had come all-over embarrassed at once. He sat up. She was gathering her clothes into her arms. She said, "Don't look at me. Please. If you be the gentleman I think you are. Don't look at me."

He sat up. He said firmly, "Bonnie. Bonnie!"

She didn't turn, just kept picking up clothes and hugging them to her.

He said louder, "Bonnie! BONNIE!"

She turned then. She had all her clothes clutched to her front and her face and neck were scarlet. She stared at him, suddenly frightened and wide-eyed. She said, "What have I done?"

"Put those clothes down and come back over here."

She said, a kind of agony in her voice, "I cain't."

"Bonnie, I just screwed you. I've seen every part of your body. There's no part of you I don't know. So quit acting silly and come back over here. I want to talk to you."

She just stared at him, biting her lip.

He said, "Didn't you hear me? Didn't you know that we screwed? We screwed each other."

She started to sob. "Oh, please . . . Please don't use that word. Please don't say that. Don't say that word."

"Why not? It's a perfectly good word. We kissed. Do you not want me to say we kissed? Or hugged? Or talked? Didn't we do all those things?"

She was slow in answering. She finally said, "Yeeeesss . . ."

"But you just don't want me to say that one word even though that was as much a part of what we did as anything. Now drop those clothes and come here. I've got some educational thoughts I want to give you."

With a sigh she dropped her arms, and her clothes tumbled to the floor. For a second she didn't move, and he could admire the curve of her slim figure and the dainty V the soft hair made where her legs met. She came back slowly, seeming reluctant. When she was close enough he put out his hand and took hers and pulled her down on the bed beside him. He said, "What happened? I thought you liked it."

8

She pulled one leg up on the bed and tucked it under her. It forced her legs to open so he could see up the inside of her thighs to the soft lips peeking through the light brownish hair. She had gone back to being unself-conscious, seeming not to notice that she had exposed herself with the movement of her leg.

She said, "I did. I liked it a lot. In fact I thought I was gonna die there at the last." She paused and examined her navel with an idle finger. "As a matter of fact I was kind of thinkin' it wouldn't be such a bad way to make a living after all. Girls have that much fun and git paid for it."

"Then you got spooked by the badge. Even though I told you I wasn't law anymore."

"Yes," she said uncertainly.

"Do you know why the badge spooked you?"

She thought for a second and then shook her head. "Well, no, I reckon not. Especially if you ain't workin' for the law no more."

"The badge made you realize that what you've been thinking of doing, going to work at the Red Rooster, is wrong. Otherwise it wouldn't have bothered you."

She looked at him, blinking her eyes. "You reckon?"

"I know so," he said. "And you didn't like it when I said the word screw, did you?"

She blushed again and shook her head quickly.

"Why not? You mean you'll do it but you don't want to say it or hear it said?"

She looked away. She said vaguely, "I don't know . . . It just seemed somehow like, like, well . . . I mean, it just sounded kind of blunt if you know what I mean."

He leaned close and kissed her gently on the lips. "Let me try and explain it to you, the difference. I said what I said for a purpose. I wanted to shock you. See, what we did wasn't just wham-bam-thank-you-ma'am screwing. We were doing what you call making love. And there's a world of difference. Making love is something two people do that care about each other, that respect each other, that have some feelings for each other."

She said shyly, "You saying you have feelings for me?"

"Now, Bonnie, let's don't get into that. There's all kinds of feelings men and women can have for each other. Some are for a long time, but others have to be for just the short haul on account of circumstances. Like my circumstances. I ain't ever in one place long enough to form no long-time feelings.

9

But of course I've got feelings for you. You'll always have a tender place in my heart. But that ain't what I wanted to talk to you about. You do, though, understand that what we did was making love? Because we liked each other and we *chose* to do it. Didn't nobody make us and didn't either one of us make the other. Do you see that?"

"I reckon. Though I did ask you to do it to me. I didn't make you but I did ask you. That might be the same thing for a gentleman like you."

He shook his head. "No, Bonnie. Nobody makes me do *anything* I don't want to do. What I'm trying to tell you is the difference between what we just did and what it would be like if you were to go to work as a whore at the Red Rooster. You wouldn't be making love then—you'd be getting screwed."

She only flinched slightly at the word. "What would make it different?"

"You wouldn't have *any* choice. None. Anybody that came in that place, if he had the money, could hand that madam two or three dollars and pick you out, and you'd be obliged to go up to a room with him and do whatever he wanted. He could be ugly as homemade sin, he could smell like a pigsty, he could be dribbling tobacco juice down his beard and wanting you to kiss him, wouldn't make any difference. You'd still have to go in that room with him and take off your clothes and do what he told you to do. And if he paid enough money you might have to do some things you couldn't even imagine right now."

He had her attention. She was staring at him. She said, "It'd be that bad? If I didn't like the feller I couldn't just say no?"

He shook his head. "Bonnie, a whorehouse ain't a social at the church where you can pick your beau. The man buys you and you ain't got no say in the matter."

She said, her voice trembling a little, "Maybe they'd see how innocent I was and kind of take it easy on me till I got the swing of the business."

He laughed out loud. "Your innocence is what is going to bring the highest price. Long as you look like you do right now, that madam is gonna work you night and day. But pretty soon you won't look so young and innocent. Pretty soon you'll get to look hard and used up, like the other whores. You'll get old before your time."

"Oh, my," she said. She looked toward the windows that fronted the street. She said, "Maybe this ain't such a good idea."

10

"It ain't a good idea at all. Now you get up and get dressed, and you and I will walk down to the depot and see which is the first train you can get that will take you home. If there's time I'll buy you some supper."

They walked out into the twilight of a fine spring evening. At the train depot Longarm found out there was a train to Fort Worth that left San Antonio at midnight and that stopped at Bonnie's little village. He bought her a ticket. When he tried to hand it to her she put her hands behind her back and said, "No. I cain't let you go around buyin' me train tickets."

He just simply took her little purse away from her, put the ticket inside, and then snapped the purse shut. He turned his back as he did so, so she didn't see the ten-dollar bill he added.

After that he walked her back uptown and bought her dinner at the best restaurant he could find. When they were through eating, there were still three hours left until her train time. He didn't say anything, just looked at her across the table. She dropped her eyes and said, "Can we wait in your room?"

When they had undressed, and were close together in the dim light coming through the windows from the half-moon hanging low in the night sky, she said, "I want to do it better this time. Will you help me to do it better? Please? I might never meet another man like you and I want to know just how to do it. So you help me."

He said, "Oh, honey, I'm going to help you. You can bet on that. And I'm going to help myself. I'm going back for second helpings and third helpings and maybe even fourths."

And then it was over and she was dressed and he was walking her through the still-lively streets to the depot. Halfway there she began to put up a squawk about leaving. She said, "Well, if you're gonna be here another day or so, I don't see why I have to leave. Why can't I stay here with you until you go? Be plenty of time at home ahead of me. Why can't I just have this little bit of time?"

He was tempted and he wavered, but in the end, his sense of honor won out. He said, "Bonnie, honey, I've got business that's got to be taken care of. And if you were to stay here, I'm not sure I could keep my mind on the job. Girl, you can be mighty distracting. And it can't go no further between us. I'm not the kind of man that will ever settle down. So you'd just be wasting your time on me."

11

"But if it's my time and I want to waste it, then that's my business."

He shook his head. "It don't work that way. Look here, there might be that ideal young man back home waiting for you right now. And if you're late getting there, why, you might miss him. I'm just a train whistle you heard in the night. You go on and forget me." He suddenly smiled. "And when you meet that right young man, it might be a good idea if you didn't let on you already knew what little I taught you. Let him think he's doing the teaching."

She hugged him and kissed him at the depot, and then he put her on the train and waited until it pulled out. Her last words to him had been, "I ain't ever gonna meet another man like you, Longarm. You've spoilt me."

He'd said, "That's kind to hear, but I'd bet money you'll feel different sooner than you think."

Then the train pulled away, and he waved her good-bye and turned around and walked back to the hotel. He'd planned on playing a little poker to while away the time, but it had gotten late and he was a little tireder than he'd expected. He figured he could establish himself around San Antonio on the morrow and the next day. From all he'd seen, they seemed to play poker night and day around the place.

Chapter 2

He awoke early even though he'd been late to bed and had no particularly pressing need to be up before the sun. It was just his custom. He could go for days with little or no sleep and then, once the job was done, catch it all back up in one long rest. He also had the capacity to be an extremely light sleeper when the occasion called for it, yet he could fall down like a log and not be disturbed by cannon fire if he wasn't needed.

The first thing he did was swing around on the bed, yawn, and then fumble around in the darkness until he found one of the little cheroots he smoked. Even on his deputy marshal's pay he could have afforded better cigars; he just happened to prefer the harsh taste of what he suspected was Mexican tobacco.

He kept fumbling around on the bedside table until he'd located a match. He struck it, took time to get his cigar going, and then lit the lamp that was on the table. The wick was trimmed too low, but the lamp still threw out enough light for him to see around the room. He yawned again and sat naked, smoking. Outside, the sun was making a false dawn, but his room was still full of shadows. One of the shadows was the absence of the girl, Bonnie. Aloud he said, "Custis, you are a stupid sonofabitch. You could have kept her one more night. One more night would not have done her honor no more damage than had already been done."

Though, in his heart, he didn't feel that he'd taken advantage of the girl. He felt pretty certain, if he hadn't intervened, that she would have eventually gotten up her nerve and walked into the Red Rooster. What would have happened after that was anybody's guess, but he would have bet money she would have ended up a mighty sad little girl with some wounds that would have taken a long time to heal.

He said aloud, "Naw, it was an even horse trade. The best kind."

And that was the way he thought of her, as a gentle, young, untrained little filly. Thinking about the pleasures he would have had by continuing his training of her got his mind excited, and that was the last thing he needed with work at hand. Still, he had liked what she'd said about never meeting another man like him. He knew he was being a vain, overaged Romeo, but at his age, it did a man good to hear such things from pretty young women.

No, it was best she'd left when she had. Get her home and get her back to her folks. She'd make out. She was smart and appeared to have breeding.

And if there was one thing he knew about it was breeding, and not just in women either. Counting pay and travel allowances, he could usually expect to clear between eighty and a hundred dollars a month as a deputy marshal. But he more than matched that trading horses when he got the chance. His main source of income, however, was playing poker with folks who thought the game was a matter of chance and not skill. A man had once said that he'd just as soon shoot it out with Longarm as try and beat him playing poker, but the people who heard the man say that knew he didn't really mean it. All you could lose in a poker game against Longarm was your money. Guns were another matter.

When the feeling moved him he reached out, put on his hat, and began to dress. First he pulled on his denim jeans; then he sat back down and put on his socks and his boots. He finished up with his shirt, making do with the one he'd worn the night before. He'd only brought two extra shirts with him, and he had to get more than two days' wear out of each, or else spend a lot of his time hunting up a washerwoman. Finally he strapped on his gunbelt, hooking the huge silver buckle into place. The buckle was oval and concave and hollow. Inside, a double-barreled derringer was held in place by a steel-spring clip. It was the kind of backup a man might never need, but if he did need it he'd need it mighty bad. Longarm didn't believe in leaving important matters to chance, recognizing that there had to be a certain element of risk in his line of work. His attitude was to eliminate as much of that element as was humanly possible.

14

When he was dressed, he walked downstairs to the dining room for breakfast. The urge for a cup of coffee was powerful, as well as the need for some ham and eggs and about a half-dozen biscuits with cream gravy. He was staying at the Gunter Hotel, which was a famous old cattleman's stopover—and one of the few places in town that didn't make you think you were in Mexico.

He got a table, sat down, and ordered when the waiter came over, asking for ham, four eggs fried sunny-side up, biscuits with cream gravy, and as much coffee as the man could carry without straining himself. His mood was good in spite of the job that faced him. It was one of the most distasteful tasks his boss, Billy Vail, chief marshal for the Colorado district, had ever set before him. He was on his way to the Mexican border, to the town of Laredo, to investigate a fellow deputy marshal. He remembered the scene in Vail's office. Vail had said, "Custis, we got a bad situation there that's got to be looked into. I know you ain't going to want the job and I don't blame you because it's a dirty one. But I got to pick you for several reasons, and all of them are good reasons, so there ain't no use in you trying to argue me out of it."

Billy had then explained. "It seems that the sheriff down there in Laredo has been taking some money to let certain parties run guns through into Mexico to supply some rebel group down there. Which particular bunch of revolutionaries is of no concern to us. They can have all the goddamn revolutions they want in Mexico, which they do, with or without our say-so. But running guns into a foreign nation without our government's permission is a federal offense. Makes it look like we're taking sides. So word got back up to the marshal's office in Austin about this here sheriff—I forget his name right at the moment—and they sent a deputy down there to look into the matter. That was about three months ago. The deputy marshal's name is Older, Les Older. Been in the federal marshal business about three years. Before that he spent a year with the Texas Rangers. Before that I don't know. He's a man of about thirty years of age. So far hasn't had a mark on his record."

Longarm had said, "So?"

"So, the chief marshal in Austin ain't been satisfied with the progress this Les Older is making. Don't like the reports he's been sending back."

"Hell, Billy, looks like he's jumping in awful fast. You say the man ain't been down there but three months?"

Billy Vail ran his hand through his graying hair. "Custis, this ain't my judgment. The chief marshal in Austin is an old friend of mine, and he solicited this office to send a deputy to Laredo to look into the matter. Obviously he can't send somebody from his crew because this Older would know them." He added, with heavy sarcasm, "And we're far enough away that there's just a chance that this Marshal Older wouldn't have heard of the famous Custis Long. The Longarm of song and legend."

Longarm gave Billy a sour look. "So the chief in Austin thinks his deputy has gone into business for himself?"

Billy leaned back in his swivel chair. "I don't recall saying what my friend in Austin thinks. As a matter of fact I don't know what he thinks. But he *wants* us to send a man down to look into the matter. Might be nothing to it. Might be I'm sending you on a paid vacation."

Longarm grimaced. "Billy, this ain't exactly to my liking. He's a brother peace officer. Why does it have to be me?"

Billy held up three fingers. "Three reasons. One, you know the Mexican border better than any other man I got. Two, you're the best man I got. Three, you don't need any reasons. Just my say-so."

"Thanks," Longarm said. He stood up and jammed on his hat. "I hope you realize the Mexican border is one dangerous place and that Laredo is the worst of it."

"My! You don't say? Hell, I'd send my granny if she could get up out of her rocking chair."

"You are an ornery old bastard, Billy. I ever mention that to you?"

"Not more than three or four hundred times."

Longarm sighed. "I guess I go incognito. At first at least."

"I reckon you do. Go on down there and mix around and act like you're a good ol' boy ain't above making a crooked buck or two. Use some of that fatal charm I hear makes you such a hand with the ladies."

"You realize it's a hell of a long ways down there?"

Billy smiled thinly. "Well, ain't that the reason they call you Longarm? More's the reason you're the man for the job."

Now his breakfast came, and he shut off his thoughts while he devoted his attention to the eggs and ham and biscuits. The cream gravy wasn't up to his standards, but the rest of it was

16

well on the side of eatable. Like all hardworking men Longarm wasn't a picky eater, but he was particular about his food. He'd always heard men say they'd eat a snake if nothing else was at hand. He'd doubted the truth of such remarks, and had finally had the chance to prove it. He and another deputy had once been left afoot and without supplies in the middle of the New Mexico desert. Finally, on the second day, they'd managed to kill a rattlesnake, which was the only game, if it could be called that, that they'd seen. Both of them had studied the snake for a good long time, but in the end had decided their more immediate need was to search for water.

Drinking his last cup of coffee, Longarm reflected wryly on Billy Vail's idea of a joke. Well, he thought, maybe it wouldn't turn out so bad after all. There was always the chance that the Texas deputy marshal had good reason for spending so much time without any action. It could well be that he, Longarm, was indeed taking a paid vacation, and then he'd get a laugh on Billy.

But he doubted it. Three months was an awful long time to spend getting the goods on just one crooked sheriff. Especially in a wide-open town like Laredo. Hell, a dedicated lawman could make one pass down the streets of that town and fill up a dozen jails without half trying. No, the greater likelihood was that the deputy had gone sour. The thought made Longarm more than a little sad. The law business was enough of a poor-paying profession without a man giving away his honor in the bargain. Or maybe not giving it away, but selling it for some dirty money, which was just about the same thing. If a man wanted money, and he had any sense, he knew that working for the federal government as a lawman wasn't the way to get it.

When he was through at the table he paid his score and walked out the hotel door and into the city of San Antonio. He had given considerable thought to just how to approach the situation on his train ride down from Denver, and he'd figured if he was hunting wolves he might as well look like a wolf. Consequently he went hunting around San Antonio, stopping at this mercantile or that, a hardware store that had a good stock of guns, even several pawnshops—of which there appeared to be more than the usual number for a town the size of San Antonio. But then pawnshops generally spoke of gamblers and desperate men and men far enough off their home range that there was no friend or family member to turn to. Longarm had spent a fair

17

amount of time in San Antone, as the natives called it, and he didn't much like it. Parts of it glittered like St. Louis, but too much of it was run-down and poor. He didn't mind that it was as Mexican as Mexico; he minded that it was a hustler's town, a bunko artist's town, a town where a man had better keep a close eye on his wallet, his gun, and his horse. Fortunately, he didn't have a horse to worry about yet, although that was a piece of business he was going to have to get tended to in the next twenty-four hours. As a federal marshal he had the right to requisition an animal from any U.S. installation, including an army post. But that would be the same as the McClellan saddle; government horses came with that big U.S. brand on the hip and he didn't want that. No, he'd buy a horse and buy it in San Antonio before he left. Horses were one good thing that could be said for the city, in his opinion. Between the auction barns and individual traders, there was as lively a market in horseflesh as was to be found anywhere in the country. And he knew a man could find good-blooded stock in the town if he knew what he was about and had the money to pay for it. But a good horse, in his line of work, wasn't a luxury. It was a necessity. Billy Vail might scream at the chit he'd turn in for what he had to pay for a good animal, but he'd understand. Besides, he was a horse or two short in his personal trading stock, so he figured it might be a good job of work to find a good animal and then let the government have the pleasure of shipping the horse home for him.

Walking, he passed the ruins of the Alamo, the old Spanish mission where a hundred or so Texans had holed up to be slaughtered by three or four thousand Mexicans during the Texas war for independence. He'd heard them called the "heroes of the Alamo," but he didn't think they were heroes; he thought they were damn fools. If he'd been in command he wouldn't have sat there, hemmed in, until he was overwhelmed by odds of better than twenty to one. He'd have gotten his men out, and then harassed and harried the Mexican army's flank until he'd worn them down to a nub. He'd have fired on them from ambush by day and by night, and never given a single soldier time enough to eat so much as a tamale or take a drink of water, let alone get sleep or hunt for provisions. Longarm didn't see anything heroic about dying needlessly. His motto was to let some other dumb bastard die for honor if he so chose; he appreciated honor and understood and valued it, but he didn't think it ought to be confused with plain stupidity.

It was at a hockshop that he found what he was looking for. He'd been searching for an older repeating rifle, a rifle that had been replaced by newer models, the kind that the U.S. cavalry might have used but which had now become obsolete, a rifle that was still serviceable and fired a common-caliber cartridge, but a gun that would sell and could be bought for a price that would make it desirable in the gun trade that was going into Mexico. In a shop near Fort Sam Houston he found an old Winchester Model 1866 .44-caliber rimfire, lever-action carbine. In that year of 1884 the gun looked every bit of eighteen years old. Its walnut stock was scarred and worn and its brass housing was scratched and nicked. He hefted it and handled it, looked down the hole in the octagonal barrel, tried the action, and found it perfectly serviceable. The hockshop owner wanted twenty-two dollars for it, but they finally settled on eighteen, and Longarm got a receipt and headed back for the hotel well pleased with his prize. It was the sort of rifle he could claim to have two or three or maybe even four hundred of, and offer to sell to interested parties for twenty-five dollars a gun, knowing that they in turn could sell them across the border for at least forty dollars apiece.

He had the rifle wrapped so as to conceal what it was. He was carrying his badge in the pocket of his jeans, and more than once he had suddenly slapped his left chest, frightened, for an instant, at the absence of the accustomed slight weight and thinking maybe he'd lost the star. Then he'd remember that the star was in his pocket and that matters were as they should be. Still, it was a strange feeling for him to be walking around without that badge after so many years. It didn't make him feel naked, just not quite whole.

He had lunch at a cantina, eating enchiladas and tacos and guacamole salad and refried beans. He had always liked what most folks mistakenly called "Mexican" food. It wasn't Mexican food, it was Tex-Mex food. If a man was in Mexico City he'd more than likely starve to death before he found a tamale or a taco. Such truck was border food, poor people's food, food made out of the cheaper cuts of meat and then heavily spiced to disguise the taste. But Longarm liked border food and he didn't get it often enough to suit him. The stuff they tried to pass off as the authentic article in Colorado and such places was a poor imitation of the real thing.

He lingered over his lunch and then had several beers, trying out his Spanish on the little waitress who had served him and several of the patrons at the bar. It became quickly clear that whatever he thought he was speaking, the people he was speaking it to didn't think it was Spanish. He'd planned to pass himself off as a man who'd been in and around the border country for some time, but he decided that, unless his Spanish got better all of a sudden, he'd better come up with a different cover story.

That afternoon he made the rounds of the auction barns. They were all doing a lively horse business, but he didn't see anything that appealed to his eye as worth the money they were asking. He did see a dun gelding that an individual trader with a small string of quality horses was holding. The man was obviously an itinerant trader because he had his little string hitched around a wagon which was loaded with traveling gear. Longarm found the man on a vacant lot near the biggest of the auction houses. He was resting in a chair and seemingly enjoying the afternoon. Longarm asked after his business and the man said, "Little early yet. Everybody that's lookin' fer a horse has got to 'vestigate them big barns first. Soon's they find out they ain't nuthin' worth buyin' in such places, that all the stock is culls er castoffs else the animal wouldn't be in a auction barn in the first place, they finally get around to folks like me who deal in a better quality of horse."

It was a sales line, but looking over the man's stock, Longarm could see there was a good deal of truth in what the man had to say. He asked after the dun, and was told the animal was a good road horse but didn't have any cow sense. The trader said, "I bought him off an ol' boy about a hunnert miles east of here, down near Houston. Damn fool was trying to use him fer cow work when the horse had never been near a head of beef, and was blaming the horse for being dumb. But he's a nice horse, still a little snorty, but if a man don't mind that he's got a nice way of going and has got some speed. I make him to be a long four-year-old."

Longarm asked the trader to lead the horse out and then hold him. Longarm walked around the horse, liking what he saw. He could tell from the size of the gelding's hindquarters that the animal had a good bit of quarterhorse in him, and he could see signs of American saddlebred conformation. He felt the horse's legs, looking for bowed tendons or other signs of

20

weakness. There were none. He stepped back and gave the horse a nose-to-tail inspection, liking what he saw. The animal was a nice dun color with the distinctive dun marking down the middle of his back. Longarm judged the horse to be near seventeen hands tall and close to a thousand pounds. The horse looked like a good, well-rounded mount. He had the quarterhorse blood and build for quick speed, and the American saddlebred influence for stamina. He mouthed the horse, and the animal didn't seem to mind too much. Peering inside, Longarm judged by the teeth that the horse was closer to a five-year-old than a four. But that was a small difference, and actually more in the horse's favor. Finally he slapped the horse in the flanks a few times to see the animal's reaction. The horse trembled, but he didn't spook. Longarm said, "You can tie him back to your wagon now. I'm done."

The trader held out the lead rope. "Two hunnert dollars and you can just walk on off with him."

Longarm scratched his neck and looked away. "Oh, I was thinking more like a hundred and ten."

The trader smiled slightly. "I don't reckon you want to buy a horse today. At least not this horse. Reckon I will just tie him back up."

Longarm watched the trader tie the dun to the wagon and then sit back down in his chair. He'd been surprised the trader hadn't countered his offer of a hundred and ten dollars. He had decided the horse was worth a hundred and a half, and he was hopeful of buying him for somewhere around a hundred and thirty-five. But he wasn't sure about that now. The trader looked like an old, experienced hand who was ready to bide his time. The trader said, "Well, good afternoon to you."

Longarm smiled. "I guess you've taken those animals for pets."

The trader shrugged. "If I don't sell this string here I'll sell it somewhars else. Besides, I'm fixing to move north and I'm more in the buying mood than the selling."

Longarm had noticed a nice-looking little bay filly. She was a bit too fine-boned and light for him, but he said, "What'll you take for the little bay filly?"

The trader looked amused. "You don't want that filly. Man of your size. That's a town horse and you know it. Kind of horse you sell to a banker that wants to ride for pleasure of a Sunday. You're looking for a using horse, a good road horse, because I

21

can see you damn sure ain't no cowboy. Why don't you go on and give me a hunnert an' eighty-five for that dun and lead him off to where you got yore saddle cached?"

Longarm said, "I got to go see a man about a train." He turned around and started in the direction of the depot.

The trader called after him, "You'll still need a horse when you get there, and you ain't gonna do no better than that dun."

Longarm said, over his shoulder, "Get where?"

"Wherever it is you be a-goin' on the train."

Longarm laughed and kept walking.

At the depot he read the timetable and discovered there was a train the next day for Laredo. He figured he'd become about as Texanized as he was likely to get, so he determined to get on down to Laredo and get the business over with. The train left the next morning at ten and arrived at three in the afternoon. He went inside the depot and inquired of the ticket agent about shipping a horse. The agent shook his head. "Ain't shipping no horses south tomorrow. All I got going that way is cattle. You can mix your horse in with them if you're a mind to."

He wasn't about to put a horse in a stock car with a bunch of slobbering, slipping, spooky cattle, and he told the agent so. The agent shrugged. "Onliest thing I can offer is you pay the freight fer a whole car. Cost you forty dollars."

Longarm said, "Forty dollars! I ain't trying to buy your railroad. I just want to get my horse to Laredo. Hell, I'll ride him first."

The agent said, "Tell you what I'll do. We got a half a car of cattle. I could wall off the car down the middle and your horse could have the other half fer hisself. Cost you fifteen dollars."

Longarm could have pulled out his badge and transported himself and his horse to Laredo for nothing. But it was his opinion a man couldn't be too careful, and if the train was going to Laredo word might just go along that there was a U.S. deputy marshal aboard.

He said, "That include my fare?"

The agent shrugged. "If you be willin' to ride with yore horse. You want to ride the chair cars it'd be another two six bits."

Longarm got out his roll of money and carefully counted off fifteen dollars. He said, "I'd druther have my horse's company than folks that ride the chair cars. But say, one thing. That's a southbound train. You make sure your crew pens them cows up

22

in the north end of that cattle car. I don't want to be smelling cow shit for five hours."

The agent said, "Get your horse here an hour early and turn him over to the stock foreman fer loadin'."

His business done, Longarm rambled back toward the center of town, managing to walk near where the horse trader was still sitting in his chair. The afternoon had cooled and evening was coming on. When Longarm was near enough he said to the trader, "Looks like you're a man don't believe in knocking off for supper."

The trader said, "Oh, I got a pot of stew made up in the wagon. I'll build a fire here directly and heat it up. Might join me if you've a mind to. Got some good sourdough biscuits working. Dough ought to be just about rize by now."

Longarm came nearer to the trader's chair and hunkered down. "You live out of your wagon, do you?"

The trader was chewing on a match. He spoke around it. "Road tradin' don't quite pay banker's wages. But it's enough for them as don't need much." He gave Longarm a sly grin. "Allows him the pleasure of sellin' his horses fer what he reckons they be worth."

Longarm laughed. "Maybe I'll go up to a hundred and twenty-five, but that's my top dollar. That dun is a nice horse, but he ain't exactly blooded stock."

The trader said, "Wa'l, you still be invited fer supper. I'm jest about to build a fire."

"Would you be a man who'd touch a drop of spirits every now and again?"

"I'm agin drinkin' in church, but I ain't ever heard of a little drop or two wronging a man's constitution."

Longarm stood up. "Well, you get the fire built and I'll step along over to my hotel room and fetch back a bottle of some pretty fair drinking whiskey. Anything else I can fetch to supper?"

"Jest yore appetite and a hunnert and eighty dollars fer that dun. Wouldn't sell him so cheap except it's beginnin' to hurt me seein' you afoot. You don't walk like a man does much of it."

Longarm had to smile. It was true. His boots were particularly high-heeled because he'd once got hung up in a stirrup and dragged and he never wanted such a thing to happen again. And while they might be effective for keeping his whole boot from going through a stirrup, the heels were hell to do much walking in.

He said, "I'll just step along and get the whiskey. That hundred-and-thirty-dollar dun looks like he can use the rest."

The trader said, "That hunnert-and-seventy-dollar horse is so gentle you could ride him bareback over to yore hotel with nothin' but the halter he's wearin'."

Longarm went up to his room and got a bottle of the branded bourbon he kept a supply of, and then stopped in at the dining room and bought half an apple pie. It was going dark by the time Longarm came up to the trader's fire. The trader had dragged out another chair from his wagon, and had the big pot of stew hanging over the fire on a tripod. Even though they were a few blocks from the center of town, they could hear the saloons and dance halls beginning to warm up.

The trader came up with a couple of tin cups, and Longarm poured them each a good slug of the whiskey. Before they drank Longarm put out his hand and introduced himself. The trader said, "Name's Teacher, Raymond Teacher. Most folks just call me Teach, or Ray."

Longarm judged him to be a man in his early fifties. He was lean and sinewy and seemed content with himself and the balance of his life. As was the custom, he didn't ask Longarm where he was from or where he was bound or what his business was. Before they drank they made a toast to "luck," and then knocked the whiskey back. The trader looked in his cup and nodded. "Mighty good drinkin' material. Better'n what they sell around here."

It was an invitation, faint though it was, for Longarm to say where he was from. But Longarm just said, "That stew is starting to smell mighty good."

They ate off the tin plates the trader had, and drank coffee laced with some of Longarm's whiskey. Nearing the end of the meal, Longarm casually asked the trader if he did any business down along the border, specifically around Laredo.

Teacher shook his head. "Not anymore. I used to buy considerable stock down there and then take it up north and sell it. I quit doing that after I got to noticing I was buying some of the same horses more than once. You know they don't brand horses in Mexico, just notch their ears in different ways. Wa'l, I finally taken notice of this one coal-black mare had a white stocking on her right front foot. I figured unless they was an uncommon

24

number of coal-black mares with one white stocking, I was buying the same horse over and over. I think I bought that one mare three times. I took her back to the last man I'd sold her to and, sure 'nough, she'd been stole about a week before. Lost money on that deal, but it was better than runnin' around the country with a string of stolen horses. Man can git his neck stretched that way. Hell, them damn Mexican horse thieves was stealin' 'em back damn near as fast as I could sell 'em. Owners never even got a chance to git a brand on 'em." He half turned toward where his string of trading horses was hitched to the wagon. "You'll notice that hunnert-and-sixty-five-dollar dun has got a brand. Duly recorded."

Longarm said, "So you don't buy horses down there anymore?"

Teacher shook his head. "Hell, I don't even go any nearer the damn place than I have to. Ain't got no reason to. Town is dangerous. Dangerous and crooked. Ain't but two kinds of men goes to the border: them as is running from the law and them that is the law doing the chasing." He gave Longarm a considering look. "You heading that way?"

Longarm said casually, "Got to pass through it. Headin' down to Monterrey. Do a little cattle business."

Teacher said, "I hear tell they got another one of them rev-o-lutions be a-goin' on down there in northern Mexico. You better watch yore hat don't pick up a few holes in it."

"When ain't they having a revolution?"

"That'd be the truth."

Halfway through the apple pie Longarm bought the dun for a hundred fifty dollars. When he got ready to leave he counted out the money to Teacher and said, "I'll pick him up sometime in the morning. Around about eight."

Teacher said, "Oh. So you'd be wanting me to grain him? I generally feed at sunup."

Longarm grinned and handed over another dollar. "Will that handle the oats?"

Teacher put the money in his pocket. "Pleasure doin' business with you, Mister Long, even if you did steal a damn good horse from me."

Longarm said, "If I could have waited another day I could have bought that plug for under a hundred."

Teacher said, "I reckon not. That hunnert and a half was my best apple-pie-and-whiskey price."

"Then I guess we're even because, as it happens, that was my best beef-stew price. Best *good*-beef-stew price. Course, a few onions in it and I might have come up a few dollars more."

Teacher said dryly, "I'll recollect that next time I'm makin' stew an' horse tradin' at the same time."

They shook hands, and then Longarm turned and started toward the bright lights around the main plaza, figuring to kill the balance of the night with a little poker. Even several blocks away he could hear the sounds of music, now and again punctured by the sound of a yell or a gunshot. He thought to himself that San Antonio was an up-and-going place—though where it was going he had no idea.

He tried three cantinas, but couldn't find a seat open in a higher-stakes game. He finally settled for a quarter-ante, dollar-limit game in the saloon attached to his hotel. He hated to play such poker because it was all luck with no strategy involved. You couldn't scare a man with a dollar bet or bluff or buy a pot. As far as Longarm was concerned, you might as well just deal the cards face up and play draw-out. But it was poker, and he figured it was better than going to bed early or standing outside and letting the moon shine in his mouth. He figured he'd used up all his luck in the women department the day before. Anything he'd find tonight would be either a professional or ugly enough to scare the horses.

There were six players at his table. Except for a young man wearing a white linen shirt and a black, soft leather vest, the rest were the run-of-the-mill workaday kind that labored at whatever they did just enough to give them money enough to hang around the saloons and drink and play cards. When their money was gone they went out and got another job, whether it was cowboying or laying iron for the railroad or carpentry or walking behind a plow horse. Which was another reason Longarm didn't care for small-stakes games; you didn't meet a very interesting class of people. He wasn't a snob, but given the option of talking to somebody with brains and some party who'd managed to lose what little he'd started with, Longarm preferred to associate with a more entertaining variety of folk, even if it was just to argue.

The saloon was noisy and smoky and crowded. Longarm lit up one of his little cigars and sat down to play some poker. Now and again he would signal to a circulating waiter, who would bring him a drink of the house whiskey. It was not up to his taste, but if a man wanted to drink he had to drink what the place was selling.

After about an hour he was starting to get bored. There just wasn't enough money on the table to make it worth his while. He could see it was exciting for a few of the players, especially a heavy-shouldered man with rough hands who was sitting next to him on his right. He sweated every pot, and Longarm could tell that the money was too important to the man. That was one of his gambling rules: Don't ever play in a game where the stakes are over your head, because then you are playing with scared money and scared money can't win.

Longarm had only made one good hand, a full house, but nobody else had drawn anything, so he couldn't draw a raise over his raise and the pot he'd won had been small. They were playing straight five-card draw with a four-card limit. Longarm had started with twenty dollars on the table and, taking a casual glance at the money in front of him, he figured he was just about even. It appeared that the only real winner was the clean-cut young man in the soft leather vest. He played with a slight smile on his face, his expression never varying, and made his bets and his decisions with a quick, sure precision.

But he was bothering the big man on Longarm's right. Nothing had been said, but Longarm could feel something amiss in the air, the smell of trouble. Once, Longarm had seen the heavy-shouldered man half rise out of his chair when the man in the black vest, in a seemingly casual motion, had pushed the discard pile farther to his right with his right hand. He'd been holding his cards in his left hand, and he'd returned his right hand to join with his left in holding his cards. Longarm hadn't seen anything amiss about the careless movement, but then he wasn't paying as close attention as he would have if there was real money on the table. But he had to keep reminding himself that what was small stakes to him might not be so for others, especially the heavy-shouldered man. Almost unconsciously he pushed his chair an inch or two back from the table and swerved it a little to the right. It wasn't much, but if he had to draw it would make a big difference. And as he moved his chair he also sat up a little straighter and extended his right leg to bring the butt of his revolver more closely to hand.

Then it happened again when the man in the black vest was dealing. The opening bet had been made and the draw called for. Longarm had drawn junk and hadn't even bothered to call

27

the opener, but had simply pitched his hand in and casually watched the game as it got played out. Three players had stayed, one other besides the young man and the heavy-shouldered man. The heavy-shouldered man had drawn three cards, the player that had opened had drawn two, and the man in the black vest had drawn one. The opener had bet a dollar and the heavy-shouldered man had raised a dollar. The bet was to the young man. The discard pile was just to his right. He made that same careless, preoccupied move again, pushing the pile away with his right hand. Only this time Longarm saw it.

As, apparently, did the heavy-shouldered man. He suddenly stood up and made a reaching motion across the table as if to catch the hand of the young man who was dealing. At the same time he yelled, "You sonofabitch! You're pickin' the discards! You pig-sucker, you're cheatin'!"

The air was heavy with menace and trouble. Longarm said loudly, "Hold on! Hold on! Let's all calm down!"

The young man was staring back at the heavy-shouldered man, seeming calm, the little smile still on his face. He said, "You better watch who you are accusing of what, fellow. And get that big paw out of my face!"

Longarm was sitting forward on the edge of his chair. He said, "Let's all sit down and take it easy. There's not enough money in that pot to have trouble over."

But he could still see it coming. The thought flashed through his mind to pitch his badge on the table and perhaps avert a killing, but he couldn't do it. He just said, "Hell, there ain't five dollars in that pot."

The heavy-shouldered man said, still pointing at the young man, "Don't care if they wadn't but two bits in the pot. The sonofabitch been pickin' at the discards all night!"

His voice was rising as he said it and his face was turning a mottled red. Longarm saw the man's hand flash back toward his side. He saw him fumble and then he could see, by the movement of the man's shoulders, that he was drawing his sidearm.

Chapter 3

Longarm rose, drawing as he did. The problem was that the man's right hand was on the side away from Longarm. Longarm leaned forward and slashed down with the barrel of his revolver as the man's hand, holding a pistol, came toward level. The blow caught the heavy-shouldered man on the wrist. He let out a startled yell, and the pistol fell harmlessly out of his hand and landed on the floor. He whirled toward Longarm, his face furious. Longarm jammed his .44-caliber revolver in the man's belly and said evenly, "Take it easy. Just hold it right there!"

"You!" the man said. He was more surprised than anything else. "What the hell you think you be a-doin'? You in with this cheat?"

The saloon had fallen silent. All the games and conversation had stopped. Longarm could see a man with a drink halfway to his mouth, transfixed, his eyes on the little scene. And out of the corner of his eye he could see a man with a tin star on his chest and a shotgun cradled in the crook of his arm hurrying toward them. Longarm said, "I ain't in with nobody in anything. I just don't want to be close when bullets start flying because one of them could hit me. *Savvy?*"

The man with the shotgun—Longarm took him to be a town marshal—had arrived at the table. He'd brought the shotgun up so that it was level with Longarm's chest.

He said to Longarm, "Put that gun down, mister."

As he replaced his revolver in its holster, Longarm said, "I was just going to do that."

The marshal said, "What the hell is going on here?"

29

Longarm said, "I think it was mainly a misunderstanding." He gestured at the heavy-shouldered man. "This gent was fixing to shoot that one there." He pointed with his chin at the young man in the black vest. "I knocked the gun out of his hand. Don't like shooting in my immediate presence. Get a gunfight going and you never know who might get hurt. You mind if I sit down while you get this straightened out?"

The town marshal, fortunately, appeared to have some years and experience on him; at least enough not to get excited. It would not have suited Longarm's plans at all to spend the night in jail until it all got explained to some judge the next morning.

He sat quietly while the marshal worked his way around the table asking details from the rest of the players. In the end he declared that the game was over with. He said, "If you men can't play poker without guns, you can't play in here. Just take your business somewhere else."

He ended up expelling the heavy-shouldered man from the premises. Longarm picked up his money and started toward the bar. The marshal stopped him on the way. He said, "Thanks. Don't take it wrong that I was pointin' this scattergun at you. Wasn't nuthin' personal. But you was the one holdin' the gun."

Longarm said, "I'd of done the same myself."

The marshal narrowed his eyes at him. "You a lawman?"

"Me?" Longarm looked as innocent as he could. "Lord, no. Whatever give you an idea like that?"

The town marshal was still inspecting him doubtfully. "I don't know . . . Way you handled yourself, stopping that fight."

Longarm said, "I told you, I just didn't want to get in the way of a bullet meant for somebody else."

"Yeah," the marshal said. "Except most folks would have dived for cover and not give a damn. You sure somewhere back there in yore past you wasn't no sheriff or deputy?"

Longarm laughed, though it came out a little hollow. "Well, I've been drunk a few times and couldn't remember what I'd got up to. But I don't believe I could have ever been drunk long enough to have been a sheriff and then forget it."

The man laughed slightly. "Reckon not. Well, much obliged. Go on up to the bar and have a drink on the house. We don't have no trouble in this town because we stop it before it gets started. Reckon you helped us out on that."

Longarm went to the bar, but not for a free drink. Instead he persuaded the bartender to find a better brand of whiskey than

30

he was serving the rest of the customers, and bought a bottle of that, got a glass, and went and found an empty table by the wall next to the street. His intention was to have a few quiet drinks and then go up to bed. He sat down and poured himself out a drink and sipped at it. It was bonded whiskey, but it still wasn't as good as the stock he'd brought with him from Denver. The only problem with that was that he and the horse trader had finished off the last bottle of his traveling whiskey. All he could hope for, and he figured it was a pretty forlorn hope, was that a man could buy a better-quality drink in Laredo. Though he was damned if he could see any reason why that should be so. More than likely it would be either tequila or rum, and he wouldn't drink either. Not unless that was all there was to be had.

So he sat there, sipping at his whiskey and looking around the big saloon. The room had roused itself after the brief quiet, and now he heard the loud sounds of drunken arguments and laughter and talk and the noise of half a dozen poker games. As he sat there relaxing, the young man in the black vest suddenly appeared. He was holding a drink and the hand holding it was trembling slightly. Longarm looked up. The young man made a motion at a chair. He said, "Mind if I sit down?"

"Help yourself," Longarm said. With his boot he shoved out a chair across from him. The young man sat down, putting his drink carefully in front of him.

The man said, "My name is Willis Howard. I come by to thank you for what you done. I reckon that man might have killed me if you hadn't of stepped in."

Longarm said, "Or you might have killed him first with that derringer you were holding under the table."

Howard grimaced. "You saw that?"

Longarm shook his head. "I didn't see the gun so I don't know that it was a derringer, but I saw you put your right hand below the level of the table, and your shoulder dipped enough to reach your boot. Didn't figure you had a *rifle* down there."

"But you weren't even looking at me. You were looking at that big blowhard."

Longarm held up a finger. "Correction. You don't know he was a blowhard."

"I read him for one. Hell, I could probably have handled it."

Longarm looked at him in disgust. "How old are you, boy? Fifteen? You plan to go on cheating you better learn to do it

31

better or you ain't going to get no older. Hell, palming cards out of the discard pile!"

Howard grimaced again. "Was I that obvious?"

"You were careless. I didn't get on you until I noticed you were catching the attention of the man to my right. But then there wasn't enough money in the game to interest me so I wasn't paying much attention. But I reckon you better not try amateur stunts like that against serious poker players. They won't bother taking the time to call you a cheater, just up and shoot you."

Howard looked at him a long second and then slowly smiled. "I reckon I was clumsy. I'm much better than that. I was like you. I ain't accustomed to playing in that small a size game. But I'd managed to go bust a few days ago in Austin and I was trying to get a little stake together. Figured the rubes at the table were too dumb to notice."

Longarm said dryly, "That's a kind of suicidal attitude, strikes me. You go to taking your opponents too lightly, and I don't care what the game is, you'll end up ass over teakettle and never know why."

"You a professional?"

Longarm paused to pour himself out another drink. The young man still hadn't touched his. Longarm wondered if his hand was trembling so bad he couldn't get it to his lips without spilling some. "A professional what?"

"Gambler. What else?"

"If you mean do I mean to make money off everything I do, then yeah, I'm a professional." He smiled slightly. "I ain't got no what you might call pastimes."

Howard suddenly ducked his head, raised his hand at the same time, and took a quick drink of his whiskey.

Longarm laughed. "Still a little shaky?"

The young man wanted to act defiant, but he looked at Longarm for a second and then shrugged his shoulders. "Yeah," he said. "I hate to admit it, but that kind of flustered me a mite. Tell you the truth, the hand I was holding the derringer with was shaking so bad I'd of probably missed. I was more than a little glad you got mixed in. What'd you do that for, anyway? Wasn't your trouble."

Longarm held out his bottle and nodded at the young man's glass. "Knock that half you got left back and I'll pour you some more. Your nerves ought to be a little improved by then."

Howard looked grateful. He finished his half a tumbler of whiskey in one gulp, and then held it out for Longarm to refill. Longarm was careful not to pour it to the brim.

Howard said, "Well, much obliged." He took down half of his second glass.

Longarm said, "You get your stake?"

Howard shrugged. "Not really. I maybe got a hundred in my pocket, or close to it. And I got a gold watch I can always get fifty on."

"And then there's the derringer. That ought to bring about twenty dollars more."

But Howard shook his head. "No, I don't sell that. I never know when I might need it."

"Well, I ain't in the advice-giving business because it don't pay. But was I you, that little popgun is the first thing I'd get rid of. There's some men that is fixed up inside to use a gun—some that ain't. I'd judge you to be one of the ain'ts. You ever shot anybody? With that gun or any other?"

The young man had put on a black, flat-crowned, narrow-brimmed hat since the game. He now took it off and set it on the table, brim down, and ran his fingers through his hair for a second.

Longarm said sharply, "Don't do that!"

Howard looked up. "What?"

Longarm gestured at his hat on the table. "Set your hat down like that. All the luck will run out. You set a hat down on the crown."

Howard stared at him for a second, and then slowly picked up his hat and turned it over so the head hole was open and pointing upward. "That's the first time I ever heard that one."

"Then you ain't been a gambler very long. Or ain't you superstitious?"

"I believe in four aces and a royal flush. Them are the only sure things I know about. And no, I ain't ever shot nobody. With the derringer or any other kind of gun. But I think I could if I had to."

"Thinking you can and *knowing* you can is the difference that can mean seven men goin' to the cemetery and only six comin' back. You better damn well be *sure* you can use it before you go to packin' a gun, derringer or not."

Willis Howard looked away. His face was moody. "Well, it don't make no difference. I'm pullin' out of here in the morning.

This damn town is full of cardsharps. That's how I come to lose my roll. I sat down in a game yesterday and thought I had me four suckers. Turned out *I* was the mark. The other four were every damn one sharps. I'm gonna head on down to Laredo on the morning train tomorrow. See if the pickings is any easier down there."

Longarm's ears pricked up. A sudden thought went through his mind. It might just be in his favor to be seen arriving in Laredo in the company of a tinhorn gambler. A bad one, but an obvious ne'er-do-well who would never be thought to be traveling with anyone respectable. It was chancy, but Longarm figured he might get a head start on being taken for a crook just by being around Willis Howard. He said, "How old are you, Willis?"

Howard looked up at him. "What the hell's that got to do with anything?"

Longarm shrugged. "You look too young to have been at this game long. Didn't mean nothing by it."

Howard said grudgingly, "I'm twenty-five. I look older usually, but I been getting too damn much sleep lately. Ain't had the money to play two or three days straight like I'm used to. You from around here? You don't sound like a Texican."

"New Mexico," Longarm lied. He paused. "I'm going to Laredo on that morning train myself. Tomorrow."

Willis Howard looked immediately interested. "Shore enough. You know the border?"

Longarm shrugged. "Some. Not the Tex-Mex border as well as I do other parts, but I been in Laredo enough. How about yourself?"

Howard shook his head slowly. "Never been near the place. Fact is, this is the fartherest south I've ever been in Texas. As far as that goes, this is my first trip to Texas."

Longarm looked at him curiously. He wasn't quite sure he'd ever met anyone as green as this Willis Howard. The young man struck Longarm as needing a guardian or somebody to help him get around. He said, having noticed a soft accent in Howard's speech, "Where are you from?"

"Tennessee. I had heard the pickings were easy in Texas so I headed down here. I had been working the riverboats on the Mississippi, but they was too many sharpers there. I don't expect to find a very intelligent species in Laredo. I hear it's just about the last stop on this earth."

Longarm looked at Howard in growing wonder. "You propose to go down to Laredo to win at cards?"

"That's what I do," Howard said.

"And you don't propose to leave it all to the laws of chance. In other words, you mean to help your luck along."

Howard said, a little stiffly, "I'm a professional gambler. I figure you are as well. You and I both know you can't just depend on luck."

"Well, you better hope like hell you have the best luck of your life. You get caught cheating in Laredo, they won't bother to kill you. They'll bury you alive." He leaned forward. "Howard, that is one of the meanest towns on the face of the earth. Are you dead certain you want to try and work that town?"

"I don't care how mean it is. I'm only interested in how ignorant the gamblers are there and how much money they got."

Longarm just shook his head. "Like I said, I ain't in the advice-giving business, but if you are going to help the cards you better know a few more tricks than what you showed in that game."

"Have no fear for me," the young man said confidently. "I got careless once. I won't again. But now then, we're both going to Laredo. We might as well ride down together."

"You got a horse?"

"No, of course not. What would I want with a horse?"

Longarm almost said, "So you can get out of town fast," but held his tongue. He said, "Well, I do. And I'll be riding in the stock car with my animal. You're welcome to ride with us if you're a mind. Save you the fare."

Howard looked a little uncertain. "Won't it be awfully messy?"

Longarm shrugged. "Not for me. But then I'm not a dandy." He leaned across and poured Howard's glass full again, and did the same for himself. Then he put the cork in the bottle and stood up. He picked up his glass, put the bottle under his arm, and said, "Well, I'm off to bed. You can look for me at the train if you're a mind." He drained his glass, and started for the door.

"Wait a minute. What'd you say your name was?"

"Long."

"Long what? Or what Long?"

Longarm was going out the door. "Just Long will do. Never cared for my given name. My old maw wasn't much of a hand at picking out names."

35

He went up to his room, undressed, and sat down on the side of the bed to smoke one last cigar and have one last drink. The bottle was about half gone. He got his cigar drawing, and then sat there staring off into space watching the blue smoke drifting toward the ceiling. He was in his hotel room, but his mind was in Laredo, speculating over just how much trouble he was going to find there. He prayed to God he wouldn't find a fellow law officer gone bad. But if he did, well, nobody had said it would always be pleasant when he hired on.

Then it was time to quit thinking. By his watch it was nearly after midnight and he had a full morning before he caught the train. Raymond Teacher had written him out a bill of sale for the dun, but he had to pick him up, get him saddled, and then get him loaded on the train. And next afternoon he'd be in Laredo.

He trimmed down the lamp until the light went out, leaving just a faint glow, and then rolled over onto the bed and pulled up the bedclothes. He never bothered sleeping with anything on and, except for cold weather, never bothered with underwear now. He'd told Billy Vail one time that he didn't wear underwear because women were always getting too excited and ripping it off him, and the whole business was starting to cost so much that he'd just given the underwear up, and Billy would be surprised what a man could save on such garments over a year's time.

Billy had just given him a sour look like he'd heard all such stories that he wanted to hear. He'd said, "If I could buy you for what the ladies think you're worth, and sell you for what you think you're worth to them, I could turn in this badge and never have to work another day in my life."

He smiled, thinking of ol' Billy. He was a good boss and a fair man, but he did indeed seem dedicated to making Longarm's life miserable.

Longarm sat on a bale of hay near the open door of the stock car. Sixty miles out of San Antonio the hills had grown smaller and smaller, until they'd finally given way to rolling plains that were flattening out with every mile. It was strange-looking country for a man who had come from the high mountains and crags of Colorado. Looking at the flat prairies, Longarm wondered jokingly if he would even remember how to sit a horse on a level surface.

36

Behind him Howard said, "Looks like home to me."

Longarm turned his head. Howard was in the corner between the side of the car and the partition the railroad company had set up to separate them from the cattle. Longarm said, "I thought Tennessee was all mountains."

Howard shook his head. "That's mostly the northeastern part of the state. Where I come from it's grasslands, like this. Though the grass is a hell of a lot better than them weeds out here."

Longarm just looked at him curiously. The man never seemed to have a good word to say about anybody or anything. "Well, if you like it so much why don't you go back there?"

Howard said mysteriously, "I got my reasons." He was dressed in a clean white shirt, though he was wearing the same leather vest. He had on corduroy trousers and flat-heeled boots. Longarm figured he had the derringer in his boot.

Willis Howard amused Longarm more than anything else. The young man seemed to take himself too seriously. It was obvious he had come from a good family, or at least a well-to-do family, by the cut of his clothes and his slightly arrogant attitude. But he appeared not to have any more common sense than a man trying to breed a mule and expecting results. That morning Howard had come flying down the tracks toward the freight end of the train, searching for the stock car Longarm and his dun gelding were in. Longarm had been leaning out the door, watching the smoke from the engine's stack, calculating how long it would be before they got started. Once the smoke started turning black you knew the engineer was building steam and departure was imminent. So he'd been able to wave at Howard, as soon as he'd recognized the racing figure, and direct him on. Howard had been carrying a fine leather valise, and was freshly barbered and shaved. Longarm had been able to smell the lilac water on him and know he'd taken time to visit the barber before they'd departed. It had caused Longarm to rub a hand over the stubble on his own face. He'd been too rushed to bother with such niceties. Besides, he hadn't wanted to look too much like an upstanding citizen when he arrived in Laredo.

At first, once the train had gotten up speed, Howard had complained mightily about the wind and the dust and the flying hay and the smell of the cattle. Longarm had just looked at him and said, "Well, if the accommodations ain't to your liking, why don't you hop off and run up to the passenger cars and buy a ticket from the conductor?"

Of course, at that time, the train had been running about forty miles an hour, so Howard hadn't answered. Now Longarm said, "What's the mysterious secret won't let you go back to Tennessee? You rob a bank?"

"Yes," Howard said. "At least I stole money from it and it was found out."

"They prosecute you?"

Howard said, looking away, "It was my daddy's bank. He covered what I stole. I used the money to learn how to gamble."

Longarm smiled slightly. "Well, from what I seen, your education ain't quite complete. Though I ain't real sure that Laredo is the place you want to continue it."

Howard said, "I've been asking around. I hear the town is as crooked as a dog's hind leg. Place like that should be well stocked with imbeciles."

Longarm nodded. "And thieves and murderers and back-shooters and the riffraff of every back alley in Texas. But they do play poker. And catch cheaters."

Howard said, "I can handle myself."

Longarm looked around at him and laughed.

Howard said, "You never have stated your business in Laredo."

"That's right, I haven't." Longarm tried unsuccessfully to spit out the open door, but the wind blew the spittle right back in his face.

"Well, what is your business in Laredo?"

Longarm looked back at him, slightly amazed. "Kid, you don't ask a man his business. If he wants you to know it he'll tell you. I recommend you learn that by heart, especially in Laredo. You go around asking folks down there their business and they are liable to show you. And their business might be shooting folks."

Before Howard could say anything the dun stamped his foot. Longarm looked the other way to the far end of the car where the dun was tied. He was saddled with the stirrups tied to the saddlehorn so they wouldn't swing around and spook the horse. Longarm didn't figure the dun had ridden many trains, but he seemed to be catching on to the business right nicely. He had his four legs spread and was comfortably braced against the motion of the train. Only when they'd started off, with all the jerks and rumblings and clatter, had he appeared nervous. The railroad had provided him with water and grain and, after a time, the

38

horse had begun eating and drinking water. Longarm had taken the bits out of the horse's mouth, just leaving the bridle loose to make it easier for the horse to eat without floating the grain out the corners of his mouth.

Longarm was well pleased with the horse. He'd led the animal over to the hotel, saddled him, and then ridden him up and down the street and around the Military Plaza quadrangle. He handled very easily and had quick speed and good movement. When Longarm had gone by to say *adios* to Teacher, the trader had offered him a five-dollar profit on the horse. The trader had said, "Ain't fair. You're like trading with another horse trader. Besides, you filled me up with apple pie and whiskey. Why don't you sell him back to me for a hunnert and fifty-five and let me catch myself some yokel don't know as much as you do?" Longarm had laughed and declined. The trader had said, "Making a mistake. Ain't no man ever gone broke taking a profit."

But now he and the horse were bound for Laredo. He'd rolled the used 1866 Winchester rimfire .44-caliber in his bedroll so it couldn't be seen, even though it did stick out a little. He figured to make that rifle his passport into whatever was going on in Laredo. His own rifle was in its boot tied to the right side of his saddle.

Howard said, "Well, the only reason I ask about your business is because I think you might be some kind of an outlaw. Ought to warn me if you are."

Longarm said in amazement, "What in the world would make you think that?"

"Well, the way you wear your sidearm, for one thing. Like a gunslinger."

Longarm just shook his head. "Son, how long have you been off a sugar tit? You go to talking like that in Laredo and they'll throw you in the Rio Grande River—wearing your hands tied behind you."

"Aww, I think you are just trying to treat me like a greenhorn. Well, I'm not as green as you think. I said I can handle myself and I can. And I don't think this Laredo is as tough as you make out. I think you're just trying to scare me."

Longarm sighed. "I give up."

A little after one o'clock Longarm got up and got a sack of food out of his saddlebags. He'd had them put up the food for him at the hotel in San Antonio. He'd pretty well figured there were damn few stops between San Antone and Laredo,

and none where there'd be time to get off and eat. The grub
was wrapped in oilskin paper, and he took a canteen off his
saddlehorn, squatted down in the middle of the car, and opened
out the paper. The hotel had given him plenty of sliced roast
beef and some cheese and biscuits. He invited Willis Howard to
join in. The young man came over and sat cross-legged on the
floor and began helping himself. While Longarm was making
himself a biscuit sandwich out of beef and cheese Howard said,
"They didn't give you no bread? No pickles or condiments?"

Longarm just stared at him. Finally he said, "Boy, I bet you
bitch when new boots creak."

Howard was busy eating but he managed to say, "I certainly
do. I've always had my boots hand-fitted from worked leather.
They better not be stiff or creak."

Leaning out the cattle car door, Longarm guessed Laredo to be
a town of some eight or ten thousand souls, though he privately
doubted that many of those souls were headed upward. But
Laredo was the kind of town that was hard to judge as to
actual size because it was so transient, with people passing
in and out at a prodigious rate. At any time there might be
twelve thousand people in the city, but only about eight thousand
of those might lay their heads down that night in their own
beds. And of course, it was impossible to separate it from
its counterpart, Nuevo Laredo, which was just the width of
the Rio Grande away. During the dry season, that sometimes
wasn't much more than a couple of hundred yards, and then
it was so shallow a man could wade across without getting his
pockets wet. The Mexican town, if anything, was bigger than
Laredo. Officially, the only way you were supposed to go over
there, especially if you were transporting goods, was across the
International Bridge, which had officials on both sides. But
everybody knew there was considerable commerce that went on
between the two towns, and the two countries, without taking
the trouble to bother with the officials at the bridge.

When the train was in the station, a couple of crewmen came
with a wooden ramp and set it up against the door of Longarm's
car so that he could lead the dun out. Once on the ground he put
the bits back in the horse's mouth, tightened the bridle, untied
the stirrups from the saddlehorn, and swung aboard. Howard
followed, carrying his valise. He looked up at Longarm. "Where
you figure to stay?"

Longarm shrugged. "Don't know. Best place I can find. Used to be a hotel here called the Hamilton, right off the plaza. If it's still there reckon I'll bunk with them. You take it easy now, Willis."

And then he touched spurs to his horse and trotted away. He couldn't, for the life of him, see how he could make any possible use of the young man, and he damn sure didn't want him around for the pleasure of his company.

The Hamilton was a large, old-fashioned Spanish-style hotel built out of plastered adobe bricks. It was easy to spot because it was right off the tree-shaded central plaza and was three stories tall. Longarm dismounted in front, took his bedroll in his arms, careful to not expose the rifle he had hidden inside, and slung his saddlebags over his shoulder. He gave the reins of the dun to a boy who had come from the stables around back, and stepped up on the big, wide porch of the hotel. Inside it was cool and dark, and the lobby was huge, with large wooden, old-fashioned Spanish furniture. He went to the desk and registered under the name of C. Long, figuring that was safe enough. The room was two dollars a night, which he thought a little high, but then the Austin district would be funding this venture and that was their lookout. Carrying his bedroll and saddlebags, he took the tile stairs to the second floor, found his room, and let himself in with the key the desk clerk had given him. The room was big enough and the bed looked like it would do. Except for the fact that the room was larger and the walls were masonry, it looked like a thousand other hotel rooms he'd seen in his time.

He dropped his gear. He did the first thing he always did when he went into a room he was going to be in for a while—looked for another way out besides the door. The hotel was built in a U shape, around a courtyard. His room was on the inside, and the two windows he had both opened out onto the courtyard. He raised one and looked down. There was no drainpipe or anything else handy to slide down; the floor of the courtyard was tiled, which would make for a pretty hard landing. The only promising feature he saw was a little clump of huisache trees right below him. If he had to jump they'd probably cushion his fall enough where he wouldn't break anything, but he'd almost certainly need a new suit of clothes because huisache trees were mostly thorns. Still, it was a way out. He always preferred to stay in an upper-story room because it made it that much harder for somebody to slip inside through the window. Unless he was

41

nearly forced to it, he'd never stay in a ground-floor room in what he considered hostile territory—which was generally anywhere he went outside of Denver.

He got the bottle of whiskey out of his saddlebags, got a glass off the washstand, and poured himself out a good measure, then lit a cheroot and sat down on the side of the bed to do a little thinking.

Billy Vail had finally shuffled around in his papers and found the telegram from the chief marshal in Austin. The sheriff's name for Webb County, of which Laredo was the county seat, was Bob Bird. The name had been troubling Longarm ever since Billy Vail had given it to him. He remembered the name from someplace, but couldn't quite get a handle on it. He knew he wasn't mixing the name up with someone else's because it was an unusual name, unusual enough to have stuck in his mind for some time. He didn't think he'd met this Bob Bird, but he figured he'd heard of him. He didn't know which side of the law he'd heard of him being on. But he had a hunch, and nothing more, that he associated the man with having spent more time on the wrong side of a tin star than the other way around.

For a long time he sat there studying over matters, trying to think of just what kind of approach to take. He expected the best thing to do was to go to hanging around the saloons, listening and asking a few casual questions. One thing that had surprised him was the news that Bird had twelve deputies, which was an astounding number for a county no bigger than Webb, especially since most of the population lived in Laredo. As a matter of fact, try as he would, he couldn't even think of another town in the county outside of Laredo, and he'd studied a map before he'd left Denver. True, the map was old and not very detailed, but it would have had to have shown a few other towns even if they were just villages.

But of course, there wasn't much to recommend that part of the border as a place to farm or ranch. The land was barren and arid, and what grass there was was nearly all down near the river. It was a country that grew a fine crop of dust and rocks and cactus and every thorn-bearing plant known to man, but there wasn't a hell of a lot of money in such produce. Laredo existed for one reason and one reason only; it was a fine place for an outlaw to make his home because it wasn't but a short hop into Mexico. It was said you could find anything you wanted in Laredo so long as it was illegal.

After a while he got up, put on his hat, and sauntered out of the hotel to go and have a look at the town, see if it had changed much since his last visit.

He first walked down to have a look at the bridge across the Rio Grande, which wasn't but a couple of blocks away. The International Bridge was a large, grand affair made out of concrete and iron and steel and floored with heavy planks. It was wide enough to drive a small herd of cattle across— which, Longarm knew, had been done more than once in the past, mostly without bothering to hold the Mexican cattle in quarantine. Such practices had gone a long way to killing a lot of Texas livestock with Mexican tick fever, which the Mexican cattle were virtually immune to.

He stood on the bank of the brown, slow-moving Rio Grande River and watched the traffic on the bridge. It was a busy place, with horsemen and wagons and pedestrians passing back and forth in a pretty steady stream. He could see the customs inspectors on the U.S. side checking the contents of wagons and buggies and saddlebags, but he doubted if the officials on the Mexican side were quite as dilligent. The *mordida,* the bite or bribe, was a way of life in Mexico, and Longarm reckoned you could smuggle the city of Chicago past the Mexican officials if you paid the right man enough.

But that wasn't his concern. His concern was what was happening on the U.S. side, and specifically what were the activities of two lawmen. He turned from the river and started back toward the center of town, most of which was built around the huge central plaza. There were businesses, saloons, whorehouses, and card houses on other streets back farther from the river, but the better places were going to be found fronting on the plaza.

The first saloon he stopped in was the Silver Dollar, which proudly announced on the sign, under its name: "Coldest Beer in Town." If that was so, then Laredo had managed to get an ice plant since he'd been there some four or five years past.

He stepped through the batwing doors of the saloon, and paused to let his eyes adjust from the light change. It was filled, he could see in one sweep of the room, with the usual run of toughs and ne'er-do-wells and gamblers that he'd expected to find. To a man they glanced up as he came in, even those involved in a poker game. They looked first at his face to see if he might be anyone they didn't want to see, and next at the way his gun rig was set up to see if appeared he knew how to use it. He never wore his holster especially low, but he was wearing a cutaway scabbard which made drawing an awful lot easier. It was a rig he only wore when he was walking around town. His other holster held his revolver much more securely and kept the gun from dropping out when he was riding.

He stepped up to the bar and asked for brandy. He was a little surprised when the bartender poured him a shot of Fundador, which was a good Spanish cognac. After good corn whiskey he preferred brandy, but he hadn't expected to get such a good brand. Then he took a taste, and realized the only Fundador was on the label of the bottle. The contents were a cheap, rotgut Mexican imitation of brandy, tasting more like rum than the smooth liquid his mouth had been expecting. He reckoned there was a bad hangover in every bottle. What they were doing, of course, was no new trick. They probably had a couple of barrels of the Mexican imitation in the back, and they just kept filling up the Fundador bottles, charging good liquor prices for popskull. If he hadn't been on a job Longarm would have called the bartender's hand on it, but he didn't want to call attention to himself, not just yet, and not in such a way.

The man standing next to him looked over, nodding at Longarm's glass. "What they don't sell to the customers they use to slick up the floors after the place closes."

Longarm glanced down at the scuffed-up floor. "Then they ought to have the cleanest floors in town. I believe this stuff is making my teeth loose."

The man laughed. "After the second one you won't notice a thing. The third one will even start to taste good. You ain't a poker player, are you?"

Longarm glanced at the man. He was a slim, even-faced man in his thirties wearing a narrow-brimmed hat and a cotton jacket. Longarm couldn't see if he was wearing a gun. He glanced at the man's hands. They were soft and looked well cared for. He noticed that the nails were trimmed evenly, except that the nail on the man's right forefinger was a little longer than the rest. It made an ideal tool to lightly crimp a card on the side so it could be felt in a deck when the man picked up the cards to deal. Longarm said, "I play, but not right now."

The man said, "They's four of us standing here at the bar looking to get up a game. Need one more. Four-handed poker ain't much good."

"Can't build a pot," Longarm said automatically. But his eyes were going down the line of men the man had indicated. They weren't the same size or build, but they looked to be just like the man with the long fingernail.

The man said, "Squarest game in town. Won't find no more squarer game you look all over town. You're a stranger, I take it?"

"Sort of," Longarm said. He smiled slightly. "Well, when I'm ready I'll sure look ya'll up. Though I heard all the games were square in Laredo."

The man started to say something, but Longarm pushed away from the bar, leaving his drink unfinished, and with an over-the-shoulder wave passed on out into the street.

He wanted to laugh. Lord, he thought, he must look like he just rode into town on a jackass. It was good, though, that he looked that green. Or maybe such types as the man with the long fingernail just hit up everyone in hopes of eventually striking gold. Willis Howard, Longarm thought, was going to have more competition than he'd reckoned on.

He continued on around the plaza, stopping in at likely-looking spots. After the second saloon tried to serve him some more of the same paint thinner, he'd switched to beer. It was colder than the ninety-degree heat outside, but not much.

As the afternoon turned into evening he gradually worked his way around the plaza, hitting nearly every saloon and card house. He didn't find out much except what he already knew, that if there were any outstanding citizens in Laredo they were either at home or out of town. But he also noticed another peculiarity that made him curious. In his long walk he didn't see a single tin star, not on the streets, not in the saloons, and not in the card houses. He found that more than a little unusual. Most towns that held a healthy element of the kind of rough trade that Laredo was full of generally kept a lawman circulating through the places where there was likely to be trouble. The town marshal in San Antonio had been a good example. The presence of a badge in such places could head off more trouble than it could stop once it got started. Longarm didn't know where those twelve deputies Bob Bird was supposed to have were keeping themselves, but they weren't where Longarm would have put them if he'd been sheriff. It might be thought that they only appeared at night, but Laredo was a twenty-four hour town, and you could have trouble in the middle of the afternoon just as

45

easy as you could at midnight. It made Longarm wonder if they might not be elsewhere, tending to the sheriff's business—say, patrolling the river to keep any would-be free-lance gunrunners from interfering with the main traffic that the sheriff was supposed to be routing. It was just a thought, but one that could stand a little more cogitating. The only way to get guns across the river in bulk was over the bridge, and the sheriff controlled that. But a few parties might try to raft over twenty or thirty or some such sum, and that would cut into the sheriff's profits, especially if it became a common practice. But a dozen deputies patrolling ten or fifteen miles in either direction could be a big discouragement to those woeful lawbreakers who were trying to dig into the sheriff's pocket.

He was still thinking about that when he went up the steps to the hotel. It was after six o'clock, and time to see what the dining room had to offer. He was wanting a steak with some vegetables, but he was hungry enough that he'd eat whatever they had.

It was a big room with maybe twenty tables, half of which were occupied. The waiters all wore white starched jackets to show this was a high-class place. Longarm found a table by the back wall and picked up the menu, glad to see that it featured steak as well as roast. What he wanted was a steak the size of a roast. The waiter came over, and Longarm was just about to order when a voice said, "You mind if I sit down?"

Longarm looked up. It was Willis Howard. He sighed and said, "No." But he didn't mean it. He wondered if he was going to have to get mean and rude to this kid to keep him from tagging along.

Willis said, after he'd sat down across from Longarm, "I see you been getting around town pretty quick."

Longarm glanced at him. "How do you know that?"

Willis said, "Because I've been watching you."

Chapter 4

Longarm stared Willis in the face for a long moment. The young man finally started to look uncomfortable, and said, "What the hell you looking at me like that for?"

Longarm said, "I was just trying to figure out how you've managed to not get your nose chopped off if you stick it in other people's business like you've been doing to mine."

Howard looked affronted. "I haven't been sticking my nose in your business."

"Oh, you haven't? Then what . . ." He stopped, and looked up at the waiter waiting to take his order. He asked for the biggest steak they had, along with potatoes and whatever vegetables could be had. When Longarm was finished, Howard told the waiter he'd have the same.

When the waiter left, Longarm said, "If you don't call watching me sticking your nose in my business, what would you call it?"

Howard said, "Good sense." He leaned forward. "I've known from the first that you've had some kind of plan in coming to Laredo. I don't know exactly what your game is, but I'm willing to bet it'll be a profitable one. You don't strike me as the kind of man goes in for chicken feed. So I've been watching you, trying to figure out what you're up to."

"And what'd you see?"

"You went in a lot of saloons."

"How you know I wasn't looking for a poker game?"

"Because you never took a hand. Just went up to the bar in every joint and looked the place over for one drink and then left. And they was all-price games going on."

"How you know I wasn't looking for someone?"

"You might have been," Howard said. "I figured you maybe already had a man down here doing the spadework. But you didn't see him."

Longarm just shook his head in amazement. "Boy, you are some piece of work. I figure you won't last another forty-eight hours in Laredo if you keep on like you've begun. I've quit killing small children so you are safe from me, but there is folks around here ain't quite so particular."

Howard said earnestly, "Look, I'd like to be in on whatever you got going. I know it's big enough for one more man. I can be of help to you. I ain't got no money to put up, but I could be mighty useful in a lot of ways."

Longarm said, "How?"

Howard looked vague. "I don't know. Nosing around, making contacts for you."

"You speak Spanish?"

Howard frowned slightly. "Well, not exactly."

"What's not exactly?"

Howard looked uncomfortable. "Well, I don't speak none to talk about. From that, I figure your business must involve Mexico. Hell, it would have to. This is the border."

The food came and Longarm began eating. And one of his rules when he was very hungry was that he'd rather eat than talk. He explained this to Howard in a very few words, and then picked up his knife and fork and went to work on a steak that nearly covered the whole platter. Besides the steak he had boiled potatoes and beans and sliced tomatoes. He finished up with coffee and a piece of apple pie. As fast as Longarm ate, though, Howard finished before him, because the young man only picked at his food.

While he was finishing his pie and coffee Longarm called the waiter over and paid his score. Howard asked if he'd paid his also. Longarm said, "No. Should I have?"

Howard said, "I just thought, since I was going to be helping you . . . I *am* going to be helping you, ain't I?"

Longarm laughed and stood up. He put on his hat. While he'd been eating he'd been giving the matter some thought. Maybe it wouldn't be such a bad idea to have the kid bird-dogging for him. Innocent as the kid looked, he might just stumble across something. He said, "Ask around and see if anybody is interested in some used army equipment."

Howard looked blank. "Used army equipment? What the hell is that?"

"Well, it damn sure ain't knapsacks or parade hats."

Howard stared at him for a minute. "You don't mean like cannon or some such? Or saddles? Horses?"

Longarm just shook his head. He took a toothpick off the table and stuck it in his mouth. "What do you think of when you think of the army?"

"Guns?"

Longarm started walking away. "Just ask around."

Howard said, "Wait a minute. You ain't told me nothin' yet. We ain't talked no business. What's my cut?"

Longarm stopped and pointed back at him. "Your cut is getting your head blown off if I see you following me again. I better not look over my shoulder and catch sight of a single hair on your head. Understand?"

He walked out into the night and headed for the biggest of the saloons, planning on playing some poker and casually asking a few questions. He found a big enough game, and passed the evening until midnight pleasantly enough, but his indirect questions about the law situation around Laredo went, for the most part, unanswered. Only one man made allusion to U.S. Deputy Marshal Les Older, and he just said, "Hear tell they is some kind 'o high-powered federal law come to town. Don't know nuthin' 'bout it, but the shur'ff's all right so long's you don't cross him. He's got some cussed mean depities, though. If you in the business of wantin' to git something acrost the river, it be best to steer clear of them."

But other than that, Longarm pretty well came up dry for the evening. He won twenty-five dollars in the poker game, but that was the only profit he could show. Lying in bed that night, he calculated he'd been on the job for five or six days and had yet to even catch sight of his quarry. Quite frankly, he was at a loss as to how to proceed. In the end it appeared he was simply going to have to march boldly into Bob Bird's office and declare himself a man with four or five hundred used cavalry rifles that he'd be willing to sell if they could be gotten into Mexico. The worst the sheriff could do would be to throw him in jail, if he was honest, which Longarm judged to be about as likely as finding whiskey in a water well. But he could throw him in jail if he wanted to appear honest, and that was a very real possibility.

Of course it wouldn't be too very much trouble to get himself out of jail. All he'd have to do would be to show his badge and have the sheriff wire Billy Vail. But then that would alert the deputy marshal from Austin and defeat the whole purpose of the venture. Yes, it was a quandary and no mistake. It had sounded so simple back in Denver. Go down to Laredo and catch a fellow deputy sticking his hand in the cookie jar. Except the crookedness wasn't right out in the open, and the only way Longarm was going to get in the kitchen, much less near the cookie jar, was to appear to be playing the same game. Now true, he did have Willis Howard out bird-dogging for him, but he put no more faith in that than a paper hat in the rain. He figured next day he'd saddle the dun, take a ride up and down the river in both directions from Laredo, and see what that turned up. The one thing he felt he had to do was take his time. Any federal officer worth his salt was going to be especially on his guard if he'd been up to some illegal activities, and the very person Older would be looking for was Longarm or someone just like him.

No, federal marshals didn't get to be federal marshals by being dumb. He had no reason to expect otherwise of this Les Older. He'd made it clear to Billy Vail when he'd left Denver that Billy shouldn't get to rushing his knitting so that he dropped a stitch if he didn't hear from him in what Billy thought was the right amount of time. Only the man on the scene could properly calculate the pace of the investigation. He went to sleep still hoping that there'd be nothing to investigate and he'd have had some paid time off. Though he was damned, given any sort of choice, that he'd have taken it in Laredo.

Next morning he had breakfast, and then got the hotel kitchen to pack him a lunch. He packed the lunch in his saddlebags, along with his .44-caliber Colt and a box of ammunition. He might not need to bust a cap the whole trip, but he'd run out of ammunition just once in his life, and he'd decided once was enough. He'd also changed his holster for the bigger one, which held a gun more securely.

Just before he left he was standing by the reception desk talking to the clerk. For as Mexican a town as Laredo there were a surprising number of hotel employees who were Anglo. The clerk was a middle-aged man with a shaggy mustache and a gossipy disposition. Longarm was taking time to sound him out about the countryside when a strikingly beautiful young woman came sweeping down the curved staircase, crossed the

50

lobby, and went out the hotel's front door. Even though she was surprisingly well turned out for such an early morning hour, Longarm could see though the thin muslin dress and all the petticoats and imagine the curves of the body inside. He said, "Whew!"

The desk clerk said, "That's Lieutenant Manly's wife. Poor lady."

Longarm looked at him. "Why poor lady? She looks to be all right."

"Yes, but the sheriff has got her husband in the pokey and he ain't likely to let him out until—" The desk clerk coughed. "Well, until he and the lady reach an agreement."

Longarm said, "You ain't talking about the kind of agreement I think you're talking about, are you?"

The desk clerk shrugged. "Depends on which way your mind runs, Mister Long. But I can guarantee you the agreement ain't about if she's willing to shoe his horse or clean his office. You got a look at her. What you reckon our good sheriff is after? And him with a fine-enough-looking wife ought to suit any man."

"What's the husband charged with? I mean, what's the sheriff holding him for?"

The desk clerk shrugged. "You mean besides having a wife that looks like that?" He turned his head and spit tobacco juice into a spittoon. He wiped his mustache with the back of his hand. "Oh, some sort of charge. Don't know that it makes much difference. Story I hear is that this Lieutenant Manly was supposed to be trying to smuggle official U.S. guns into Mexico, his sidearm and his carbine."

Longarm looked troubled. "Why doesn't his wife wire the military? This sheriff hasn't got any authority over an army officer."

The desk clerk said, "Lieutenant just retired. Or served out his hitch or resigned or something. Anyway, them was his guns. Officers has to buy they own guns. I know that much. He was supposed to be heading into Mexico to be a military advisor to either the main government or one of the rebel bunches. Hell, I can't keep up with it."

Longarm glanced toward the door. "So what's his wife doing?"

The desk clerk shrugged. "Not much she can do. She's been to see the mayor and the city council, but they don't give a good goddamn. Hell, everybody in this town is scairt of Bob Bird and

51

that army of deputies he's got. I reckon she spends most of her time begging the sheriff to let her husband go without paying the price he wants." He spit again. "Ain't going to do her no good. That sorry sonofabitch don't care how bad he hurts folks. Eventually she'll have to give in. She's been here at the hotel for about a week, and her money has to run out sometime."

Longarm said curiously, "You say everybody's scared of the sheriff. You don't seem to be."

The desk clerk laughed harshly. "The bastard is my brother-in-law. I wouldn't let it out except everybody already knows. Married to my sister, treats her like dirt. But I'm one of five brothers and Bird knows that if he messes with any of us, the rest of us will blow his goddamn head off and the consequences be damned."

Longarm said casually, "Did I see what I thought was a U.S. marshal around here the other day?"

The desk clerk's eyes went dead. He spit again. "I wouldn't know about that."

Longarm said, "I was just thinking. A U.S. marshal has got federal power anywhere. He could get that lady's husband out of jail."

The desk clerk said, "Like I told you, I wouldn't know nothing about any federal officers. We like to tend to our affairs ourselves. Keep them in the family."

"Can't beat that," Longarm said. "It was just a thought."

He went around to the stables and got his horse. The livery boy had him saddled and ready. Longarm flipped him a small coin, but he still checked the girth and the adjustment of the bridle. Then, once aboard, he pulled his Winchester Model 73 out of the boot, levered a cartridge into the chamber, and then put the hammer on safety by putting it on half-cock.

He rode north out of town and then turned west. There was no discernible road, but then none was needed since the country, except near the river, was as flat and featureless as a tabletop. Occasionally he'd send a lizard scurrying, or now and then a snake wiggling through the sand, but other than that, and the cactus and thorn bushes and greasewood and cedar, he and his horse appeared to be the only living objects on the dry plain. He put the dun in a slow lope, switching his head back and forth as he rode. It was hot, hot and still. Off to his left a scraggly line of willows and small oaks followed the line of the river, but other than a few clumps of stunted mesquite and post oak, there was no shade to speak of. "What a country," he said aloud. "If I owned Laredo and Hell, I'd rent them both out and balance on the head of a pin for eternity."

After half an hour he pulled the dun down to a slow walk to let him have a blow in the heat. He figured he'd covered about four miles and, except for a few burros and a few poor-looking cattle, he hadn't seen anything bigger than his shadow. He was beginning to doubt his theory about the deputies patrolling the river to keep individual gunrunners from going into business for themselves. But then he'd been riding at least a half mile away from the tree line that snaked along with the Rio Grande, and there could have been a half a dozen men hidden in the shade of the trees that he wouldn't have seen. Even deputies of Bob Bird probably had better sense than to just sit out on the scorching plain when there was shade to be had.

Still, he hesitated about making directly for the trees. He had an idea that the kind of deputies that Bob Bird hired hadn't been on the right side of the badge very long, and were just as likely to shoot anything that moved as not. Riding blindly into the trees and surprising one of them might be a quick way to get fatally wounded. He figured the best idea would be to ride on a few miles farther and then, coming back, cut in nearer the tree line. That way, if there were so-called lawmen lurking in the bushes, they'd have at least gotten a sight of him before and wouldn't be startled.

He put the dun back into a slow lope, and continued on for what he reckoned to be another half an hour. As he rode he came to the conclusion that if nothing else good came out of this job, he'd at least picked up a good horse. He was liking the dun more and more every time he stepped aboard the gelding. He was responsive, alert without being snorty, and quick to the rein, and appeared to have both speed and endurance. On top of that, all of his gaits were smooth. Longarm didn't necessarily need smoothness in a horse, because he'd been born with what was called a good "seat," but it was a pleasure to be able to relax on a new animal and not get any unpleasant surprises.

A bit farther on he decided he'd come far enough from town. From all appearances his theory about the deputies had been shot to hell. He wheeled the dun left and cut down toward the tree line, aiming to ride along just in what little of its shade he could find. He figured the dun was about due a drink, and soon he would stop and have himself a bite of lunch. He was perhaps fifteen yards from the trees when a horseman suddenly burst into the clear, reining his horse to a jolting stop and pointing a double-barreled shotgun at Longarm. By the time they both got their mounts stopped only about five yards separated them. The man said, "Hold it right there, *hombre*! And be damn careful with yore hands!"

The man was roughly dressed, wearing a slouch hat, worn jeans, and a short leather jacket. But there was nothing shabby about the shotgun; it gleamed blue with good care. Longarm didn't see a badge on the man's chest, but he guessed he was a deputy in spite of his scraggly looks. He doubted seriously that Bob Bird recruited his help from the upper crust of society.

The man said, "Git yore hands up!"

Longarm said, "This is a new horse. I ain't sure he'll stand if I let go of the reins."

"Then keep both yore goddamn hands on yore saddlehorn. An' don't you flinch, *hombre,* er I'll take the biggest part o' yore head off with this scattergun."

Longarm said, "You robbing me?"

The man said, "I'll be astin' the questions. What the hell you doin' here?"

"Just riding," Longarm said. He was watching the man closely, trying to catch sight of a badge underneath the short jacket. It was the kind of a jacket that *vaqueros,* Mexican cowboys, used in the thorny brush of the border country to keep from getting their shirts torn off their backs.

The man said, "In this heat? What do you take me for, a damn fool? Er are you a-tryin' to kill yore horse?"

Longarm said mildly, "I said I was just riding, looking the country over."

The man jeered at him. "You some kind of idjit? Who'd ride fer pleasure to look over this here country? No, I reckon you was doin' a little scoutin' around. Ain't that about the size of it?"

"Look here, who the hell are you pointing that shotgun at me? What business is it of yours what I'm doing?"

"You never mind about my bid'ness. You rode outten Laredo, din't you?"

Longarm nodded. "Yes, if it's any of your business. You planning on robbing me? If you are you ain't gonna get much."

"I kin see that," the man said. He gestured with his shotgun. "That's a good-lookin' horse. Where'd you steal 'im?"

Longarm was starting to get angry. He knew this was a crooked lawman, and he knew his job was to get information off the man, not make him mad, but he couldn't help himself. He'd been playing docile just about as long as he figured he could stand it. He said, "Goddammit, I bought this horse. And I got the bill of sale back at the hotel to prove it."

"Shit!" the man said. "Bum like you buyin' a two-hunnert-dollar horse. Don't make me laugh."

Longarm hadn't shaved in three days, nor had he changed his clothes since he'd left San Antonio. He'd figured the best idea was to fit in as best he could with the grubby border hardcases. But for a man who took pride in his appearance, it had not been a pleasant experience. He said, "Look here, what right you got to ask me these questions?"

"This right," the man said. He raised the shotgun slightly. "You want to argue with it?"

Longarm just stared back at the man. Underneath him the dun shifted restlessly. The noon sun was beating down fiercer than ever. He said, "Are you the law?"

The man said, "I'm any goddamn thang I want to be. What hotel you claim to be stayin' at? Where you got this here bill o' sale?"

"The Hamilton."

The man laughed outright. "Yeah, an' I bet they give you the best room in the house. They wouldn't even let you *in* the Hamilton Hotel, much less rent you a room. You stole that horse an' I kind of like him." He motioned with the shot-gun. "How about it if you just step off him and get down on the ground. Jest git down off that horse an' lay on yore face in the dirt. I'll take that horse and find out who he belongs to."

Longarm said, "Goddammit, I told you I bought this horse! If you're law, show me a badge."

The man let his horse came a step closer to Longarm. Very little distance separated them. The man said menacingly, "I done tol' you fer the last time to git offen that horse!"

Longarm said, "If you're law you'll go back to town with me and I'll show you the bill of sale."

For answer the man slowly pulled the hammers back on the double-barreled shotgun, using his thumb to cock them one at a time. They made an ominous sound in the quiet of the dry plain. Each one went *clitch-clack.*

Longarm put his hands halfway in the air, his arms raised only slightly so that his right hand was not quite to his shoulder. He said, "All right! All right! I'm getting down. Take them hammers off cock!"

The man said, "I'm a-gonna count to three. An' you better figger I ain't real good at countin'."

Longarm shifted his weight to the left stirrup and began to raise his right leg. He held the saddlehorn with his left hand as his right leg came almost horizontal to the ground and his body tilted to the left. The position he'd started in, with his right hand just below his shoulder, made the draw almost automatic. With no perceptible movement that the man could see Longarm drew his revolver and, still hiding the gun with his body, fired under his left arm. The slug took the man square in the breastbone. Even over the roar of his revolver Longarm could almost hear the solid thunk as the slug hit. He turned his head in time to see the heavy bullet virtually flip the man backwards off his horse. The shotgun seemed to fire of its own volition as the man went down, both barrels scattering shot harmlessly toward the sky.

Longarm stepped to the ground. The dun had trembled at the gunfire, but he stood his ground.

The man's horse had run off at the shooting, and was standing thirty yards away, fitfully cropping at the grass, such as it was. Longarm walked carefully over to the man, his revolver at the ready. It was an unnecessary precaution. Two yards away it was clear the man had pointed his shotgun for the last time. Longarm holstered his revolver and then looked carefully around. He didn't know how far apart Bird stationed his deputies, if indeed he did so, but sound would carry a long way in the dry air, and he didn't want to be caught unawares by another rider suddenly bursting out of the trees.

No one was in sight. He leaned over and pulled back the man's jacket. There was no tin star, but the man's shirt's left pocket was buttoned and there was something inside. Longarm undid the button, reached inside, and came out with a deputy sheriff's badge. It was clear the man was a peace officer when it suited his purposes, and wasn't when he was working the other side of the law. He slipped the badge back in the man's pocket and buttoned the flap. Then he straightened up and looked around again. There was still no sign that anyone had heard the shots. But he thoughtfully walked back to his horse and exchanged the revolver he'd fired the shot with for the one in his saddlebags that hadn't been fired. It was a minor precaution, but Longarm wasn't one to take chances that didn't need taking.

For a moment he stood thinking as to just how he wanted to handle the matter. He could get on his horse, ride away, and act like he'd had no part in the incident. More than likely he'd be successful with such a maneuver. But there was a chance, small though it might be, that there was another deputy lurking just inside the tree line waiting to see what he was going to do.

He decided to tend to his horse and eat some lunch. He mounted, caught up the reins of the deputy's horse, and rode down to the river's bank. While the horses drank, he rummaged around in one side of his saddlebags and found the lunch the hotel had put up for him. It was nothing but flour tortillas and dried beef, but he made a good meal out of it and washed it down with water from his canteen. He figured he'd have to be mighty thirsty to drink out of the Rio Grande. He figured more bodies had floated down the river than any other stretch of water in these United States.

As he ate, he realized that the smart idea would be to take the body back into town. He felt almost certain no one had seen him shoot the deputy. If an ordinary citizen had seen him they'd most likely keep their mouth shut, and even if they didn't, it would be his word against theirs. Bringing the body in would look proper for his story that he'd just happened upon the dead man and had done his duty as he saw it.

And he had to figure that if another deputy had seen him he'd already be under arrest. He'd been standing by the river for upward of ten minutes. That was plenty of time for any law, no matter how clumsy or timid, to have gotten in behind him and put a gun to his back.

But the main argument for taking the dead deputy in was that it would give him a chance to meet Bob Bird. There was a chance that Bird might try and give him a hard time or accuse him of the killing, but he felt pretty confident of getting out of any such situation. So far as he could see it, the pluses of the situation far outweighed the minuses. There was another plus. He'd at least reduced the odds against him by one. They'd been fourteen to one against before the deputy had got too pushy. Now they were down to thirteen to one.

He mounted his dun, took the deputy's horse on lead, and rode back to where the man lay. He dismounted, leaving the dun several yards away, and led the deputy's horse toward the body. For a few minutes he let the horse smell around the dead man. The smell of blood spooked some horses, and he didn't want to be in the midst of loading the body when the horse decided to get the jitters.

After he felt sure the animal was calm enough to handle the chore, Longarm dropped the horse's reins to the ground and planted one boot firmly on them, then got the deputy under the shoulders, and lifted and worked him until he had him lying sideways across the saddle. Longarm was sweating hard by the time he had the body placed just so. The man wasn't especially big and Longarm was strong, but deadweight always seemed to weigh about twice what it ought to. Longarm had handled a lot of dead bodies in his time, and they always seemed to be uncommonly heavy.

After he had the body in place, he took the man's own lariat and trussed the body tightly in place so that it wouldn't slip or slide around or fall off.

After that he looked the ground over carefully. There were enough horses' hoofprints, as well as prints of some cattle, to make it impossible for anyone to read off the ground exactly what had happened. Neither his horse nor the deputy's horse left any distinct prints. There would be no way to say that a third man had not been there, or even a fourth or fifth.

When he was sure he wasn't forgetting anything important he mounted up, took the deputy's horse on lead, and started for town.

He was about three miles from Laredo, riding about a quarter of a mile away from the river, when he saw a rider suddenly come charging out of the tree line, bearing down on him at a hard gallop. Even at the distance he could see the man was carrying a carbine sideways across his lap. The man was wearing a red and white checkered shirt and a red bandana. When he got within hailing distance he hollered, "You thar! Hold up!"

Longarm reined his horse in and stopped, waiting for the man to approach. He had no doubt it was another one of Bird's deputies. The man jerked his horse to a skidding halt until only ten yards separated him from Longarm. The horse came on, sawing his head against the bridle and dancing sideways. When the man finally got the animal under control he was almost right next to Longarm. Longarm could see the deputy's tin star worn in plain sight. Obviously this one didn't work both sides of the river. He also noticed how young the man was, younger-looking even than Willis Howard, though this young man was blond where Willis was dark. He said, holding his rifle but not pointing it at Longarm, "Who you be an' what you got thar?"

The dead deputy and his horse were on Longarm's off side, away from the young deputy. Longarm gave the horse and its cargo a glance. He said, "Name's Long. I found this man laying on the ground about six miles back. Appears to have been shot. I'm carrying him into Laredo to the sheriff."

"Wa'l, who is it? You know the man?"

Longarm shook his head. "No. I'm a stranger in these parts."

The deputy dismounted. "You jest hold it right there. I'm a deppity shu'rrf an' it's my bid'ness to look into these matters."

Longarm watched while he walked around the two horses and took the dead man by the hair and raised his head. His mouth dropped open. "Gawd A'mighty damn! This here is Lester Priddy! Hell, he's a deppity shu'rrf his ownself!"

Longarm said, "Ain't no more."

The deputy looked up, his eyes wild. "You watch yore mouth, feller."

Longarm thought idly about the advantages of dropping the odds down to twelve to one, but decided two dead deputies in the same day might be stretching matters. He said, "He ain't got no badge on. Least he didn't when I found him."

The deputy in the red bandana raised up the body of the late Lester Priddy and rummaged around under the dead man's jacket. In a moment he came out with the tin star. He held it up. "What'n hell you be callin' this?"

Longarm said, "I be calling that what he wasn't wearing when I found him. Where'd you find it?"

The blond man looked slightly sulky. "Was in his pocket." Then he flared up again. "But that ain't none o' yore concern. Now then, what be yore name?"

"Long."

"Whar you from?"

"Around. Right now I'm staying over in Laredo."

"Wa'l now, you jest tell me how you come to have a hand in this business."

"I found the man. That's all. I didn't figure to let him lay out in the sun and rot, so I tied him on his horse and figured to take him on into town to the sheriff. Then I met you. That's all I know."

"You jest come along an' there ol' Lester was layin' in the dust?"

"No, it wasn't exactly like that. I'd been out riding. All morning, as a matter of fact. Near about noon I turned my horse down toward the river to water him and get myself a bite of lunch. I had settled down and had finished eating, and was laying back with my hat over my face, kind of dozing, when I heard what I took to be shotgun blasts. Went off loud so I knew they was close. Well, that got me sittin' up and looking around. Then I heard another shot. Just one. Sounded like a pistol to me."

"Then what'd you do?"

"Well, I didn't do nothing right away. I got in behind a tree and tried to see in the direction of the shots, but there were too many trees in the way. So I just sat there."

The young deputy looked angrier than ever. "Goddamn coward. An' ol' Lester probably layin' out thar bleedin' to death. You might have saved him if you'd of got off yore dead ass an' done a little somethin'."

Longarm said, almost wanting to smile, "And I might have got shot also."

"You say you hear'd two shotgun blasts? Lester carried a scattergun."

Longarm pointed. "It's in the gun boot. I found it right beside him. Both barrels had been fired."

The deputy walked around Longarm's horse and got on his jittery mount. He still looked like a man hunting for someone to take his mad out on. He contented himself with raising his rifle in Longarm's general direction. "By Gawd, we goin' in and show the shu'rrf this sorry bid'ness. An' you better not try nuthin' neither, er you'll be upside down on yore horse, by Gawd."

Longarm said, as seriously as he could, "I was trying to help. I'm still trying to help. But I wish you'd quit waving that rifle around at me. It frightens me."

The young deputy said, "Wa'l, you jest see you tend to yore p's and q's. You jest lead on off. An' don't fergit I'm right behind you with this here cannon o' mine."

"Yes, sir," Longarm said.

Chapter 5

Sheriff Bob Bird said, "Now you be a-tellin' us that you was jest out riding 'long near the river when you hear'd these shots an' come out and found my deputy dead?"

Longarm said, "That's right."

The sheriff said, "You was just ridin', lookin' at the country. That right, Mister . . . uh . . . ?"

"Long."

"Mister Long. You tellin' us you rode ten miles west of town to take a look at country that looks the same if you be one mile out of town er a hunnert?"

"But I didn't know that," Longarm said. "I told you I'm a stranger here."

"Uh-huh," the sheriff said, fixing Longarm with a doubting eye.

They were in the jailhouse, in the sheriff's office. The sheriff had the biggest lawman's office Longarm had ever seen, at least outside of a big city. The jailhouse itself was two stories, and half the first floor was given over to desks and chairs and benches for the deputies' use and for whoever else might have business at the jail. The sheriff himself had a walled-in office over in one corner that was the size of an average parlor. Because two of its walls were glass, it reminded Longarm of the office of the president of a bank, one where the president could see that none of his hired hands got careless with the bank's money. He figured it was the same way for Bob Bird; he could sit in his office and look out and make sure that none of his hands got careless about anything, especially dangerous prisoners.

Bob Bird was about the primmest and neatest thing Longarm had seen in the dusty, dirty border town. He wasn't much over five feet tall, and was lean as beef jerky. Even in the heat, he was wearing a white shirt with starched collar and cuffs and a string tie, and had on a lightweight frock coat. If Longarm hadn't known better he'd have sworn the man was wearing a bowler, a hat he'd only seen in some big cities in the East. But closer inspection showed it to be a round-crowned, narrow-brimmed black hat with a lighter silk ribbon around the brim of the hat and a silk hatband. Just looking at him, Longarm decided he was not a man to be taken lightly. Any man mean enough or tough enough to walk around a town like Laredo dressed like that would have to be reckoned with.

On top of everything else he had a neat little pencil-thin mustache that came straight across his upper lip.

Bird said, "An' you say you had no business other than riding up the river to look at the country. What was you looking to find?"

Longarm shrugged. He was playing evasive, hoping the sheriff would turn out to be smarter than he looked. He wanted him to figure out that he'd been searching the river, looking for a good place to, say, cross a couple of wagonloads of guns. But he didn't want to give him any help. He wanted to hear Bird say that he didn't allow any free-lance gunrunning, that any gunrunning that got done got done through the sheriff's office.

But he had to let the sheriff bring it up because he wasn't supposed to know the sheriff was crooked. Over in the corner the young, blond deputy, who Longarm had found out was named Billy Wayne Pilgrim, was sitting in a straight-backed wooden chair he had tilted back against the wall. He had his hat shoved forward so his eyes weren't quite visible. Longarm had decided the boy did that because it made him look like a man you didn't know for sure whether or not you ought to fool with or get too loose around. He had tried to slyly question Longarm on the way back to town, asking him virtually the same questions over and over.

Sheriff Bird said, "What's yore line of business, Mister Long?"

He said, "Oh, I'm kind of a trading man."

"What do you trade?"

Longarm shrugged. "This and that."

The sheriff studied Longarm for a moment. Bob Bird had washed-out, pale-looking blue eyes. Longarm had seen those kind of eyes before. They usually went with a man who'd long ago lost whatever good he'd ever had in him. Longarm thought of them as killer's eyes. Behind them you generally found a brain that was pickled in greed.

Bird said, "What would be a tradin' man's interest in the countryside, Mister Long? That'd be the business of a farmer or a man with cattle, wouldn't it?"

Longarm said casually, "Oh, I like to know pretty well where I am. Same reason a man will look to see where the back door is when he goes in a house." He threw that out as bait, wondering if it would encourage Bird to bite.

Bird said, "You do that, Long? Check for a back door when you go in a house?"

"Don't most folks?"

Bird said, "Not no honest folks that I know of."

Longarm said comfortably, "Just a habit, I reckon."

Bird said, "You mind if I examine your sidearm, Mister Long?"

"Not at all," Longarm said. He pulled out the revolver with the nine-inch barrel and handed it across.

From the corner Billy Wayne said, "It ain't been fahred, Shu'rff. I smelt it nearly right soon as I come up on this feller."

Bird turned a cold stare on his deputy, and the young man fell silent. Bird continued to look at him until Billy Wayne brought the front legs of his chair to the floor with a thump. He straightened up, looking uncomfortable, looking like he wished he'd never called attention to himself.

Bird turned his eyes back to the desk. He took the revolver from Longarm's hand. If he'd been going to smell the barrel, the intrusion from Billy Wayne now kept him from doing so. Instead he flipped open the gate to the cylinder and spun the cylinder. "I see you carry six cartridges to the cylinder, Mister Long. Ain't that a little dangerous? Ain't you a little scairt of shooting yore leg off?"

Longarm said, "Colt just come out with a modification on that model. It's got a floating firing pin, as they call it, so it won't accidentally set off a cartridge in your holster. Takes the full force of the hammer at full cock."

Bird said, "Now ain't that innerestin'. Though it seems that a new idea like that would be of more interest to a lawman than a man like you." He eyed Longarm. "Or a man on the other side of the law."

Longarm said, "Army's got 'em. The cavalry at least. Fact is I traded for that gun."

Bird hunched over his desk, coming closer to Longarm. "You trade in guns, do you, Mister Long?"

Longarm said, nodding at his revolver, which Bird had put on the desk in front of him, "I traded for that one."

Bird said, "Well, suppose you tell me all about it once more. 'Bout how you rode clean out there in the middle of nowhere to have you some lunch down by the river."

For what he reckoned to be the fourth or fifth time Longarm told the story he'd invented. He finished by saying, "And I would reckon it was at least five minutes or better before I came out of the tree line after I heard the shots."

"You ain't a very curious man."

Longarm said, "I've found tending to my own business is a much healthier way to get by."

"An' you didn't see no rider or riders taking off? Even in the distance? That land out there is flat as the top of this table. You can see for miles. How far can a man get in five minutes?"

Longarm said gently, "They could have ducked into the tree line and been out of sight in seconds. Or they could have ridden upstream and crossed the river."

"So you jest laid in the bushes while my deputy was layin' thar mortally wounded."

Longarm said, "He wasn't wearing a badge. I didn't even know he was a deputy until this officer"—he nodded toward Billy Wayne—"told me who he was. His badge was in his pocket."

Bird fell silent, looking off out into the big office where a couple of deputies were lounging around. He said, "You say you're stayin' over at the Hamilton Hotel."

Before Longarm could answer, Billy Wayne said, "He's thar a'rright, Shu'rrf. I done checked. Even the way he looks, he's registered. I . . ."

This time Bird turned in his chair and gave Billy Wayne a full-faced stare. The deputy shut up. Longarm wondered if all of Bird's deputies were such slow learners.

When Bird turned back to Longarm he said, "You planning on being here awhile?"

Longarm said, "Well, I come to do some business. I figure to be here until I get that tended to."

"An' that's tradin' business."

Longarm nodded. "Yessir, it is. That's what I am. I'm a trading man. Trade nearly anything."

Bird said, "I don't believe you've ever gotten around to sayin' exactly what it is you've come to trade."

Longarm said, "Well, I don't know what yet is the reason I ain't said. See, the way I work is to go to an area an' see what folks are looking for, what they need. If I haven't got it I go back and see if I can find it. *Savvy?*"

Bird nodded. "Oh, I *savvy* all right, Mister Long. When you reckon to know what it is you might be bringing to town to trade?"

Longarm reached out, picked up his revolver, and put it in his holster. He could tell the interview was coming to a close. He said, "Hard to tell. Hell, I ain't been in town long enough to get cleaned up."

Bird put both his palms on his desk top. "Yeah, I noticed that. You planning on riding up and down the river anymore?"

"I might," Longarm said. "Any objections?"

Bird shook his head slowly. "But you might want to be kind of careful and not do anything looks suspicious. We patrol that patch of land along this side of the river pretty closely, and I got some deputies as will shoot faster than they ast questions. You may not have noticed it, Mister Long, but this is a rough stretch of country. Man can get hisself in trouble around here without half trying."

"I reckon he could at that," Longarm said. He turned his head just as a man came in through the double front doors off the street. He was a tall man, well set up. Through the glass Longarm could see the flash of the gold six-pointed badge that exactly matched the one he had hidden back in his room. He had very little doubt in his mind that he was looking at Les Older, the U.S. deputy marshal out of the Austin office whom he'd been sent down to investigate. The man fit the description Billy Vail had given him to a tee.

Bob Bird had quit talking. He was looking at Longarm. Longarm swung his attention back to the sheriff. He said, "What?"

"I said you was to hold yourself handy. Might be we'll lay hands on a suspect. Could be you got a glimpse of somebody without quite realizing it."

Longarm said, "You're not telling me to not take any more rides along the river, are you?"

Bob Bird said, "That'd be up to you."

Longarm put on his hat and stood up. "Reckon I'll go along to the hotel and get cleaned up. Would you know if they got a barbershop handy?"

Billy Wayne said, "One right there in the hotel. Git a bath an' nearly anythang."

Before Bob Bird could give him a look or say anything, the door to the office opened without anyone bothering to knock. Longarm turned. Les Older was standing there. He looked past Longarm to the sheriff, and said, "Am I walkin' in on somethin' ain't none of my affair?" But Longarm thought he said it without really giving a damn whether he was or not.

Bob Bird said hastily, "Naw, naw, Les. We're jest tryin' to git to the bottom of a little trouble. Somebody gunned down Lester Priddy out at ten mile." He nodded at Longarm. "This feller here brung the body back. Said he hear'd the shots, but claimed he was hid back in the bush an' never seen nuthin'."

Older turned his brown eyes on Longarm. "That right?"

Longarm said easily, "That's right. Except I wasn't exactly hid. I just didn't see no point of coming out in the middle of a gunfight."

Older looked to be about thirty years of age, as Billy Vail had said. He was an even-faced man with thin lips that didn't look accustomed to smiling. He was wearing a lightweight blue shirt that was splotched under the armpits from sweat. His hat was the same color as Longarm's, pearl gray, except the brim was wider in the Texas custom. What startled Longarm was that Older was wearing an ivory-handled revolver. He didn't recall ever seeing a man, outside of a New Orleans gambler, walking around wearing a sidegun with ivory grips. It was the sign of a dandy, but Older wasn't dressed like a dandy. He thought that if anyone should have been wearing ivory grips, it should have been Bob Bird. Which might well be the case, because Longarm hadn't seen the sheriff's sidearm. His coat covered it sitting down, and he had yet to stand in Longarm's presence.

Older looked at the sheriff. "Reckon it was somebody trying to carry something across the river?"

Bird cut his eyes at Longarm as if to signal to Older that he didn't want to talk about the subject in front of a stranger. "I don't know. I would reckon. Lester shore as hell can't tell us. He got plugged dead center."

Les Older looked back at Longarm. "How'd you happen to be there?"

Bird answered for him. "Claims he was riding to look the country over. Said he taken him a picnic lunch, and was settin' on the riverbank eating it when he heard the shots. Lester must have cut down on them." He jerked his thumb at Longarm. "This feller said he heard two shotgun blasts, and both barrels of Lester's double-barreled 12-gauge was fired. I've sent Roy to pick up Jack at two mile and ride on out there, and see if they was any blood sign in case Lester hit one of them or their horses. If they was more than one."

Older said, looking at Longarm, "Did you tell Roy and them to look for sign of this here feller havin' his picnic lunch?"

Bird said, "I done that."

Older was looking Longarm over from boots to the crown of his hat. "I ever see you before?"

"I don't know," Longarm said. "I travel around a good bit. You might have. I just come in from San Antonio."

Bird said, "Man says he's a trader."

"Oh, yeah? What's he trade?" He asked the question without taking his eyes off Longarm's face.

"Says he trades whatever folks are looking for. Says he'll trade anything."

Older was still staring at Longarm. "Reckon he's in the gun tradin' business?"

"Says he's traded guns."

"Reckon he was out there at ten mile tradin' guns?"

Bird shook his head. "Billy Wayne says he saw him riding out in the morning. Didn't have nothing with him. Then Billy Wayne saw him coming back with Lester's body. I'm satisfied. But he ain't goin' nowhere anytime soon. Stayin' over to the Hamilton."

Older said, "That's right handy. So am I."

Longarm deliberately looked at Older's badge. "United States deputy marshal. Ain't that a lot of gunpowder for a little burg like this?"

Older gave him a flat look. "I wouldn't be concerning myself about federal business was I you. What's your name?"

"Long."

"What's the rest of it?"

Longarm shrugged. "Never cared for my given name. Just use the initial C when I have to sign." He looked back at Bird. "You gentlemen mind if I leave? I'd like to get cleaned up. Ain't every day I lug in a deputy sheriff."

Older hesitated for just long enough to let Longarm know he was the one making the decision. Then he slowly stepped out of the doorway. "Stay handy."

Longarm said, "I'll be around. The sheriff has already give me the word. Besides, I ain't done any business yet." He smiled deliberately at Older and walked past him.

Outside, he stood on the boardwalk, lit a cigar, and watched the traffic on the dusty street. Now that he'd met Older the job didn't seem so distasteful. He was ready to bet a year's pay that the deputy marshal was as crooked as a Mexican road. And he didn't figure that Older had been corrupted by the little dandy in his funny-looking hat either. He figured Older had been doing a little taking in one way or another a long time before he met Bob Bird. It was clear from the way they acted around each other that it was Older giving the orders. And from the way he'd said to Bird, "Reckon it was somebody trying to carry something across the river?"

Now that was just downright cute. Couldn't come out and say, "Reckon it was somebody trying to run guns?" Longarm had to smile. He felt like a small child who'd just had a word spelled out in front of him he wasn't supposed to know about.

But he still hoped that Older wasn't dirty, even though every instinct he had told him he was. Well, if he was and if Longarm could catch him at it, the job wouldn't be near as onerous as it had appeared it would be before he'd met Mister Older. There might, if he worked it right, be just a little pleasure in the task of taking Older into custody. Normally, Longarm was not a man who let his feelings interfere with his work. A lawbreaker was a lawbreaker, whether he was likeable or not. But he hadn't particularly cared for the superior way Mister Older had looked him over or the disdainful way Older had treated him.

It was a bad sign for Older—though he didn't know it—that Longarm was already thinking of him in his mind as *Mister* and not as *Deputy Marshal*.

He didn't know what he was thinking of Sheriff Bob Bird, because every time the man entered his mind he wanted to laugh. And that was a dangerous practice. The man might be a preening little banty rooster, but he still wore a gun, and he had eleven more men on his payroll who did also.

Longarm went over to the hotel and up to his room and got a complete change of clothing, then went next door to the barbershop-bathhouse. He took a bath first, and handed over his dirty clothes to a Mexican washerwoman, who was conveniently set up right behind the bathhouse, and then went into the barbershop and got a shave and his hair trimmed and his boots blacked. The whole matter came to a dollar and six bits, not counting having his clothes washed and ironed. They'd be brought around to the hotel later. The funny thing was that the bath was the most expensive part of the whole business, that is, if you wanted fresh water. Which he did. He'd never seen the point in bathing to get clean in somebody else's dirt. But the bath alone had cost a silver dollar. It seemed uncommonly high to Longarm, especially since it was not an expense he could turn in for remuneration. But a man could get a passable steak dinner for a dollar, less in some places, and when soap and water went to getting in the same price range as eating material, then something was bad wrong with the economy.

He went back to his hotel feeling much refreshed by the bath and the shave and the change of clothes. He'd trailed outlaws for days when there was no chance to wash his face, much less shave or take a bath or change clothes. But that was part of the job and unavoidable. When he could, he preferred to be able to walk into a room without sending his scent in ahead of him.

He was about to cross the lobby to go into the bar when he saw the beautiful young wife of the ex–cavalry lieutenant. She was just descending the stairs and starting for the front door. On a sudden whim he stopped. As she came up to him he took off his hat and said, "Mrs. Manly, my name is Long. I know I'm butting into business that is not mine, but could I speak with you for a moment?"

Up close she was even more beautiful than he'd thought that morning. Her perfectly heart-shaped face was framed in a lace-trimmed bonnet, and the dress she wore traced perfectly the curves of her hips and the swell of her breasts. Her bodice was open at the neck and caught with an ivory cameo pin. The skin of her neck was almost as milk white as the cameo. Just looking at her made a copperish taste well up in his mouth.

She stopped and said, with a Southern accent, "Have we met, suh?"

"No, ma'am, but I've heard of your troubles. I'm an ex–cavalry officer myself. Rather I should say I'm an ex–federal officer myself, though I say cavalry because my work did involve mounted activity."

She fixed him with deep blue eyes. "So you have heard of the humiliating predicament my husband has been placed in by this rogue of a sheriff."

"Yes, ma'am, I have."

"Do you have any official position in this town, Mistuh Long, where you might be of assistance in bringing this unfortunate affair to the proper authorities?"

He shook his head. "No, ma'am. I wish I did. All I can do is give you some advice. I've heard that what your husband is accused of doing is not illegal. All ex-officers are allowed to retain their sidearms. Your husband was within his rights whether he was going to Mexico or Halifax."

She colored slightly. "I'm afraid the right or wrong of the matter has nothing to do with it. We are . . . I should say, I'm . . ." Then she blushed deeply. "It's something I can not speak of, suh. All I can tell you is that this so-called sheriff here is an unmitigated scoundrel."

Longarm said gently, "I understand the situation. My advice is that you seek the assistance of federal officers who have more authority than the sheriff. I would suggest you wire the War Department or the nearest fort, which I believe would be in San Antonio. If not that, then I suggest you wire the chief marshal in Austin and appeal to him for help."

"Suh, are you aware that there is a federal deputy marshal in this very town?"

"I am. Have you appealed to him?"

"I have. I have stated my case, and I have come within an inch of telling him what the sheriff is demanding to release my husband."

"And what did he say?"

"He said there was nothing he could do. He said he had no jurisdiction over the sheriff." She colored again. "But he gave me advice—he advised me to do as the sheriff wanted." She looked Longarm straight in the eye. "I'll die first."

Longarm looked at her for a long moment. "Mrs. Manly, be strong about this matter. I think it will be resolved sooner than you think. Though I'd recommend you not mention what I've said."

"I'm on my way now to lay siege to the mayor again. But I must say, I have never seen such a pack of cowards in all my life as this whole infernal town seems to be occupied by. Yours is the first kind voice I've heard."

"I'm going to make an effort on your part, Mrs. Manly. I just ask you to be patient and do nothing outlandish for the next couple of days."

He watched her leave, admiring her now for more than just her beauty. For another moment he stood, savoring the scent of her perfume that still lingered in the air. Finally he turned for the hotel bar, where he'd made the happy discovery that it was at least one place in town that carried a good grade of whiskey.

The door was just off the lobby and he stepped inside. It was late afternoon, but the place was quiet and almost deserted. Most of its clientele came from the hotel, and they were a more elegant lot than the motley riffraff that frequented the saloons and card houses around the plaza. He signaled the bartender to bring him over a bottle of whiskey and a glass. Then he settled back to have a quiet smoke and a pleasant drink and do a little thinking. But he'd gotten no more than half a glass down, and had barely gotten a cigar lit, when Willis Howard came in the door and made straight for his table, pulling out a chair and sitting down without invitation. Longarm said, "You still alive? That means you either ain't been playing poker or you ain't been cheating."

Howard signaled for the bartender to bring him a glass, and then, when it arrived, poured himself a drink out of Longarm's bottle. "I been doing all right. But mainly I been working on our business."

Longarm gave him a look. "*Our* business? I wasn't aware you and I was in business together."

Howard leaned forward and lowered his voice conspiratorially. "You know, them things we talked about. That military equipment what brought you to town."

"So?"

"I been asking around."

"You what?"

Howard put up a hand. "I been mighty discreet. Asking on the QT. Asking the right people. Kind of letting the word get out."

71

Longarm looked at him. The man was a born fool, but there was no real harm in him. He half listened as Willis went on describing his activities around town. Most of Longarm's mind was on Mrs. Manly and her problem. The hell of it was, if he hadn't been on an assignment that was on the "QT," as Willis had said, he could pull out his badge and jerk Lieutenant Manly right out of that jail. The transportation of firearms across an international border was a federal offense, and Bird had absolutely no jurisdiction.

Of course Older did, and he must have known what Bird was up to. Just thinking about a U.S. deputy marshal standing by and watching while some little worm like Bird pulled such a dirty trick made Longarm get angry all over again. He knew the last thing you wanted to do was get angry in a fight, but it was one thing to be a crook and take money to look the other way; it was quite another to be so goddammed depraved you'd let a wonderful woman like Mrs. Manly be raped by a pipsqueak like Bird.

Longarm said, "What?" Willis had just said something he hadn't quite caught.

Howard said, "I was askin' how much of this here military equipment you had. You never said exactly."

Longarm said, slightly amused, "Quite a bit, Willis, quite a bit. Any buyers you get lined up, you can tell them we can more than supply their needs."

Then he filled Willis's glass again, finished the whiskey that was in his, shoved the cork in the bottle, and got up. "I've got to get along."

"You going to eat supper in the hotel?"

"Ain't decided," Longarm lied. He shoved away from the table and walked out of the bar, signaling the bartender with the bottle that he was taking the whiskey with him and to put it on his account. The bartender nodded back. Longarm had sweetened him up with a two-dollar bill before he sat down.

For the next couple of days he just hung around town trying to think of a way to get at the sheriff, or to make something happen that would allow him to bring up the transporting of guns across the border. He didn't feel he could just march into the sheriff's office and hit him up with a proposition. He didn't think even Bob Bird was so dumb he wouldn't smell a rat in that sort of an approach.

So mostly he hung around bars and saloons, playing a little poker and listening. Occasionally he would catch sight of Les Older, but the opportunity never quite presented itself for them to have words.

Nothing he could overhear or find out pointed directly at the illegal transportation of guns across the border. It was an odd situation. The matter seemed an open secret, but no one ever talked about it in detail. It was frustrating to Longarm to know that it was probably going on right under his nose, but he couldn't very well look under every wagon sheet of every vehicle that crossed the bridge. But he knew that Older and Bob Bird didn't have deputies strung out along the U.S. side of the river to keep goods from being smuggled in.

He was sitting on a bench in the middle of the plaza one day, staring across at the courthouse and the massive jailhouse, thinking over the problem, when he saw Willis Howard flanked by two men coming directly toward him. As they got nearer, walking between the trees and water fountains, he saw that the two men were sheriff's deputies. He'd never seen them before, but they were wearing badges plain enough. And then, when they were about thirty or forty yards away, Willis pointed directly at him and said, "There he is! That's Mister Long! That's him right there."

Longarm stared in some curiosity, wondering what Willis had gotten himself up to now. And then both of the deputies were drawing their sidearms and pointing them his way. They were only about ten yards away by then, and one of them said, "You there! Hold right still! Don't you dare try to run!"

Longarm stood up slowly as they came up to him. "What in the hell is going on?"

One of the deputies said, "Your name Long?"

"Yeah. So what?" He looked back and forth from the deputies' faces to Willis Howard. Willis looked scared and ashamed and uncertain.

The deputy who was doing the talking made a motion with his revolver. "You better get them hands up. Git his iron, Virgil."

Longarm slowly raised his hands. The deputy named Virgil reached over, pulled Longarm's revolver out of its holster, and stuck it in his belt. Longarm's first thought was that it had something to do with the shooting of Lester Priddy. But that didn't explain Willis Howard's part in it. Longarm looked at the spooked young man. Willis Howard was showing enough

73

white in his eyes that, if he'd been a bronc, Longarm wouldn't have gotten within a half a mile of him. He said, "What the hell have you got me into now?"

Howard said, "Nothing but what you told me to do."

Longarm frowned. "Told you to do what?"

" 'Bout that military equipment."

One of the deputies had moved to take Longarm by the arm. He shook loose. "I can walk on my own, thank you. Where we going?"

Virgil said, "We is takin' you to see the shur'ff. Yore partner here done be doin' some mighty high talkin'. An' you'll be talkin' to Shu'rff Bird."

Longarm gave Howard a disgusted look. "You damn fool. What'd you do, go up to the law and talk about what I told you to be careful with?"

The other deputy laughed. "You shore got yoreself a hell of a bird dog, mister. That's prezactly what he done."

Longarm shook his head sadly, but inside he was more than a little pleased. Maybe now he would make some progress.

Chapter 6

They sat like they had the time before, with Bob Bird perched on a big chair behind his big desk with his strange-looking city hat on and his little mustache bristling. Longarm sat comfortably across from him in a large wooden chair with arm rests. He'd taken off his hat and set it on Bird's desk. Longarm and the sheriff were alone in the office. The deputies had brought Willis Howard in and Bird had listened to what he had to say, apparently for the second time and obviously for Longarm's benefit. Then Bird had cleared the office, telling the deputies to lock Howard up and then go find themselves something to do to earn their pay. As Willis had been led out of the office he'd given Longarm a frightened, appealing glance. Longarm had just shrugged as if to say, "What can I do?"

Longarm had been glad to see that Bird was going to talk to him alone. He took it as a sign that the sheriff might be interested in talking some business about illegal rifles.

But Bird didn't say anything for a long time, just eyed Longarm in what Longarm took to be Bird's idea of an intimidating stare. Longarm got out a cigar, lit it, and dropped the match on the sheriff's floor. He said, "You arresting me, Sheriff Bird?"

Slowly, like a wagon wheel sucking out of deep bottom mud, Bird said, "I'm a-talkin' to you."

Longarm said, "Your deputies brought me in here when I didn't want to come and they took my revolver away from me." He pointed with his cigar. "You got it in your right-hand desk drawer."

Bird narrowed his eyes. "Long, you was in here the other day. I didn't believe what you said then, an' I don't believe

75

what you think you're a-gonna tell me today."

Longarm pulled on his cigar. "Well, then, ain't much point in me sayin' anything. But you said you didn't believe what I said the other day. You better not be trying to tie me in with the killing of that deputy. I told you what I saw. And what I heard."

Bird waved his hand. "Thet ain't what I mean. We found yore picnic lunch. I ain't got no doubt thet Lester was kilt by party or parties unknown. But I don't believe you was ridin' along that river to look the country over or fer fun. I reckon you had a purpose and I reckon that purpose was to look for a wagon crossing." He suddenly sat back, almost disappearing in his big chair. "Now. What do you think of that?"

Longarm shrugged. "I don't think anything of it. What would I want with a wagon crossing?"

Bird leaned forward. "Long, the time fer bullshit is over. Yore assistant has been goin' 'round town talking about military equipment. And you yourself have described yoreself as a 'trader.' Now what does that come down to except a man who is lookin' to smuggle this here 'military equipment' into Mexico. Huh?"

Longarm flicked the ash off his cigar. "First off, that kid ain't no assistant of mine. I wouldn't trust him with a bucket of water if my hat was on fire. He ain't got no sense. He's just a cheap, tinhorn gambler that I got out of a scrape in San Antonio because I didn't want to get caught in no crossfire. *If* I was looking to do some business—and I'm always looking to do some business— it wouldn't be with no jackrabbit like that. I know what he told you and your deputies, but it ain't got nothing to do with me."

Bird leaned farther forward until his head was halfway across the desk. "He told *me* that you'd told him that you traded in used military equipment and you'd make it worth his while if he could find you a buyer." Bird suddenly leaned back again. "Now. What do you think of that?"

Longarm just shook his head. "The damn fool kid has been pestering me ever since San Antonio. He wanted to know what I did and I told him I dealt in used military equipment. Ain't no law against that. But why in hell would I ask him to find me a buyer in Laredo? Does he look and act like somebody *you'd* ask to find somebody interested in military equipment?"

Bird said casually, "Long, we ain't quite as dumb down here as you've got us figured. We do know they is a couple of revolutions goin' on acrost the border."

Longarm took a puff of his cigar. "I've heard something about that, seems like."

Bird smiled thinly without showing any teeth. "What would this *military equipment* of yours consist of?"

Longarm shrugged. "Oh, whatever a man with connections to the War Department could get that they didn't have no use for. Not worn-out stuff, just used. Canteens, knapsacks, military saddles." He yawned slightly. "You know, stuff the cavalry uses. Not counting horses."

Bird said softly, "Guns? Carbines?"

"Tsk, tsk, tsk, Sheriff. You know as well as I do that it's against federal law to sell firearms to a foreign power. Though I do hear there's a pretty good market for 'em amongst some of them revolutionaries. I hear some of them peasants is having to make do with old muzzle-loading smooth-bore flintlocks. I hear repeating rifles fetch a right nice price down there in Mexico."

"Well, before you get any ideas, let me tell you that me and the sheriff in Brownsville and the one in Del Rio have got this border locked up for three hundred miles. You might want to keep that in mind next time you take it into yore head to go ridin' an' lookin' at the river."

"Seems like a waste of manpower to me. Any fool knows Laredo is the only direct route to Monterrey, at least by road. And if you've got heavy wagons you better go by road. And any fool knows that Monterrey is one of the headquarters of the revolutionaries under Carranza. I don't know what them sheriffs in Brownsville and Del Rio are playing at, but they sure ain't gonna attract no business, not like you could down here. Big rail yard here to receive materials. Straight road to Monterrey. You're the one doing the job."

Now it was as laid out as plain as he could make it without directly committing himself. The next move would have to be up to Bird.

Bird fiddled around for a moment, looking at his fingernails and rearranging some papers on his desk. "You say you got connections at the Department of War?"

Longarm nodded. The fish was nibbling at the bait. "Yeah, me an' an old buddy that go way back. He's in charge of selling off certain articles to the highest bidder. Of course he's the one decides who is the highest bidder."

Bird said casually, "I suppose he handles cavalry carbines as well."

77

Longarm nodded. "Yes, as a matter of fact he does. At least them that have been replaced by a newer model. I believe the Winchester 73 is now the official cavalry rifle. I believe it replaced the Model 1866. Course that's just what I hear. But they both fire standard .44-caliber ammunition."

Bird sat slowly back in his chair. "What kind of condition would they be in, these Model 1866 carbines?"

"Serviceable," Longarm said. "They were all retired in good working order. They ain't new, but just because the stock of a rifle has got a few nicks and scratches don't make the rifle fire no worse."

Bird was rubbing his hands together and staring off into the corner. "Wonder how many of these rifles could be had in a batch."

"That would depend on the price. See, this friend of mine goes to considerable trouble in deciding who the highest bidder is he sells the guns to. He kind of thinks he ought to be rewarded for all that effort on his part. If you get my drift."

"Yes," Bird said. "But you still ain't said how big a lot of these rifles might be had."

Longarm crossed his legs and folded his hands around one knee. "They get sold in lots of five hundred. I reckon a thousand could be negotiated for."

"At what price?"

Longarm smiled slowly. "At what price to who? To me? To you? Or to the rebels down there in Monterrey? Seems like you be talking about several prices here."

Bird shifted around uncomfortably. "What the hell do you care? You got a interest in some stupid revolution between a bunch o' greasers?"

"Naw, I got an interest in how much money I can make. You telling me you might know a way to sell those guns to that bunch of greasers?"

Bird looked even more uncomfortable. "I might. If the price was right."

Longarm looked at him a long moment, calculating. "I hear repeating rifles delivered just across the border are bringing a pretty good price. I hear you can get thirty-five, forty dollars apiece for guns in fair shape. Is that about what you hear?"

Bird said stiffly, "Could be."

"Only one thing . . ." Longarm said. He let the thought hang in the air.

"What?"

"Well, you may not care about them guns crossing the border, and it's a damn cinch that I don't, not if I can make some money at it. As far as I'm concerned them Mexicans can kill themselves off as fast as they can buy bullets. But the other day right here in your office I met a gent that might care. In fact he might care a hell of a lot considering he's a U.S. deputy marshal. Smuggling guns is just right up his alley. That's federal duty. And I got reason to believe he ain't just passing through because I have seen him in town several times since me and him had a little talk here in your office. He makes me kind of nervous."

"Don't worry about him."

"Don't worry about a federal marshal? Like hell I won't. He's the kind puts folks in prison."

Bird leaned over the desk. "If I tell you not to worry about him, then don't worry about him. Er are you hard of hearing?"

"No, ain't nothing wrong with my hearing. What I'd like to hear right now is for you to say we might could count on his help in this matter. That would make matters a sight easier."

Bird's face got grim. "I ain't gonna tell you again that that marshal ain't none of your affair. Now, I want to hear about the price of these guns."

Longarm wanted to keep pressing Bird about Les Older, but instinct told him to let it wait for another time. "Why don't I give you a look at what we're talking about."

Bird's face came instantly alert. "You got a sample?"

Longarm nodded. "Got it right handy. Why don't you come over to my room at the hotel after supper. Say, around seven o'clock. You can have a look. After that we'll know what we're talking about."

"What room you in?"

"Room Two-twelve."

Bird pulled open his right-hand drawer and took out Longarm's revolver. He handed it to him without a word. Longarm dropped it into his holster, and said, "Been an enlightening talk, Sheriff. Hope it turns out profitable for the both of us."

Bird looked at him. "You know, you ain't the first gun smuggler I've seen. Ever' one of you comes down here with the same idea—gettin' by me. Well, it ain't never happened and it ain't never goin' to. I run this town and that bridge and all the land along the river on this side. Ain't nobody goin' to smuggle so much as a derringer into Mexico without I have a hand in it.

79

Long, I knew what and who you was the minute I laid eyes on you. Ridin' up the river fer pleasure. Shit!"

Longarm said casually, "I hear you got an ex–cavalry officer in here tried something on you. Met his wife at the hotel."

Bird's eyes suddenly got hard. "Mister Long, was I you I'd mind my own business in that matter. In fact, was I you I'd stay away from the lady and not listen to a word she has to say."

Longarm shrugged. "Ain't no skin off my ass one way or another."

"Keep it that way."

Longarm turned for the door, but the sheriff's voice stopped him. "What do you want me to do with your assistant? Or helper?"

Longarm laughed lightly. "I done told you. He ain't got nothing to do with me. If you've got the space I'd keep him in jail. Be cheaper that way."

"What do you mean cheaper?"

"Like I said, he's a tinhorn gambler. You let him out and it won't be long before somebody catches him cheating at cards and blows his head off. Then you got the expense of burying him. But do what you like."

Bird sat back. "I think I'll let him out."

Longarm opened the door. "I'll be in my room at seven o'clock."

"I'll probably bring a deputy with me."

"Hell, bring whoever you want. Ain't no law against a man having a cavalry carbine in his possession. Though if you bring that U.S. marshal I'm not going to remember a thing about what we talked about here today."

Bird looked irritated. "Goddammit, I tol' you to leave that marshal to me."

Longarm closed the door behind him and walked out of the jail. He paused to relight his cigar, and then started across the plaza to his hotel. It was going on for five in the afternoon and he was as dry as bleached bones. He wanted a drink and, strangely enough, another bath. But he reckoned the need for the bath had come from being around Bob Bird as long as he had.

He went to his room instead of the bar. He had some heavy thinking to do and he didn't wanted to be interrupted by anyone, especially if that anyone was to turn out to be a newly freed Willis Howard. In his room he poured himself out a good tumblerful of the whiskey he'd gotten from the downstairs bar, and then got a chair and sat it in front of the window that opened onto the courtyard. He had the chair turned backwards, and he straddled it and looked down into the courtyard at the clump of huisache trees, wondering if the hour might come when he had to trust to their thorny branches to break his fall while making a hasty exit.

He took a sip of whiskey, and then got out another cigar and lit it. When it was drawing good he dipped the chewing end in the whiskey, and then stuck it in the corner of his mouth and stared out into space.

The problem was the sheriff. He was in between Longarm and his real target, Les Older. Longarm had to figure some way to get Older included in the deal or he wasn't going to accomplish anything. Of course he could arrest the sheriff. Hell, he could do that the minute the sheriff walked in his room and made him an offer on the rifles. But that wouldn't fetch Les Older.

No, he had to figure a way that would allow him to deal directly with Older. He had not the slightest doubt that the sheriff was conferring with Older about this new development, maybe at that exact moment. Older was the boss. He had to be. The sheriff couldn't operate without his permission and cooperation.

But how the hell to get Bob Bird out of the way so he could offer Older the cookie jar and see if he'd stick his hand too far inside and get it caught? That right there was the crux of the matter. He had to get rid of the sheriff.

He could kill him, but he hated to do that. Not that he didn't think the sheriff needed killing, if for no other reason than the despicable trick he was trying to pull on Mrs. Manly. No, he just couldn't kill him in cold blood, and he couldn't see any way he'd be able to provoke Bird into a fight where he could kill him and be able to live with it the rest of his life.

He thought a while longer, running over various ideas in his mind. Hell, he didn't need the sheriff out of the way but for a few days. Maybe he could arrange for him to be called to Austin. But that would involve using the local telegraph, and Longarm had a hunch that there weren't many messages that came or went that might be of interest to the sheriff that the telegrapher didn't tell him about. And if Longarm was to wire the chief marshal in Austin to send for Bird, more than likely Bird would know about it fifteen minutes after he did. And then the game would be up.

He took the cigar out of his mouth and took a long pull on the whiskey. There had to be a way; it was just a question of thinking about it. Maybe if he went out and snooped around the sheriff's house, he might find him and Older having a palaver and he could make something incriminating out of that.

Hell, he thought, he was just grasping at straws, and not very big straws at that. He poured himself out another tumbler of whiskey, downed it in two gulps, and gave the thinking up as a bad job. It was near six o'clock, time to go down and eat some supper and then get back up to his room for his guest. Maybe Bird would give him some kind of opening that would suggest a line of action, say something or drop a hint of some kind. The easiest solution, he thought, would be to just provoke both of them into a fight and settle the problem right then and there. But he had a feeling that Billy Vail would frown on such a solution.

He met Mrs. Manly on the first landing of the stairs. Even though it was hot as a whorehouse in hell, she always managed to look cool and collected with every hair in place. But all the composure in the world couldn't hide the worry in her eyes. She stopped as she saw him. She was carrying a dainty little lace handkerchief, and she used it to daub at her brow. He could tell from the shape of her light gingham gown that she had surrendered a few petticoats to the heat. He swept off his hat as he came up to her. "Mrs. Manly, I was just thinking about you. Have you made any progress?"

Tears almost came to her eyes. "What kind of town is this? What kind of place? The sheriff is a brute and the mayor is a coward, suh."

Longarm put out his hand and touched her shoulder. "Mrs. Manly, if you can just hold for on a few more days I think matters will right themselves."

She said, "But I have so few funds. I . . ." She stopped again and dabbed at her eyes. "Mistuh Long, I have no business being a bothuh to you with my troubles."

He smiled as gently as he could. "Believe me, Mrs. Manly, you are no bother. Fact of the matter is you are a spur, an inspiration."

She looked at him questioningly. "As what? I don't understand you, suh."

He smiled again. "Never mind. Some day I'll explain. Right now you go along and don't worry your head about this matter. I believe I can tend to it. But you musn't speak to anyone about it. Especially any law officers. And that includes that U.S. deputy marshal."

She said, frowning, "You are a puzzle to me, suh."

"That's what my wife says." He didn't have any wife, but he thought it would make him sound more respectable and trustworthy to her.

She shook her head. "The thing is, I don't know what to do next. I have exhausted all the avenues of hope I can think of."

"Don't do another thing. Just go along to your room and bathe your face in some cool water."

He watched her walk off down the hall to her room, and then descended into the lobby and went over to the desk. The clerk he had become friendly with was on duty. Longarm asked him what Mrs. Manly's bill was standing at.

The clerk gave him an amused look. "Mighty pretty young lady, Mrs. Manly."

"Her looks ain't got a damn thing to do with it. I just don't much like to see a bully get his way."

The clerk reached under the desk and came up with a ledger. He turned pages until he came to the right one. "Bit over fourteen dollars. She's been signing for her meals. Chargin' 'em to her room."

Longarm reached in his pocket for his small roll. He kept the biggest part of his greenbacks in the little pocket in his boot. He peeled off a twenty-dollar bill and laid it on the counter. "That ought to pay her up and give her a few more days. Let me know when you need more."

The clerk picked up the bill and looked at it. Then he looked at Longarm. "The sheriff ain't going to like this much if he hears about it."

Longarm gave the clerk a flat look. "Neither will I."

The clerk laughed. "That sonofabitch ain't gonna hear nuthin' from me. My slop-suckin' brother-'n-law. He's gonna hit my sister about one time too many, and then I ain't gonna care anymore what he can do to me."

"He bad about knocking her around?"

The clerk's face went cold. "The only lucky thing fer that woman is he spreads it around amongst his girlie friends. Otherwise he'd of beat her to death a long time ago. The little shit."

"Why does she put up with it? There is such a thing as divorce."

"In this town? With him sheriff? You *are* a stranger. But I'm glad to see you helpin' that young wife. I was thinkin' 'bout riggin' the books, but I'd of probably got caught. Bird owns part of this hotel. And she ain't supposed to have no money."

Longarm had been leaning against the desk. He pushed away. "Maybe she sold a piece of jewelry."

The clerk smiled. "That's just what I heard. That'll piss the hell out of Bird."

"I got to get supper. Then don't be surprised if your brother-in-law shows up to pay me a visit."

The clerk gave him a strange look, but Longarm just walked away and went into the dining room. It was late and the room was almost empty. Thankfully, Longarm noted, Willis Howard was not in evidence. He ordered a shot of whiskey to start, and then hurried his way through a steak and some fried potatoes with gravy. The rest of Laredo ought to be buried and forgotten, but Longarm couldn't find anything to complain about the hotel except what he'd just learned, that Bob Bird owned part of it. But then that shouldn't have surprised him. The man probably owned a piece of everything in town. Between Older and Bird, Longarm couldn't recollect two men he was more anxious to bring to justice. He paid his score and then went back up to his room, got the Model 1866 out of his bedroll, and propped it against the washstand.

He was sitting in the chair by the window with a glass of whiskey in his hand when the knock came a little after seven o'clock. He called out, "It's open."

He watched as the knob was turned slowly and the door pushed open all the way. No one came in. Then, after a second, Bob Bird stepped into the entrance and looked around. Longarm wanted to laugh, but he just said, "It's all right, Sheriff, ain't nobody here but me and I'm just having a drink of whiskey. Care for one?"

Bird was still looking left and right. "Never touch it. Fouls a man's system."

Longarm took a sip. "Probably does. Probably what's wrong with me now."

Bird finally stepped into the room, closing the door behind him. He had the right skirt of his black frock coat shoved back so that the handle of his revolver was exposed for a quick draw. Longarm noted, with some interest, that it too was ivory-handled. He didn't know if Older was imitating the sheriff or vice versa. He said, indicating a chair at the foot of the bed, "Take a chair."

Bird walked slowly around the room, taking his time. He glanced at the Model 1866 rifle Longarm had leaning against the washstand, but he didn't touch it. Finally he sat down. Longarm said, "Care for a cigar?"

"Don't smoke," Bird said. He glanced over at the rifle. "That it?"

Longarm spoke around the cigar clamped between his teeth. "That's it. Ain't spanking brand-new, but the rifling is in good shape and so is the firing mechanism. And it's got a big U.S. branded right on the stock and a little one on the brass breech plate. They are surplus government cavalry carbines, put out to pasture by a newer model. Least that one is. But that one is just like the rest I can get."

Bird got up and walked over and picked up the rifle. He hefted it for a moment and then sighted down the barrel. Next he levered the action and snapped the trigger on an empty chamber.

Longarm said, "Action still smooth as silk. Actually, I think it gets better after a gun has had a little use."

Bird didn't say anything. He levered the action open so that the hammer was all the way back, reversed the gun in his hands, and holding the stock end toward the overhead lantern sighted down the inside of the barrel. He said, "Little rust."

Longarm said, "Don't start knocking the goods with me, Sheriff. It ain't going to have a damn thing to do with the price." He got up and walked over to the sheriff, took the rifle from him, and peered down the inside of the barrel. The rifling still looked in good condition and he didn't see any rust, except around the mouth of the barrel. He handed the gun back to Bird. "I don't see any rust inside. Besides, ain't it good enough for them greasers?" He bore down hard on the word. He didn't care for it himself, but the sheriff seemed to.

Bird said, "I won't argue with you. You guarantee the rest in this good a shape or better?"

Longarm looked down at him. Though actually, the sheriff was taller than he appeared behind his desk. Standing, Longarm judged him to be about five feet, six inches tall. He either had a high desk or a low chair. Longarm said, "Well, I don't know about that. I ain't going to get the chance to go through and hand-inspect every one of them. I told you they was sold as surplus in lots of five hundred. But what I've seen looks to be the same as that rifle. I just picked it out at random before I started down here."

He walked back to his whiskey and his chair and sat down. Bird replaced the rifle against the table and then sat back down. "How much?"

"How many?"

"Five hundred."

"Five hundred, delivered right in the rail yard, will cost you twenty-five dollars apiece. If my arithmetic is right that's twelve thousand, five hundred dollars."

Bird said, without smiling, "No, twenty dollars each. That's all."

Longarm laughed. "Hell, Sheriff, you're supposed to be on the right side of the law. If you're aiming to rob me why don't you just pull out that pearl-handled six-gun and do it right."

Bird said, bristling, "Ivory. It's ivory."

"What's the difference?"

"I didn't come here to talk about the grips on my sidearm. I'm telling you now I will pay you ten thousand dollars for five hundred of those rifles delivered right here in Laredo. All in, no delivery charges, no nothing. You give me the rifles, I give you the money and you leave town."

Longarm looked at him thoughtfully for a moment. "You wouldn't be trying to sucker me, would you, Sheriff? You wouldn't let me bring those rifles down here and then arrest me for smuggling guns. You wouldn't do a feller thataway, would you?"

"You said yourself that it wasn't illegal to have a surplus U.S. cavalry carbine in your possession on this side of the border."

Longarm thought a moment. "Yes, that's true. And I will have a bill of sale from the United States government, Quartermaster Corps, Department of the Army, saying I bought them rifles fair and square. But I ain't taking no twenty dollars apiece for them."

"That's all I'm going to offer."

"Then we ain't going to do any business. Those rifles will cost me a little better than fifteen dollars apiece by the time I get them delivered here. You want me to make twenty-five hundred dollars while I know damn good and well you are going to ship them guns to Mexico, and probably no more than just across the border, and make at least twenty dollars apiece for ten cents' worth of trouble? Hell, I just *look* stupid."

"You came down here with the idea of smuggling those rifles across the river, didn't you?"

"I ain't got no comment about that."

"An' now you see that that can't be done. So it's deal with me or don't deal at all. Twenty-five hundred is a hell of a lot better than nothing, especially for a saddle tramp like you."

Longarm smiled slightly. "You don't mind calling a man names, do you?"

"I might see what you call yourself if I throw you in that jail across the plaza. Give you time to think."

"On what charge?"

"I don't need a charge."

"That's right, I forget. You've got that young Lieutenant Manly over there on no charge."

Bird bristled. "Jest cain't seem to mind yore own bid'ness, can you?"

"You said it's deal with your or don't deal at all. Well, you know, that old knife cuts both ways. Maybe it's deal with me or don't deal at all. I got the inside connection."

"What makes you think we ain't got a connection?"

"For that many guns?" He gave a short laugh. "I'm an ex–cavalry officer. You don't look much like one. I bet you've been dealing twenty rifles here, thirty there. I could even bring a thousand down if the money was on the table."

"You're a pretty cocky bastard for a man as far off his range as you are, Long."

Longarm decided to press Bird even further. He wasn't afraid of Bird arresting him because that wasn't going to happen, not unless it was for the murder of the sheriff himself. But he had to know about Older. "You said *we* got connections. You talking about yourself and that U.S. deputy marshal?"

"Who *we* is ain't none of yore goddamn business. You want the twenty dollars a gun or not?"

"I'll take twenty-two-fifty. That still leaves you at least a profit of seventeen-fifty a gun. If not more. But then I recognize you got to pay off them officials on the Mexican side, though I doubt that comes to more than a hundred dollars for a wagon train. Then I recognize that you got some other expenses, keeping them twelve deputies in cartridges. Hell, it would probably break the town if they had to arm and outfit that small army. Say, does anybody ever take notice that your little army don't spend no time around town? I walked these streets for two days and never saw a badge. Had to ride down the river before I ran across a deputy. Don't nobody find that kind of odd?"

Bird said, "I'll give you twenty-one dollars apiece fer them rifles an' that's my last word on the subject."

Longarm poured himself out a little more whiskey. He took time to take a sip before he said, "Twenty-two bucks a head and you let that Lieutenant Manly out of the jug."

Bird rose a half an inch off his chair. His face flamed red. "I don't reckon you got sense enough to keep yore nose outten whar it don't belong. Might be you'd like to join up with that *ex*-lieutenant in the jug, as you call it."

"Listen here, Bird," Longarm said. "You might as well quit threatening to throw me in jail. You might do it after I get those rifles down here. And I'll be watching for that and might just fix it so you can't. But you ain't going to do squat when you have a chance to make a mighty healthy profit. You might as well figure his wife ain't ever gonna give in to you. She'd druther rot and die first."

"I guess you've got your eye on a little bit of that tail. That it? You promised to help her and she'd spread her legs for you?"

Longarm said evenly, "No, that ain't it at all. I got to talking to her one day in the hotel, and it runs out I served with her husband's older brother. He's out of the cavalry now, but he's kind of part of my connection to those rifles."

Bird said, "All right. She's so goddamn important to you I'll give you twenty-one dollars a rifle and let her husband go."

Longarm was not bargaining in earnest. It was all sham. He was playing a part. But he had to play it properly to keep Bird convinced he was a gun smuggler. He laughed. "You reckon that girl is worth five hundred dollars to me? You ain't thinking with your head, Sheriff. If you'd throw her husband in at twenty-two the rifle, well, then, so much the better. But it ain't worth coming down to twenty-one to me. And I ain't even trying to bed her, like you are. Nope, twenty-two is my price."

"It's too high."

"What the hell is all this argument about one dollar? So you'll be making eighteen dollars a rifle instead of nineteen. So what? I mean . . ." He suddenly stopped and slapped his forehead. He said, "Hell, what am I thinking about? Of course, you got a partner. That deputy marshal. So you wouldn't be making eighteen dollars a gun, you'd only be making nine. Or maybe even less than that. The marshal taking the lion's share, Sheriff?"

Bird stared at him for a long second. "You want to sell some guns or not?"

"That's what I come for."

"Then you just worry about your end."

Longarm half smiled and cocked his head. "Fact of the business, Sheriff, that's what I'm doing. That U.S. marshal worries me considerable. Now, like you say, ain't illegal for me to have them guns on this side. And I did buy 'em. And I'll have a bill of sale to that effect. But them guns is federal property, U.S. property. Oh, sure, I got some paperwork that looks right enough for a local sheriff. But that marshal ain't local and federal business is his business. They got a prison in Leavenworth, Kansas, where they put people who fool around with the United States government, if you get my drift."

Bird said, gritting his teeth, "The marshal is my affair. Getting the rifles here is yours. When can you have them?"

Longarm appeared to think for a moment, then said, "Two days. Three at the most."

"Fine," Bird said. He stood up. "Then we have a deal at twenty-two dollars apiece."

Longarm said, "Cash on delivery, Sheriff. I'll deliver them guns in a boxcar in the rail yard. You give me the money and I'll give you the key to a sealed boxcar. By the way, that's eleven thousand dollars."

"You'll have to give me some notice. I don't have that kind of money just laying around."

"I'll let you know while the banks are still open. But I want that marshal there. I want to be damn sure he can't arrest me for something he's a part of."

Bird just stared at him, and then turned around and started out of the room. Before he could open the door Longarm said, "I ain't as big a fool as you think I am, Sheriff. I know damn good and well this marshal has got to be a part of this matter. You wouldn't be fool enough to be trying to smuggle guns across the border with him hanging around. So you just bring him along and I'll sell him a key for eleven thousand dollars and nobody's the wiser. I ain't selling guns, just a key."

Bird said, "The guns will be inspected. We won't just be taking your word for it."

Longarm said, "Once you got the key and I got the money I'll stand around as long as you want. Except don't expect to arrest me. I'll have an opinion about that. And if any shots get

89

fired you will most likely catch the first one."

Bird just stared at him, a long, calculating stare. Then he stepped through the open door and was gone.

Longarm lifted his glass to the place where the sheriff had been standing. He said, "*Salude, el jefe.* I think I better get to know you a little better, beginning with your home life." He took the half tumbler down at a gulp, and then got his hat and went downstairs. The friendly desk clerk had gone off duty, or else Longarm would have asked him a few interesting questions. Instead he just went on out the front of the hotel, bound for the railroad depot and the telegrapher's office. It was a good long walk, maybe a quarter of a mile, in his high-heeled boots, but it seemed like less trouble than going around and getting his horse rigged up and then putting him back. It was closing on nine o'clock and, if he hurried, he'd have time for some poker before midnight.

It was pleasant walking along. The heat of the day had faded and there was a good breeze blowing. He strolled down the boardwalk, past the all-night saloons and whorehouses and card houses, wondering which one Willis Howard was about to get himself killed in. But that was Willis Howard's problem. *His* problem was luring Les Older out into the open, and he wasn't altogether sure that he'd accomplished that with the sheriff. Well, all he could do was go down to the telegrapher's and put another piece of cheese in the trap.

Chapter 7

At the telegrapher's he wrote out a carefully thought-out wire. It was just addressed to Billy Vail, Denver, Colorado. No mention was made of Billy's title nor was any office or address given. He pretty well knew that the Denver telegraph operator would recognize Billy's name, and would get it to him in a hurry because he intended to mark the wire urgent. In block letters he printed out his message on the telegraph form. It said:

IMPORTANT YOU WIRE QUARTERMASTER GENERAL FORT SAM HOUSTON SAN ANTONIO STOP URGENT YOU REQUEST HE SEND ME IMMEDIATELY FIFTY CARBINE CRATES CORRECTLY LABELED STOP SEND ME IN SEALED BOXCAR STOP URGENT STOP URGENT STOP URGENT NEED DAY AFTER TOMORROW STOP DIRECT AS SIGNED STOP

                                                    C. LONG

He gave it to the telegrapher to send, not particularly worried that the man could interpret enough from it to pass on any information to Bob Bird. Bird wouldn't know if the crates were empty or full. If he asked, Longarm just intended to tell him that it was code and he wasn't about to wire in the open for five hundred carbines. And if the sheriff wondered who Billy Vail was, he'd tell him that Billy was his partner and, other than that, it wasn't any of his business. He also wasn't worried, should Older somehow see the wire, that the deputy marshal would recognize Billy Vail's name. There were just too damn many marshals and too damn many names. And no reason to know them all.

The wire cost him a little over a dollar and a half. He went around to the depot side to see the freight agent. The man was sitting under a double lantern working over some papers at a small table. Longarm told him he'd just ordered some goods to be shipped to him in a sealed boxcar and wondered what the procedure was for that. The man yawned and pushed his green eyeshade a little farther back on his forehead. "You just tell me where you're staying and yore name and I'll get word to you. Then you come down and I give you the onliest key will open the door of that car. It ain't real hard."

Longarm turned to leave, and then turned back. "Have you got a fast freight going out of here? Night or day?"

The agent said, "One leaves every night at midnight. Don't stop until it pulls into the yard at San Antone."

"What time does it get made up?"

"It's *finished* making up by eleven o'clock. It o-riginates from here so we got all day to get it hooked up. But it pulls out at midnight on the dot. That is one train what leaves on time."

Longarm left and started the walk back to the plaza. On the way he passed several wild, noisy, cheap joints full of *vaqueros* and *pistoleros* and *desperados*. Listening to the commotion as he walked, he reflected that a man wouldn't have much trouble finding trouble in such places. One wrong word or wrong look or maybe nothing at all would do it.

It started him on a line of thought. The sheriff was in his way and he couldn't figure out how to get rid of him short of killing him. Maybe, he thought, he could spirit him out of town and hire some *pistoleros* to hold him for a time. It probably wouldn't cost much, and it would allow him to approach Les Older acting like he knew more than he really did. Either one of two things would happen. Either Les Older would implicate himself by agreeing to buy the guns or he'd try and arrest Longarm. If he did the first Longarm would arrest him, and the second couldn't happen because Longarm was on an official investigation.

He wondered, walking along in the night air, if Bob Bird and Older discussed matters or if Older just gave the orders. He was willing to bet that Older had told Bob Bird exactly how high he could go on the rifles.

It only stood to reason. Older didn't need Bird to smuggle guns into Mexico, but Bird damn sure couldn't do it on his own with an honest U.S. deputy marshal on hand.

He came to the door of a saloon he favored for poker playing, but hesitated. What he needed more than poker was a long spell of thinking, and he couldn't do that while he was concentrating on the cards. He decided the hell with it, and headed for his hotel.

The night clerk was Mexican. As Longarm stopped to get his key the clerk said, a tiny smirk on his face as he turned to the keyholes, "Señor Long, you have the note. From a very pretty lady, I thenk."

He handed Longarm his key and the note, which was sealed in a dainty blue envelope. Longarm turned it over in his hands. It just said, "Mister Long," on the front. He nodded at the clerk, giving him a little bit of a hard look because of the smirk, and then walked toward the stairway. He went up a few steps, waiting until he was out of view from the lobby, and then tore open the envelope. In a dainty feminine hand was written, "Mister Long, though the hour may be late I would so kindly appreciate seeing you at your earliest convenience." It was signed, "Belinda Manly." Below was her room number, 224.

He stood for a moment, thinking. He didn't quite know what he might be getting into, but the lady certainly sounded like she wanted to see him pretty urgently. By his watch it was nine-thirty, but she had written, "though the hour may be late." She couldn't make it much plainer than that that she had something of consequence to talk to him about. He hoped she wasn't going to ask for a progress report on getting her husband out of jail, because he didn't have one to give her, at least not one he could tell her about. With all his heart he wished he could reveal to her his position as a U.S. deputy marshal so that she could know, if she could just be patient, that it was all going to work out fine.

Well, he decided, there was only one way to find out what it was she wanted, and that was to go and see. He climbed the stairs to the second floor, walked down the hall past his room, and drew up in front of 224. For just a second the thought flickered across his mind that it could be some sort of trap set by Bob Bird, but then that didn't make any sense. Bird didn't have to lay traps for him; Longarm was standing right out in the open, a clear target for anyone who had reason to shoot.

He knocked lightly. He didn't want to arouse the floor and be seen entering her room. The door was opened immediately, almost as if she had been standing there waiting. She was dressed in a blue lightweight satin wrapper. It did very little to hide the curves of her body. She said, "Mistuh Long, thank you. Please come in."

There was a slight urgency in her tone. He hurried in and stood in the middle of the room and looked around. The room was exactly the same as his, yet it had a feminine quality that he couldn't explain. He thought it probably came from the scent of her body and her perfumes. She said, "Please. Sit down."

He took off his hat, but he shook his head. "Mrs. Manly, I don't reckon it would look good, you being a married woman and all, me staying too long here in your hotel room."

"Right now, suh, that is of no concern to me. I fear that the time is running out for me and my husband. And after I found out that you had so kindly paid my hotel bill I felt like I had to speak to you. I . . ."

She stopped. Whatever it was she wanted to say just wouldn't come out. He said, "Now, Mrs. Manly . . ."

"Belinda, please."

"Mrs. Manly, whatever is troubling you, I wish you'd tell me. I just want to help."

She came a step closer to him. He was uncomfortably aware of her perfume and the beauty of her young body. "Oh, I know you do. It was such a kind thing when you paid my hotel bill. Such a kind thing. Perhaps you already know it, but the sheriff has all our funds. I came to this hotel with his permission. But ever since he has incarcerated my husband he's used it as a threat against me. Sometimes he calls me to his office and sometimes he leaves messages for me at the desk."

Her eyes started to brim up.

He said, "Hold on to yourself now. Crying won't do no good."

"You're right," she said. "I'm sorry." She held the back of her hand to first one eye and then the other. "He left a message today saying I only had two more days to make up my mind. After that he's going to send my husband to prison. I—"

And then she did begin to cry, very softly, almost without sound. He reached out and took her arms with his hands. "Mrs. Manly, he can't send your husband to prison."

He was aware that she had put the palms of her hands on his chest, just letting them rest there lightly. He immediately dropped his hands from her shoulders. "The sheriff hasn't got any authority over a federal crime, and if your husband was guilty, which he's not, the sheriff couldn't do anything about it. Besides, he couldn't go to prison without a trial. He's just trying to scare you, that's all."

She was looking up in his face. He felt she hadn't heard a word he'd said, and he felt very uncomfortable. She said, "Mistuh Long, I don't know what your part in this is. All I know is that you've been very kind. And if I have to give myself to someone, I would hope it were you. The thought of that little beast touching me is near more than I could bear. But if it would free my husband I could surrender myself to you."

He looked down at her in amazement. "Mrs. Manly, that is a very courageous thing for you to offer to do for your husband. But believe me, I have no influence with the sheriff. In fact, I cannot abide the man myself."

She was looking up at him, her lips slightly parted, her breath slightly elevated, the blue of her eyes so deep Longarm felt he could almost swim in them. She was beautiful, she was naive, she was scared, and she had completely misunderstood why he had paid her hotel bill. And he was not the sort of bastard that would take advantage of such a young lady in such a situation. He put on his hat. She said, "You're not going?"

"Yes, I am, Mrs. Manly. I stick around here and I'm liable to weaken and do something I'd never forgive myself for. I give you my word of honor your husband is not going to prison. And I give you my word that they are not going to turn you out of this hotel. And I give you that same word of honor that this whole mess will be over in two or three days."

"Suh, you are a gentleman."

"Well, I don't know about that." Then he dug in his pocket, took out a ten-dollar bill, and laid it on the bed. "We can't have you walking around without a few dollars in your purse."

Her hand flew to her mouth. "Oh, I couldn't! That would make me feel like a . . . a . . ."

It made him think of Bonnie back in San Antonio. God, it seemed like a month had passed since then. He smiled. "It can't make you feel like anything but what you are, a lady, because we didn't do anything."

She looked up at him, blushing. "Suh, you are teasing me."

He smiled again. "Yes, yes, I am. You need to do a good deal more laughing and a lot less crying." He touched her shoulder. "This will all work out. You wait and see. Bob Bird likes to scare people because he's a bully. But he's not really very frightening. You don't have to be afraid of him."

"I saw him go in your room earlier tonight. That's what made me think you had business with him."

"Ah," he said. "So that explains all this." He smiled. "And here I thought it was my good looks."

"But you are!" she said. "Handsome, I mean."

He laughed out loud. "Mrs. Manly, I do believe you need glasses."

"I'm sorry." Her eyes searched his face.

"For what?"

"For thinking you were in league with him. It is an insult to a man like you that I should even dream such a thing. But I'd seen you around the jail and then I saw him in your room."

"Don't think another thing about it."

She said, looking at him directly, "But I still mean what I said."

He half smiled. "Right now you do. Right now you are alone and frightened and half out of your wits for a way to turn. When your world gets right side up again you'll think different."

"I don't think so," she said.

He touched his hat brim with his forefinger. "Good night, Mrs. Manly. I'll just slip out. You don't need to come to the door." He gave a half smile. "You ain't exactly dressed for public viewing."

He left her staring after him, and walked down the hall to his room, and let himself in. The first thing he noticed was that the surplus cavalry rifle was not quite in the spot he'd left it in. Someone had come in to make an examination of the trading goods while he had gone to the railroad depot. He guessed that the man was wearing a U.S. deputy marshal's badge. Though not for long, not if Longarm could help it.

His first act, after pouring himself out a drink of whiskey, was to get Mrs. Manly's letter out of his pocket and strike a match and put flame to the delicate paper. He didn't see any reason in the world for anyone else to read that note. Then he lifted his glass and said, "Lord, don't tempt me like that. My flesh is weak and can't stand no real heavy strains." Then he drank the tumbler down in one gulp, gave a little shake of his head, poured himself out another glassful, and sat it on the bedside table. After that he sat down on the side of the bed and took his boots off. It was only a little after ten o'clock, pretty early for him to be going to bed, but he was tired from all the plotting and figuring and thinking, and besides, it wouldn't hurt him to catch up on a little of his sleep. He took off his hat and then his shirt and then his gunbelt, and hung it over the bedpost nearest to his hand. Finally he lit another cheroot and sat there on the side of the bed, thinking and smoking and relaxing and having an occasional sip of whiskey.

After a time his mind and body started to relax, and he got up and propped a chair under the door handle. He'd never known too many hotels with very secure locks. He set the other chair in front of the first. In case somebody did manage to get in the room, it would give them something else to trip over. He went back to the bed, took off his jeans, sat down, and then rolled back, and pulled the thin sheet over his body. He was starting to go to sleep when he thought of the telegram he'd sent Billy Vail. Longarm reckoned it would give the old goat more than just a moment or two of puzzlement wondering what he was up to where he needed fifty empty gun crates. Well, maybe it would keep Billy awake a few nights. God knows, Billy had given him duties that had kept *him* awake often enough.

But then, nobody put a shotgun to your head and said, "Here, sign right here. You're going to be a U.S. deputy marshal." Man had a choice. And when you had a choice you gave up your right to complain. You might bitch a little, sure, but you couldn't *complain*.

Longarm awoke earlier than usual, and with time to kill before the hotel restaurant opened up. He strolled out into the plaza and took a seat on one of the benches to watch the sun come up. The air was as cool as it would get, and the town about as quiet as it ever got. Only the occasional sound of a random gunshot, along with a drunken yell or two, disturbed the peace. On the streets near the plaza he could see Mexican *peons* hurrying along, either driving burros laden with some kind of cargo or riding them. As the sun got up and began to turn the air a soft yellow, he saw women coming up from the river with loads of wet wash on their heads. He reckoned it was their business, but he couldn't see the point of washing anything in the Rio Grande and calling it clean. There were plenty of public water wells and cisterns scattered about, but he reckoned these women had been washing clothes in the river for so long that it just never occurred to them to do it any different.

Then he spied a figure he wasn't especially interested in seeing: Willis Howard, coming out of a saloon right directly opposite the bench that Longarm was sitting on. His path, if he was going to the hotel, would take him almost directly by Longarm. Longarm thought of getting up and trying to sneak off, but knew he'd run into Willis sooner or later, so he figured he'd get it over with. He had a powerful taste for coffee in his mouth, and had just been about to start for the hotel when he'd seen Willis. But if he did, Willis would just come sit at his table, and that would be even worse than a meeting in the open air.

He watched Willis coming on. The young man looked like he'd had a rough night. His collar was undone and his shirt was wrinkled. He walked like he was either slightly drunk or there was something the matter with his legs. As he got closer, Longarm could see the stubble on his face. Likely he'd been playing poker all night and drinking. And likely he felt like merry hell. If he did, Longarm thought, Willis might be more interested in getting to bed than in talking.

But he soon saw his hopes were pointless. Willis was heading toward him on a straight if slightly unsteady line. He finally arrived at the bench and stood right in front of Longarm. He said, "What'd you do that to me for?"

"Do what to you?"

"Get me thrown in jail like some common villain."

"I never got you thrown in jail. You managed that trick all by yourself."

"You was the one told me to go out and ask around about who'd be interested in buying some military equipment."

Longarm said wearily, "No, I never told you to go out asking anybody about buying anything. You pestered me about my business and insisted on having a part in it until I said you *might* go out and inquire around about parties interested in surplus military equipment. But I *damn* sure didn't tell you to go and ask a couple of deputy sheriffs! That was your own idea. Though what put it into your head is beyond me."

Willis stared at him blearily. His eyes were bloodshot and his hair was tousled. Even in his young face Longarm could see the outlines of little pouches under his eyes. Willis said, "Well, I just want you to know that I ain't gonna do no more askin' around for you. Do you know they fined me five dollars?"

"What for?"

"Didn't give me no reason. Just fined me."

Longarm shook his head. "Well, that's a pity. Tell you what. I'm just about to go in for some breakfast. Be glad to buy you some."

But Willis shook his head. "I'm goin' to bed. Been up all night. Playing poker."

"Did you win or lose?"

Willis thought for a moment. "I don't know. But I didn't get caught cheating, I'll tell you that. I think I won because I got money in every pocket."

Then without another word, he started toward the hotel, still staggering slightly. Longarm turned to watch him. He appeared tired more than drunk. Finally Longarm stood up and stretched and yawned. His mouth and belly were about ready for a pot of coffee and half a dozen fried eggs and ham and biscuits with cream gravy. And when he'd finished that he figured he might have a piece of apple pie if there was any room left.

That afternoon he commenced on a plan that had been in his mind since the night before. The desk clerk he was friendly with, the sheriff's brother-in-law, was on duty. Longarm waited until the desk was clear of customers, and then sauntered up and put an elbow on the desk top. He said, "You doing all right?"

The clerk smiled slightly. "Pretty well considering the bullet holes."

Longarm said, "Yeah, them are tiresome."

"Hear you got a lavender-scented note yesterday evening."

"You don't know how good it makes a body feel to know that his business is kept strictly confidential around here."

The clerk laughed. "An' you also had a visit with my brother-'n-law. You open yore window and let the place air out after he left?"

"Speaking of the good sheriff, where does the man live? I might need to pay him a visit."

The clerk's face changed slightly. He said, with an edge in his voice, "You mean where does he sleep when he ain't bunkin' in with one of his *putas*? You mean where he goes when he feels the need to give my sister a damn good whumpin'? You mean that house he makes her stay in seven days a week so she won't git into town an' be an embarrassment to him on account he's got to act nearly polite to her in public?"

Longarm shook his head. "He's a hell of a man, ain't he?"

"Yeah." The clerk studied him. "Of course I ain't quite figured you out yet, Mister Long. You a friend of the high sheriff's? If you are I don't reckon I want to be as friendly with you as I have been."

Longarm smiled thinly. "Well, I can't tell you about my business because some parties might think it's illegal. But I'll just say that, where the sheriff is concerned, I ain't exactly got his best interests at heart."

"If you git a chance to skin him, pull a little skin off him for me. If I was a braver man I'd do it myself. But he's already locked me up once for telling him my mind. It wasn't no church picnic."

"Reckon I'd be taking my life in my hands if I went out to his house?"

The clerk shrugged. "First place, I doubt you'll find him there. But he don't keep no guards around if that's what you mean. Place is kind of a small ranch, but the sheriff is way too busy to fool with a bunch of cattle. Besides, somebody would just swim over from Mexico and steal them."

"So where would his house be?"

The clerk pointed toward the door of the hotel. "You go out the river road. West. It ain't marked, but it's the only road heading that way. Kind of starts right there at the southwest corner of the plaza. Then you just follow that on out of town and go on for about two miles, little more, and you'll see a white house set off from the road back toward the river. It's a fair-sized house, about six or seven rooms. It's made out of adobe brick and whitewashed just like all the big houses around here. Red tile roof. There's a barn made out of sawn lumber, but it ain't painted. There's a little corral just to the right of the house when you're facing it. He usually keeps two or three horses in there. And there's a little shack just behind the main house where my sister's maid sleeps. Though what she needs with a maid beats the hell out of me. I think she's one of my brother-'n-law's *putas* that he wore out and is givin' her a place to sleep and a few pesos. But you can't miss the place. Not another house on either side for a mile. Only man out there is an old Mexican does handiwork around the place. I'd like to ask you why you don't just see him in his office or in your room or in a saloon, but that wouldn't be any of my business so I won't ask you."

"I always found you could size a man up better if you saw how he lived."

The clerk looked at him. "Shit."

Longarm smiled. "And two makes eight."

The desk clerk was looking at him steadily. He said, "You may not think I mean this, but I hope you're going out there to ambush the sonofabitch."

Longarm shook his head. "Ain't my style. I figure he needs killing, but I ain't got reason enough to. What's your sister's name?"

"Shirley. If you see her tell her I said hello. My name is Mac, by the way."

They shook hands formally. Longarm said, "Well, glad to finally meet you. Anything you want me to carry out to your sister?"

Mac shook his head. "Naw, she's got most of what she needs. Except for a good man. Like I say, I don't figure you'll find him out there. But I don't know for sure. I ain't allowed around the place. Maybe things have changed."

"You can't go see your sister?"

Mac smiled. There was no humor in it. "Naw. According to the sheriff I put the wrong ideas in her head."

Longarm gave a low whistle and a little wave and walked out of the hotel. He stood a moment on the sidewalk determining what to do with the balance of the afternoon. He figured to go out to Bob Bird's house late, maybe as late as nine-thirty or ten o'clock. He wanted to catch the man relaxed, off his guard, not expecting callers. He wasn't certain in his mind what he intended to do, but he could feel the well of impatience rising in him to get something done and get something done in a hurry. Too much time had passed. He knew Older was guilty; it was just a matter of proving it. And his plan was to either get Bird to implicate the deputy marshal, or get him out of the way so he could go directly at Older.

But just exactly how he was going to do that was still unclear. One thing, he knew for certain he couldn't approach the man the way he had a mind to do in town, not with him surrounded by deputies. He had a feeling now that Bird wasn't a very strong man, nor a very brave one either, for that matter. Little strutting blowhard bullies seldom were.

There was something else, though, that he wanted to discuss with the sheriff. It had been on his mind ever since he'd learned that Bird owned a share in the Hamilton Hotel. Beginning with that, he'd begun to piece together little snippets of conversation that he'd heard that made him believe Bird had an interest in more of the town's businesses than just the hotel. And it made him wonder if Bird was just a real good businessman or if he'd dealt himself in because he was sheriff. It also made him wonder if maybe Older was part of more than just the gun smuggling. Well, there were two people who knew that for sure, and he figured to have a talk with one of them no later than that night.

But meanwhile, he thought he'd kill the time with a mild poker game. He didn't want to get into anything heavy because his time was limited and he wasn't carrying that much money. He figured he had about thirty dollars in his pocket, and knew he had an even two hundred dollars. He walked across the plaza and went into a card house called the Square Deal. He doubted it was, but he reckoned a man could call his place of business anything he wanted, even if it was a lie.

The place was about half full. In the back there were several faro and blackjack tables, both games he didn't particularly care for. Up front were the poker games, so he walked around noting the size of the play and looking for an open seat. One finally came open in a five-dollar-limit game. Just before he sat down he noticed that Willis was playing at the next table and, judging from the pile of money in the pot, it was a sizeable game.

For the next hour or so he put all other thoughts out of his mind and concentrated on the game. His luck was about average. Once he trapped two players, both holding small straights, in a good pot, and beat them both with a king-high heart flush. The pot was nearly a hundred dollars, but he figured he'd put in at least thirty dollars of that.

A little later he was deep in the middle of a hand of straight draw poker, drawing one card to two pair, trying to make a full house, when a commotion started at the table where Willis was sitting. Longarm looked over quickly, certain that Willis had finally been caught once too often. To his surprise Willis wasn't involved. Two rough-looking *hombres* were standing, facing each other and shouting threats. Willis was just sitting, his hands folded before him on the table, looking innocent and disinterested. After a second he glanced over and saw that Longarm was watching him. He just winked and shook his head. The fight had quieted down. A burly man had come over and said something to the two players, and they'd either settled their differences or decided they weren't in the right place to have an argument.

Longarm boxed his cards and began to look at them one at a time. He'd gone in with a pair of tens and a pair of fours. The first card he looked at was a four. He squeezed the next one into view. It was a ten, followed by another ten and then another four. The fifth card was the ten of spades. He looked up and said, "Now, what was the bet? Five dollars? I raise that five dollars."

By seven o'clock he figured he'd won something over a hundred dollars. He got up to go to the hotel to get some supper and get ready for his trip out to the sheriff's ranch. Willis caught him on the boardwalk just outside the door. Longarm said, "You mean ain't nobody killed you yet?"

Willis said smugly, "I don't cheat anymore—don't have to. These poker players are so dumb I don't have to cheat. I'm up almost five hundred dollars right now."

Longarm said, "Then you better come eat supper with me and put that five hundred in yore hip pocket and keep it there."

But Willis said, "I can eat anytime. I'm on a hot streak right now."

Longarm laughed. "You sound like a sucker. You mean you're playing on luck? Hell, ain't nothing can cool off as fast as a hot streak in cards. Unless it's a whore once she gets your money in her hands."

Willis said, "I reckon I been gambling long enough to look out for myself."

Longarm started toward the hotel. "Good luck."

He was eating late and the selection was limited, but he was able to get some good roast beef with gravy and mashed potatoes and boiled *jicima*, which was kind of a Mexican turnip. He finished the meal off with a shot of brandy and two cups of coffee. After that he went up to his room. All the Mexican desk clerk had for him this time was just his key, no little blue envelopes. But the act of stopping at the desk brought back the memory of Belinda Manly dressed in just that light wrapper. The thought of her made his throat swell and his jeans get tight in the crotch. She was some beautiful woman, and he reckoned her being so near and yet out of reach was torture for her husband. Well, that might all come right in the very near future. Maybe in a matter of hours.

About nine o'clock he went around to the stables behind the hotel and called for his horse. By now the stable man knew that he liked to saddle his own animal, so he just brought the dun out with the saddle riding on the horse's back. Longarm checked the bridle, then girthed the horse and swung aboard. The horse responded instantly to the light touch of his spurs. They went past the hotel, rounded the south end of the plaza, and struck the road that Longarm felt sure was the one Mac had described.

It was a nice night, pleasant and cool with nearly a full moon showing. The horse snorted once at the moonlit shadow of a tree, but very shortly settled down to a slow lope. As he rode Longarm wished he had a more definite plan in mind. He had nothing to hold over the sheriff's head except physical fear, and he reckoned he'd use that to get what he could out of Bird. He wasn't going to expose himself as a deputy marshal; just a trader wanting to deal with the ramrod, the boss, so as to get a better price. And he was going to make it clear to Bird that he knew that party to be Les Older, and that the sheriff had the chance to save himself a hell of a lot of pain if he'd give the information up without any prompting.

It was not a tactic you'd find in the deputy marshal's handbook, and it wasn't a method he'd want to tell Billy Vail about, but he felt the situation was important enough and drastic enough to warrant drastic measures. Marshals just couldn't afford to have rotten apples going around wearing the badge. It discredited the whole service.

So even though it was not to his personal taste, he was going to employ some extreme measures.

About twenty minutes out of town he could just distinguish a white house set off toward the river where Mac had said it would be. He got out his watch and, in the moonlight, was able to see it was just about nine-thirty. He put spurs to his horse and rode on the half mile, until a little road turned off to the left toward the house. He pulled his horse down from a trot to a walk and proceeded slowly toward the ranch house, taking his time, his eyes flickering back and forth looking for any sign of movement. The place was still as a graveyard.

The house was a one-story affair, low and rambling. Longarm could make out the dim glow of a light in what he took to be the center of the house, the parlor or sitting room.

He rode even more slowly toward the place, now stopping every few yards to look and listen. He saw the corral and saw that there were three horses in it, but they were just standing around quietly; they didn't seem as if they'd been ridden recently.

Ten yards away he could see that there was a screened-in porch along the front of the house. He rode the dun up to a hitching post, dismounted, and tied the horse loosely. If he had to leave in a hurry he didn't want to have to be fooling with any knots. He walked carefully up to the door of the screened-in porch. Behind it he could see the main door to the house, a big, heavy affair. He didn't know if he should knock on the door of the porch or let himself through and knock on the big door. He finally gave a tentative rap or two on the flimsy screen door. Nothing happened and he doubted he could be heard inside. He opened the porch door and walked across the board floor to the big door. He loosened his revolver in his holster. He had switched back to the gun he usually carried, the one with the six-inch barrel, and he was wearing his cutaway holster. He put out his hand and knocked lightly on the door.

Nothing happened.

He knocked again, and this time he heard sounds inside. In a moment a woman's voice said, "Who is it?"

Longarm cleared his throat. "My name is Long. I'm here to see the sheriff. Here on private business."

The door swung open and a woman stood there. The room inside was brighter than it had appeared from outside. He reckoned she must have some sort of curtains over the windows.

She said, "I'm Mrs. Bird. Can I help you?"

He took off his hat. "No, ma'am, I don't reckon. My business is directly with the sheriff. Do you know when he might be in?"

She seemed to be inspecting him very closely. Only then did he notice she was wearing a robe and, underneath that, some kind of nightgown. He could see the lace of the gown sticking out from the open collar of the robe.

She said, "Well, I'm not sure. Why don't you come in and wait? I bet you'd like a cup of coffee. Or maybe a drink."

He looked at her. He couldn't tell much about her body in the robe, but she was a comely woman in the face. The light was on her side so he couldn't see her as clearly as she could see him, but he judged her to be no more than thirty years old. He said, "Well, ma'am, I wouldn't want to put you to no trouble. I see you are rigged out to go to bed. I can just wait outside here for a spell."

She said, "Oh, nonsense. I usually get undressed right after supper so as to be more comfortable. God knows I'm not going anywhere. No, you come on in here and wait. Do you take whiskey?"

"I didn't think your husband held with strong drink."

"He don't hold with a lot of things. But what he don't know won't hurt him." She stepped back and held the door wide. "Just come in."

He hesitated for only a second. Something told him he was going to be doing more than waiting, but he couldn't imagine doing anything with the sheriff's wife. Maybe she was just naturally friendly, but it seemed to his ears that he'd heard more than just an invitation to a drink and a chair.

He stepped across the threshold and she shut the door behind him.

Chapter 8

She sat him down in an overstuffed morris chair and then disappeared from the room. He looked around. Even though the place was supposed to be a ranch house it was elegantly turned out. The walls were paneled in some kind of shiny wood, and there were hand-woven carpets on the tile floor and an overhead lamp fixture that held at least six brass-based lamps. All of the furniture was large and heavy and looked expensive. He didn't know what the sheriff's job paid in Laredo, but he didn't figure it would cover the price of such fixings.

Mrs. Bird came back with a glass in each hand. She'd poured him a good tumblerful of amber-colored whiskey. She had the same, but he noticed she'd watered hers some. She sat down in a parlor chair just across a little table from him. Now, in the light, he could see that she was indeed a very attractive woman. But there was a kind of sadness about her face that kept the beauty from getting all the way out. He noticed that the robe she was wearing was brocaded silk. In San Francisco he'd once seen such a robe, and it would have taken him a month's pay to buy it.

He'd tried to get up when she'd entered with the whiskey, but she'd waved him back in his chair. Now she sat, delicately and demurely, with her legs crossed, openly studying him. She said, "You're not from around here. I don't mean that I know that because I've never seen you. I mean it because you don't sound like you've been in this hellhole long. Your language is too good. And you've got a little bit of an accent."

"Well, that kind of surprises me, Mrs. Bird. That part about me having an accent. Much as I've traveled I figured to have lost it. No, I'm originally from the Arizona Territory."

"Call me Shirley. I hate 'Mrs. Bird.' In fact I hate the name Bird."

He began to feel uncomfortable. He knew enough about this woman to know she couldn't be very happy, but he didn't want to listen to her complaints. For something to say he said, "Your brother Mac says to tell you hello and to let me know if you need anything. I'll get word to him."

Her face lit up at the mention of her brother. "Dear Mac. He's as trapped as I am. I wish he'd leave here."

That left him with nothing to say. He'd been waiting for her to drink first before he tasted his whiskey, but she was just sitting with the glass in her hand. He lifted his and said, "Well, here's luck."

It brought her back. He'd seen her go off in her mind, but now she lifted her glass also. "Yes," she said with just a trace of bitterness, "here's to luck. Let it be the good kind for a change."

He had the definite feeling that he was not where he should be. He had hoped to find Bird at home and then entice him outside and drag him off somewhere for a little prayer meeting, but that hardly seemed possible with his wife there.

She said, without the trace of a smile, "Are you one of my husband's crooked friends? Most of the men who come out here to see him are involved in some crooked business with him."

It caused him to blink. This woman was what you called direct. "Mrs. Bird, I reckon I better run on along. I'm just a trader in surplus military equipment. I'm trying to sell your husband some rifles. It's completely honest."

She smiled sadly. "I wasn't trying to insult you. I was insulting my husband. I don't often get the chance, especially with a gentlemen of your obvious character. I don't see many gentlemen, Mister Long, so you'll have to forgive me."

He couldn't tell if she was slightly drunk or just a woman so beaten down and bitter that she didn't seem to care what she said. But what he couldn't figure was, if she was so unhappy, why she didn't run for her life. He leaned forward and said, "Mrs. Bird."

"Shirley, please."

"All right. Shirley. Shirley, your husband is the sheriff. You just said a kind of surprising thing to me and I'm a total stranger."

108

"You really must forgive me." She looked at the glass in her hand. "I guess I could blame it on this, but I really haven't had that much. Not of whiskey. I've had plenty of Sheriff Bird." She bore down on the last two words with a viciousness that was almost physical. "Like I say, I don't often get a chance to talk to a man of breeding. Not that I'm claiming that for myself. We moved here from Houston some years back. Believe it or not, this was once a civilized place. My father came down here to be town marshal. Then Bob got elected sheriff." She looked away.

"Shirley, your husband is the law here."

She laughed. "My husband is the *out*law here. The main outlaw here. The biggest crook of them all. The only difference between him and the rest is that he runs the jail and sometimes he puts some of the little crooks in it. He's the one belongs in it."

"Shirley, you shouldn't be telling me this." The woman had him baffled. She was obviously not drunk, and she certainly didn't sound like she was off her rocker. She was telling him what she was telling him for a reason. Maybe that reason was just to get it off her chest. Or maybe she was hoping it would be repeated back to her husband and cause him to let up on her for fear of what all she might say. It had him puzzled.

She suddenly put the glass to her mouth, drained it, and set it on the little table. Then she stood up and untied the sash of her robe and let it fall on the floor around her feet. She stood before him in a very thin nightgown. He could see the clear outline of her breasts and the black patch of hair that rose from between her legs. She said, "Take me back in the bedroom. It's just down the hall and through the door."

He was so startled he almost dropped his glass. He said, the words sounding stupid even as they left his mouth, "What for?"

"To hold me. To be tender to me. To treat me like a woman."

He swallowed and reached nervously for his hat, which was sitting on the floor at his feet. "Shirley, is this some kind of a setup? Me and your husband ain't exactly friends. I know I may look stupid, but I ain't coming in a man's house and taking his wife back to the bedroom. If he ain't already back there he could be along pretty shortly. And catching me with you would be all the reason he'd need to shoot me in the back." He stood up. He was conscious that he was still holding the glass of whiskey in

109

his right hand. He leaned forward and set it on the table that stood between them.

"No, this is not a setup. You can search the house. He's not here and he won't be back tonight."

"Then how come you told me he would and that I should wait?"

She took a step toward him. "Because I wanted you to stay." Her voice suddenly went intense. "I stay here all day by myself, all night by myself. I'm going crazy. But worse, I'm being wasted." She was close enough to touch him, and she put her hand up to his cheek. "I'm so hungry as a woman that I'm dying. I need you. I want you."

"Hell, lady, you don't even know me."

"Oh, I know you all right. You're a good man. You're kind and you're gentle. And you're handsome." She saw his disbelieving look and said, "I know you don't understand and I know this is coming at you pretty fast. But I've had to learn to judge people in a hurry. Living with Bob is like living with a stick of dynamite always ready to go off. So I've gotten very good with people." She laughed bitterly. "Unfortunately five years too late, or I'd of never married the good sheriff, who only wanted to use me and my daddy and our money."

He said, troubled, "But if you feel that way, why don't you leave?"

She laughed without humor. "You think I haven't tried? What do you think he's got so many deputies for? I've left, but they've always caught me and brought me back. And then Bob made sure I was very, very sorry I'd ever tried it. Besides, this is my ranch. My daddy left it to me."

He shifted uncertainly. God knows, the woman was tempting. He could feel the pulse in his throat, feel the copperish taste in his mouth. "The man could walk in here with a shotgun at any minute."

"Take me back to the bedroom. It's a strong door and you can lock it from the inside. I swear to you that there is no danger." She grabbed his shirt and pulled him toward her until his face was just at hers. She leaned forward and kissed him with her full lips, her mouth opening slightly, her tongue flicking out to find his.

His breath was coming hard. "All right. But it's crazy."

She took his hand and they went through a door off the parlor, and then down a short hall and through another door and into a

110

big bedroom that was softly lit by one lantern.

He said, "Shirley, you know you don't want to make love with me so much as you want to get back at your husband."

"Like hell," she said. She put her arms around his neck and kissed him again. Even through his clothes he could feel the soft warmth of her body. She said, when their lips parted, "He can freeze in hell. I'd take ten beatings from him for one night with you."

"Well, then I don't guess the reason matters, does it."

"No. You can lock the door if you want."

He turned and shoved the heavy door closed and locked it with a big key. There was a sliding bolt and he shoved that home. It would take somebody a good little while to get through such a door, and meanwhile, there were two good-sized windows a body could make an escape through.

He turned around, and she was standing by the bed, naked. A head of steam had been building in him from the night before in Belinda Manly's room. Over and over he had remembered her standing there without that wrapper. And when Shirley had first stood up and taken off her robe, his mind had immediately raced to Belinda. He had thought, somewhat distractedly, that it was odd how things came in bunches. Sometimes he went weeks without a woman, and now all this had come, beginning with Bonnie in San Antonio.

He started walking toward her, taking off his gunbelt as he did. She was a very comely woman, not a beauty like Belinda Manly, but there was a ripeness about her that was even more appealing than Belinda's young perfection. Other than a very thin veneer of flesh, she was probably still the same woman she'd been ten years ago. Her breasts were firm and full and erect, and her hips flared out from long, straight legs.

He walked to her and past her, the saliva thick in his mouth, and laid his gunbelt on the table beside the head of the bed. Then he sat down and slowly pulled off his boots, still staring at her, his eyes switching back and forth from her breasts to the little soft mound that grew the black, curly hair. He had put his hat back on, and now he took it off and laid it by the side of the bed. He took his shirt off and dropped it on the floor. Then he stood up and began unbuttoning his jeans. She was standing there, beginning to tremble. All of a sudden she dropped to her knees in front of him and, using both hands, jerked his jeans down past his knees. Then she took him in her mouth. The sensation was so sudden and overwhelming that he grabbed her head with his hands.

Then she sprang up and lay down on the bed on her back, her legs open, holding herself open with her fingers. She said, her voice choked, "Now! Take me, now!"

He jerked his jeans the rest of the way off and flung himself on her. She guided him inside her. She began to moan as he thrust rhythmically, deeper and deeper into her. He could feel fire running all through his body; even his toes were tingling. Her breathing was coming faster and faster. She had her legs wrapped around his hips and was using her heels to drive him harder and faster. Her arms were around his neck, holding his mouth glued to hers. Her tongue entered his mouth in rhythm with his thrusts. He could feel them both beginning to sweat. The room, the bed, the air seemed like it all was on fire.

And then it was over. He expired with a jolt and a yell and then a long moan. For a few moments he just lay on top of her, inert, while the tips of her soft fingers stroked gently up and down his back. Finally he rolled off her, rolling to the side where his revolver and gunbelt lay on the night table. He said, still a little short of breath, "I'm sorry. I know it was too fast."

"Don't be. Something that wonderful shouldn't last too long. It can't. You don't want to get too used to it. You want it to be something you can just dream about later and wonder if it really happened the way you remember."

Now he was sitting up cross-legged, smoking a cigar and putting the ashes out in a glass of water on the table. She'd gone and brought him a tumblerful of whiskey, and then crawled up to sit beside him on the bed. He drank and smoked while she gently massaged his testicles, hoping to arouse him again. He said, "I think you're beating a dead horse, Shirley. I think you emptied the barn."

"Oh, God, to be able to look forward to that just a few nights a week. How wonderful that would be."

He had to turn his head a little to the right to see her full in the face. He said, "Shirley, something I don't understand. I know you hate Bob Bird, but doesn't he do anything to you? I can't call it making love, but doesn't he have you on occasion? Hell, I don't see how any man could be around a woman like you and keep his jeans buttoned all the time. Pardon the language, but I didn't know any other way to say it."

112

"Don't worry about words. Believe me, the girls know just as many as the boys and maybe a few more." Then she wrinkled her brow for a second. "Yes, at first we made love. When he was courting me I really thought he loved me. I didn't love him, but he was ambitious and knew how to make people like him and my father thought it would be a good match. But then he changed." She shook her head. "My God, how he changed when he started getting a little power. But now, of course, he never comes near me. I'd kill myself first. The sight of him makes me sick." She suddenly laughed. "I actually threw up on him once. God, did I get a beating for that." She shook her head. "Now he just contents himself with telling me, in great detail, what he does with his whores, his girlfriends in town. He thinks I care." She smiled grimly. "I thank heaven every day for those girls. If I could I'd send them Christmas presents."

"Why don't you get out of this? You can divorce him."

She looked at Longarm. "I can? Find me a way. I managed to make it to one lawyer; idea nearly scared him to death. What is your first name? I can't keep calling you *Mister* Long after what we've done."

"Just Long will do. I never cared for my mother's choice in given names."

"All right," she said. "Anyway, Mister Long, I don't think you can understand how powerful Bob Bird is here. He controls this town. He controls the local judge."

"But there's a federal circuit judge. There has to be one."

She shrugged. "Find me a lawyer first who'll file the papers."

He said cautiously, "I hear there is a U.S. deputy marshal in town. Couldn't you go to him?"

It sent her off into peals of laughter. "Now that is funny. The arrival of that federal marshal nearly gave my dear husband a heart attack." She laughed again. "Do you know that he came home and started packing? He was going to take all his money and run for Mexico. But then I said, 'Why don't you try and buy him off? Like you've bought off everyone else.'" She frowned. "Hell, I didn't know it would work. I thought federal marshals were supposed to be above corruption. I was just trying to help my dear husband stick his head in the noose. But damned if the marshal didn't turn out to be crooked." She pointed in the general direction of the parlor. "They sat right in there and made the deal. Right here in this house, with me listening."

She looked at him and held out her hand. "Give me a sip of that whiskey."

He handed her the tumbler, and she took two quick sips and then handed it back to him. He took a pull and set the glass on the table. He said, "You heard them?"

"Bob treats me like a piece of furniture. Who would I tell? And what good would it do?" She stopped for a second and then said, "I did get the satisfaction of watching Bob grovel. He's not the boss no more. That deputy is. Bob is scared to death of him, and for once I don't blame him. He scares me too."

Longarm said, with studied casualness, "Have you ever . . .?"

She gave him a wry smile. "No, but I think I could have if I'd wanted. And right in front of Bob too. I've even thought of it that way. Really rub his nose in it. Show him what kind of man he really is. But I couldn't do it. That damn deputy makes me as sick as Bob."

She had stopped massaging his testicles and now was lying back on her side. He ran a hand over her belly and on up to her breasts, touching them with his fingers until the nipples came erect. He said, "You asked me if I was one of your husband's crooked friends when I came in. Isn't that a little dangerous?"

"I apologize for that. But I knew you weren't the minute I laid eyes on you."

"You've certainly got a lot of faith in your judgment. You don't call Bird a crook, do you? To his face, I mean?"

Her hips were starting to move slightly as he continued to caress her. "Sure I do. When he comes here, which he seldom does, thank God, I can tell by the look on his face if I'm fixing to get a beating. So I get my licks in when I can." She shrugged. "Might as well."

"Have you ever thought of blowing the sonofabitch's head off?"

"Ooooh . . ." she said, "That feels good. Don't stop. Yes, I've thought of it. But I'm no good with guns. I'd just make a botch of it. Oh, keep that up." She moaned a little.

"What do you mean, he owns the town?"

"Well, he doesn't exactly own it. But he makes all the whore-houses and gambling dens and saloons pay him so much to stay open. If they don't he goes in with his deputies and finds something wrong and arrests everyone."

"And is the deputy marshal in on that too?"

"Oh, my God, yes. In fact I think he makes Bob give him the biggest part of it." Her hand came out to touch him between the legs. "But I think they make the most money smuggling into Mexico. You know that I don't care if you tell him any of this. Especially what we've done and are about to do again."

He slid down beside her. "I don't think you're going to have to worry about your husband too much longer."

She had her mouth close to his ear. "Are you going to shoot him?"

"No," he said. "But I think he'll get in trouble with a federal marshal."

"That's what I've been hoping," she said. "That fellow Older is about five times as smart as Bob. I keep hoping he'll just get rid of my bastard husband. Put your hand right there for a second. Oh, yes! Oh, yes!"

She rolled over on her back, carrying him with her. She said, "Now! Please, now! Oh, hurry! Get in me!"

It was after midnight when he finally left. She clung to him at the door and kissed him over and over, and made him promise to come back as soon as he could. She said, "God, I feel light as a feather. I feel like I'm floating. Oh, God, do hurry back. Nights I know he's not here I'll have the whole house lit up so you can see it from town."

Back in Laredo he put his horse away and then went up to his room, his head full of all he'd learned that night from Bird's wife. And it all wasn't about the sheriff either. As he took off his shirt he could smell the scent of her still rising from his skin. She was as fine a woman as he'd met in years and he had to figure that Bird, on top of being a crook, was just plain crazy not to feel himself lucky to have a woman like Shirley. Maybe, he thought, Bird ought not to be put in prison, but left out in the middle of a desert somewhere where he could go quietly crazy by himself without posing a threat to anyone else.

Longarm got undressed, and sat down on the edge of his bed to have one last drink and a few puffs of a cigar. It had made him sad to see the sadness in Shirley, to see a woman like that watching her life go down the drain. Well, she was soon going to be free of Bird if he had anything to do with it. And maybe, once rid of that snake, she'd have enough life left in her to go on and find some happiness. She was tough, but she wasn't tough in a fight-back kind of way; it was more a sort of resilience that allowed her to take the blows and the insults and the deprivation and still hang on. Well, he would do what he could for her. Then he smiled at the ceiling. And for himself also. He did not plan to leave town without another small sampling of Shirley.

And then there was Belinda. Lord, he didn't reckon he'd ever been on a job where there were more damsels in distress that needed rescuing. Wasn't nothing in the handbook about rescuing damsels in distress, but he reckoned the clause about keeping the peace applied to the matter.

Finally he yawned, stubbed out his cigar, finished the last of the whiskey in his glass, and turned off the lamp and rolled back into the bed. For a second, before sleep overtook him, he dwelled on the events of the evening. As far as he was concerned, it was the best laugh on Bird he could think of. Bird had a woman's husband locked up so he could get at her. And meanwhile he was getting the horns put on him right there in his own house. Longarm reckoned he didn't know of a more deserving fellow for it to happen to. His mind strayed to Willis Howard. So now the young man had given up cheating in favor of depending on luck in poker. Well, certainly playing luck was a lot safer for the young man, but he rather expected it would prove a great deal more costly, money-wise, in the long run. What that kid needed, Longarm decided, was a hardheaded wife and a job clerking in a mercantile store. He went to sleep dreaming of the mountains of Colorado and wondering when he was ever going to get back to that cool, crisp air and crotchety Billy Vail.

About three o'clock the next afternoon he was sitting in the lobby of the hotel, smoking a cigar and watching the passersby. Mac had discreetly asked him if he'd gone out to see Bird the night before, and he'd said that, yes, he had gone out there but that the sheriff hadn't been home, so he'd come back to town and played a little poker. Mac had asked after his sister and Longarm had, discreetly, said she looked fine, but he'd only spoken to her for a moment. Mac had given him a look, but he'd returned it innocently enough.

Now there wasn't much to do but sit and wait. He was doing just that when he saw a young boy of some thirteen or fourteen years come in the front door and go up to the desk. The boy was carrying an envelope. He asked Mac something and Mac pointed Longarm's way. The boy came over to where he was sitting. He said, "Do you be Mistuh Long?"

"I am."

The boy held out the envelope. "I's a messenger clerk for the railroad. This here note is to tell you that yore sealed boxcar is in. The number of the car is in that envelope."

Longarm opened the envelope and pulled out the little note that said it was from the Texas and Rio Grande Railroad Company.

The boy shifted his feet. He said, "Course thet's jest yore 'ficial notice. What you got to do is go down and see Mistuh Allbright. He's the freight superintendent. He's the one kin give you the key to yore car. See, you got to heve the key 'cause the car has got a lock on it. Thet's why they calls it a sealed car. An' Mistuh Allbright'll give you the key an' tell you whar yore car is spotted. That thar note ain't nuthin' but the 'ficial notification which I'm the one brangs to you."

Longarm nodded and looked grave. "Well, that's an important job you got there. Now, reckon you could do a job for me?"

"'F it don't take too much time from my 'ficial duties fer the railroad."

Longarm said, "I want you to carry a message to the sheriff for me. Reckon you can do that?"

"Don't see why not," the boy said. "I's mighty good at takin' messages."

Longarm got up and walked with the boy to the door of the hotel. He pointed to the bench in the middle of the plaza where he generally sat. He reached in his pocket and took out a half-dollar and gave it to the boy. It was a considerable tip, and the boy's eyes got big as he took it. Longarm said, "You run over to the jail and tell the sheriff that Mister Long . . . Can you remember Mister Long?"

"You betcha."

"Well, you run over there and tell the sheriff that Mister Long will be waiting on that bench at four o'clock to see him. If the sheriff ain't there you tell whatever deputy is on duty the message. Now you can handle that, can't you?"

"You betcha, sir."

"Well, run along then."

He watched as the boy went flying out the door and across the plaza, heading for the jail. When the boy disappeared behind one of the shade trees he turned and went into the bar and ordered a single drink. He took his time drinking it, sipping it down

117

slowly. He was letting his mind go blank. There was no point in trying to plan until he saw Bird because any plan would depend on how the sheriff wanted to play it.

When his drink was finished he squared his shoulders, went out of the hotel, and crossed the plaza and sat down on the bench. He didn't know how long a wait he was in for, but he didn't have anything better to do than try and put Bob Bird out of business.

The sheriff was twenty minutes late. He came strutting across the plaza from the jail, looking neither left nor right, and came to a stop in front of Longarm. He said, without greeting, "Well?"

Longarm smiled up at him, trying to see if the horns the sheriff had growing out of his head were visible. He reckoned only he and Shirley would be able to see them. He said, "You might as well have a seat, Sheriff. We got a little talking to do."

Bird said, "You picked a hell of a place to have a meeting. What the hell was wrong with yore hotel room whar we talked before?"

"Well, once probably wouldn't draw no notice. Twice might get folks to wondering what we was up to. No, I figured if a man was gonna have a parley about smuggling guns over into Mexico, and making a lot of money in the bargain, the best place to talk was right out in the middle of everywhere." He patted the empty part of the bench. "Why don't you take the load off yore feet. This might get interesting."

Bird sat down reluctantly, but he only sat on the edge of the bench, holding himself stiff, not really looking at Longarm.

Longarm said, half laughing, "You trying to act like you don't know me?"

Bird said, through his teeth, "Git on with it."

Longarm took a moment to relight his cigar. When it was drawing he said, "The guns come in."

Bird looked at him sharply. "They're here? In Laredo?"

Longarm nodded. "Sitting right down there in the rail yard in a sealed boxcar." He took the note from the freight agent out of his pocket and showed it briefly to Bird. Then he took it back and put it in his pocket. He didn't want to give Bird time to memorize the car number. The car might be sealed, but it could be broken into. He said, "Guns are in there resting nice and easy. All me and you has got to do is work out the arrangements."

"What arrangements?"

"Well, I want to make sure you understand this is cash on the barrel-head. I'm sure you're a right nice feller, Sheriff, and just as honest as the day is long. But I'm gonna want to see the color of yore money while you are looking at my guns. *Savvy?* And I want to get this over with in a hurry. I've taken a great hankering to get back up north toward my part of the country. I don't seem to get along so well down here. Maybe it's because I don't *savvy* the lingo so good. You reckon about eleven o'clock tonight would suit you?"

Bird said, tight-lipped, "Are you crazy? It's after four. The banks are closed. Where would I be able to get eleven thousand dollars in cash?"

Longarm put his head back and laughed. For the life of him he couldn't understand how a little worm like Bird had talked Shirley into marrying him. "Tell you what, Sheriff, why don't you just make a swing around these joints along the plaza. I bet you could collect eleven thousand in about a half an hour."

Bird said coldly, "What are you talking about?"

"I'm talking about all the times I've seen your deputies come in a saloon or a card house with an empty sack and leave with a full one. You know what I'm talking about. Hell, I wasn't in this town twenty-four hours before I knew you were lopping the top off every joint in town. Hell, what's the point of being the sheriff in a rat's nest like Laredo if you can't make it pay?"

"You got a big mouth, Long."

"Yes, and that's another good reason to get me out of town. If it ain't payday at the joints, why, just take it out of your office safe. Or get it off that U.S. deputy marshal."

Bird said tightly, "Your mouth is getting bigger and bigger, Long."

"Well, meanwhile, let's get our business done. If the time suits you you show up at the south side of the freight yard, where they make up the trains. I'll be there, waiting. You give me the money and I'll give you the key. After that you won't have to worry about how big my mouth is, and I won't have to worry about how small your jail cells are. *Comprende?*"

Bird stood up. "All right, but those guns will be examined."

"Long as you got the money you can take them apart for all I care. And make sure your count is right on the money. You going to bring a lantern or you want me to?"

"Suit yourself," Bird said.

He was starting to walk away when Longarm said, "And don't forget that deputy marshal. I want to make damn sure he's there when the money changes hands and he can verify it was a straight deal."

Bird whirled around. "I told you to leave Marshal Older out of this. This is between you and me."

Longarm slowly shook his head. "No, it's not. And ain't no use in your lying about it. If anything he's the boss of this operation. I don't want to make this deal and then get arrested fifty miles up the road for selling stolen army rifles. Because by then you'll have the bill of sale. You *savvy*? I want the marshal in on this. That way I'll feel right nice and safe, and I won't have to be explaining to no *other* federal officers where I got eleven thousand dollars, and if I got them for surplus cavalry carbines where is the bill of sale. So you just bring the marshal. Won't take up much of his time."

Bird said, "No."

Longarm shrugged. "Then we ain't got a deal, and I'll just go down to the railroad and get those guns shipped to Del Rio. You've already told me the sheriff up there and in Brownsville was part of the plan. Ain't no skin off my nose. Just a matter of a few more days. And what's time to a hog?"

Bird stood there biting his lip for a moment. "You're being a damn fool about this. He ain't gonna like it."

"Then he can get his guns somewhere else." Longarm suddenly hunched forward. "Bird, let's you and me get something straight. I ain't a goddamn bit scared of you or your deputies or that marshal, for that matter. You want to do business, we do business my way. I don't trust you and I don't trust no marshal that would work with you. You try anything with me, there'll be an awful lot of dead folks around here before I go down. I been in this business a hell of a lot longer than you and I know how to protect myself. So you show up tonight with the money *and* the marshal and we'll do business and I'll be gone. *Savvy?*"

Bird gave him a cold, murderous look. He opened his mouth to say something, but then closed it and turned on his heel and walked away.

Longarm called after him, "Has your charm and good looks worked on that young lady yet?"

Bird didn't pause to turn around or answer. If anything, his gait increased. Longarm watched him hurrying away, and then laughed and stood up. He figured he'd get a drink and then ride out to the railroad depot.

Chapter 9

The freight agent gave Longarm another slip of paper showing he was authorized to open car number 178P46T and a key about the size of a small wrench. Longarm took it and said, "I wouldn't want to carry this around in my pocket for a long spell."

The freight agent said, "That's so folks can't get them duplicated. You just try and take that to a locksmith and get another one made. First off he'd know it was a railroad key, and second, he wouldn't have enough brass on hand to make one. A sealed car is a sealed car and we intend to keep it that way. You wait until you see the padlock it fits."

"What? Takes two men to lift it off?"

"Not quite. But it is a piece of work."

"Now where will that car be spotted?"

The agent showed him a map of the freight yard on the wall. "It'll be settin' off by itself on this little siding. Right next to it is that midnight train that pulls out on the dot. So don't be leaning up against that sucker when she cranks up or you're likely to get ground to sausage. But you ought not to have no trouble finding yore car. It's settin' right there if you'd like to go on back there and take a look."

"Can I ride my horse back there?"

"Well, yeah, if yore horse ain't tangle-footed. They's many a rail and switching block between here and there. You could come in from the south end, but it's fenced off to keep out kids and them as would find a place to sleep in a boxcar. There's a little path through there, but you got to know where to find it."

"I'll make it all right. I got a sure-footed horse that don't spook easy."

Longarm went outside, mounted the dun, rode him around the long freight building, and set a course toward the south end of the freight yard. Because Laredo was a terminus and a turnaround point it was a big yard, with any number of trains in the midst of being broken down or made up, and there were groups of cars scattered all over the place, with here and there a yard engine chuffing and puffing as it worked to bring a whole train out of a lot of links and pieces. Over to the north Longarm could see the big engines that could pull a hundred cars sitting patiently on their northbound tracks waiting for the little yard engines to fetch up their cargo. The whole place was alive with the sounds of engines and men shouting and cars banging together as they were coupled up. The dun pricked his ears back and forth as a particularly loud piece of noise caught his attention, but a pat from Longarm's hand seemed to settle him down.

The yard was a busy place. He hoped it wouldn't be quite so busy at night. There were several ways the meeting that night could go, and he figured at least two of them would create noise. Not that he thought it would be noticed. There should be enough noise being made in the yard to cover a pitched battle. And anyway, this was Laredo, the kind of town where it was a whole lot safer to tend strictly to your own business.

He located the car fairly easily. It was standing near a wire fence on the south side of the yard at the very end. He could see the beginnings of the town from where it was located. The car itself was standing on a rusty stretch of track. Even before he got to it Longarm could read the car number, done in white against the dull red paint. He rode up to it, dismounted, and tied the dun to the sliding door handle. Then he took the key and inserted it into the bottom of the enormous bell-shaped padlock. The key turned easily and the gate of the lock snapped open. He removed it from the hasp and slid the door back, the movement making the dun dance sideways. With the door open he leaned inside the car. The floor came just midway between his belly and his chest. It was gloomy dark inside, but he could make out the gun crates stacked neatly at one end, taking up about half the car. He leaned in a little further and struck a match. The U.S. ARMY markings were clearly visible on the long, flat crates. Anybody looking would think they contained ten rifles each. He clambered up in the car and lifted the end of one of the crates. It was appropriately heavy. Someone had had the good sense to put the weight of ten rifles in each one either in lead or bricks or something. And the crates were nailed so secure and were of a heavy enough construction that it would take more than an idle effort to open one.

He climbed back out of the car, slid the door home, then picked up the lock and replaced it in the hasp. He took the key out and put it in his saddlebags. On the next track a long train was being made up, and the clanging and banging as the cars were coupled together were making the dun nervous. Longarm untied the horse and mounted. For a moment he sat the jittery animal, familiarizing himself with where everything was. It wouldn't be so easy to see in another six hours, and he wanted the advantage on Bird, and whoever he decided to bring, of knowing the locale.

Finally, satisfied he knew which way to jump if he had to seek shelter, he turned his horse and rode north until he could turn out of the yard and hit the road back into town.

It was dusk by the time he got back into town. Since he'd be using his horse that night he just tied the dun in front of the hotel. He loosened the animal's girth and made sure he could reach the water trough. The dun had been expecting to go back to the stable for a meal of oats, so he gave a little snort of displeasure and stamped one foot. Longarm said, "You'd get spoilt with just a little help, wouldn't you?"

He took his saddlebags up to his room, and took time to hide the freight car key between the mattress and the springs of his bed. Then he took time to shave and wash his hands and face and neck before going down to supper. As late as he was, he expected to find the place deserted, but Willis Howard was sitting at a table staring down at a plate of stew. Longarm sat down across from him. The young man barely looked up. His beard stubble was black, his eyes were bloodshot, and his face was long enough to reach the floor. Longarm said, "What's the matter, Willis? You look like you've lost your last friend."

A little life came back into Willis's face. "I wish it was my last friend. More like my last dollar."

"Oh? What the hell happened? These Laredo poker players turn out not to be as dumb as you thought?"

"They seem to have got a considerable education overnight. I've lost over four hundred dollars since this morning. Don't seem to matter what I do, play them tight, bluff, try and buy pots, anything. I went about four hours an' never won a nickel."

"That'll happen." The waiter came up just then, and Longarm took time to order the beef stew. He added, "And bring me plenty of bread. And I'll have coffee and a shot of brandy."

Willis said dismally, "I got to make a comeback tonight. I'm down to just a little better than two hunnert dollars."

"You look like you need some sleep more than you need to hit the poker table. You ought to take a rest. You can't think as well when you're bone tired. And you look like you're about to drop over."

"I got to win that money back. This bunch of fuckin' hicks ain't gonna outplay me. Shit, if I have to I'll go to workin' those cards."

Longarm just looked at him. "Willis, you're a grown man. And if you don't know that you're about half on and half off the horse, ain't my job to tell you. But I will point out that you never was much good as a cardsharp. You try it when about half your head is asleep, somebody will put the rest to sleep for you. Forever."

His meal came and Longarm ate, not with haste, but not wanting to spend any more time with Willis than he had to. When his stew was done he drank a cup of coffee, and then chased it with a shot of brandy and got up. He said, "Go to bed, Willis. Catch up tomorrow."

Willis looked up at him. "It's a matter of pride. I am from a distinguished family. I will not be beaten by such riffraff."

Longarm just shook his head and walked away. He was not predicting a successful night for Willis Howard.

In his room he pulled the chair up to the window and sat down to look out at the night and do a little thinking. He had to figure that Bird was going to try something, but he didn't know exactly what. Therefore he had to be ready for just about any play that might come his way. One thing he was going to do for certain was to get there at least a half an hour early so he'd be able to spot, in advance, how much company he would be having.

He wasn't certain about Older, wasn't certain if he would show up or not. If he did, then the play would come from the deputy marshal. Bird wasn't dangerous by himself, but Older didn't get to be a deputy marshal by being a slouch with either a gun or his brain. Just because he'd gone crooked didn't make him any less smart. No, Older was the danger. If Bird showed up with a deputy, or even two, it wouldn't be much to worry about. They'd be acting on orders, Older's orders, and he didn't

126

think they'd try and gun him. They might try and steal the rifles because he was going to refuse to deal without Older on the spot, and he'd make that clear from the beginning. If they didn't like that, well, he reckoned he'd just have to cut the odds down a little more.

But he felt sure Older would show up. He'd made it as clear to Bird as it was possible to make anything, clear enough for even someone like Willis Howard to understand, that no Older, no deal.

But then, Bird wasn't very smart. Maybe Older would send Bird along first just to check out the situation. Then, if everything looked okay, he'd make an appearance.

Longarm stopped thinking. Looking back, he recollected that nothing had ever gone the way he'd viewed it in advance. Best to do it the way he always did, just pick up his hand and play the cards he'd been dealt. He couldn't predict what Bird or Older was going to do. And they couldn't predict what he was liable to get up to.

But he had one big advantage; he knew who he was and they didn't. And when he pulled that badge out of his pocket and pinned it to his shirt, the game was going to take an all-new turning.

About ten o'clock he went downstairs and out the front door and untied the dun. He mounted up. The quickest way to the railroad station was straight north from the hotel. But he didn't head that way. Instead he rode around the hotel like he was taking his horse to the stable, and then went on past the stable and circled town to the east before he turned back north to head for the freight yards. He didn't know if Bird was watching him or not, but he didn't figure it hurt any to take some extra precautions.

He rode up to the freight office, and then turned into the gate that led into the huge yard. It was a moonlit night with at least a three-quarter moon in the starry sky, but he still took it slow and careful, his horse acting hesitant about where he put each hoof down. Longarm figured it was about a half a mile, in a winding way, back to his car. It was hidden, now, by the long freight that was just about completed and that would be pulling out at midnight.

He came around the caboose of the long freight, stopped his horse, and studied the area around the solitary car with the gun crates in it. When nothing moved or showed itself, he touched his horse with his spurs and moved slowly and gently down the line of cars. That afternoon he'd noticed the lading bill on his car. It was in a little metal envelope about three feet up the side of the car at the very front. He'd looked inside and found a kind of lading bill on stiff carboard. It had said, "DEST LAREDO CONSIGNED LONG." He figured that was so that the railroad hands, when they were switching cars and trains around, could see where a car was bound and hook it in to the right train. It seemed to him like a piece of information that might be useful. As he rode along by the long freight train he stopped and examined several of the little boxes that contained shipping instructions. Most of them were bound for San Antonio or Houston or Dallas, and most of them were to different companies or different individuals. But he was surprised to find a few scheduled for towns way up north, and even some for California. He figured the ones heading for California had to go pretty near Colorado, and he couldn't think of anything he'd rather do than stow away on such a car and get on home.

But there was still too much work to be done.

He rode his horse over to the boxcar that, for the moment, belonged to him. Or at least it did so long as he had the key in his boot. He debated about tying his horse close, but then changed his mind and rode the animal around to the off end of the boxcar, and dismounted and tied the animal to a handy ladder that went to the roof of the car. The key was uncomfortable in his boot, and he leaned down and took it out and shoved it in his left-hand jeans pocket. Then he walked around to the door of the car, leaned back against its dusty side, got out a cigar, and lit up. He didn't figure Bird would be on time. Other than that, he didn't know what to figure. He didn't even know if the bait was strong enough to draw the man. Older might smell some sort of trap and decide to just pass on the rifles. But it was a powerful amount of money to allow to just walk away. Especially since he'd let them know he could get more guns, get as many as they wanted.

The yard was relatively quiet, with only the occasional sound of an engine venting steam or ringing its bell or the banging together of cars. But the sounds were mostly distant, coming from the other end of the yard. The train he was standing next to was so long that its tail end curved back to the west, while way up ahead its engine was pointed north. Longarm could feel a slight tremor in the earth as the big engine that would pull the hundred freight cars was slowly backed into place to be coupled. He could tell from the sound of the engine that it really didn't have steam up yet and was just moving under minimum power.

He finally grew impatient waiting and got out his watch. It was a quarter after eleven. He was beginning to get the feeling that Bird wasn't coming. And if Bird didn't come, then neither would Older. He figured to give it fifteen more minutes, and then give it up as a lost cause and try and think of something else. In point of fact he could arrest Bird any time he wanted to for holding Lieutenant Manly without authority, and Older as well for participating in the miscarriage of justice. But the charge against Older would be a weak one, one he might well walk away from. It would probably get him kicked out of the federal marshal service, but Longarm wanted more than that. He wanted the sonofabitch in prison.

Then he heard the faint *clink* of a shod hoof on steel. A moment or two later he could definitely make out the sound of at least two horses headed his way. They were coming from the direction of the freight depot, so the long freight train was between him and them. He loosened his revolver in its holster, ground out his cigar on the rocks beside the rail, and got ready for company.

A few minutes passed, and then he saw two horsemen round the caboose of the freight and head his way. He could tell by the size of one of them that Bird had decided to show up. But they were too far away and the light wasn't good enough for him to recognize the other as Older.

He let them come on until they were about twenty yards away. Then he called out, "Hold it right there. I'm afoot. You two might as well be also."

They had stopped at his words, but now they came on a few more paces. He was about to call out again when he realized they were looking for someplace to tie their horses. They pulled up some twelve to fifteen yards away and dismounted. The short man handed his reins to the other rider. That, to Longarm, was a bad sign. Bird wouldn't be expecting Older to tie his horse.

The short man waited until the other man had finished with the horses and joined him and then together they started walking toward him. He could hear the crunch of their boots as they walked over the rocks that had spilled down from the roadbed. Now they were close enough and Longarm could recognize the sheriff. The other, he thought, might have been one of the deputies that had grabbed him up and taken him to see Bob Bird when Willis Howard had propositioned them about "military equipment." He could see that Bob Bird was carrying a small cloth satchel.

Well, he thought, this was going to be a pickle. If Bird had brought the money but not Older, it was going to seem a little strange him turning down the money just because the deputy marshal wasn't there. On his part, he really wasn't doing anything illegal, not if he'd supposedly gotten the guns legally. But he'd planted the idea in Bird's mind that the paperwork on the rifles might not be all that straight, and that he didn't want to run the risk of being arrested for dealing in stolen goods unless the marshal himself was involved.

He said, when they were only a few paces away, "I see you, Sheriff, and I see what I take to be the money. Where's the marshal?"

Bird said, "Whar's the guns?"

Longarm inclined his head to the left. "Right in that box-car."

Bird took a couple of steps forward. "It's got a big padlock on it. How'm I supposed to know they is any guns in there?"

Longarm reached in his pocket and pulled out the key. "I take this key and open it and shove the door back and then you can see."

"Well, do it."

"I asked you where the marshal was?"

"You git that door open an' then we'll talk about the marshal." He shook the satchel. "I got the money right here. By rights that's what you ought to be in'rested in."

Longarm thought for a second. It couldn't hurt to open the door and shove it back and let Bird see the boxes. He might even let him send the deputy up into the car to heft one, making sure they weren't empty. He said, "All right. Since you don't trust me and I don't trust you, we'll take it a step at a time."

He moved to the door of the boxcar, put the key in the lock, twisted it, and then removed lock and key and laid them on the ground. The door was on steel runners. With his left hand he gave the door a shove. It slid open. Longarm stepped back. "Have a look."

Bird started toward the door, and then realized how high off the ground the floor of the boxcar was. He stopped a few yards from Longarm and motioned the deputy forward. He said, "Take a look."

As the deputy stepped toward the door Longarm backed up a few paces. He didn't want the man getting too close. So far all the guns were still in their holsters, and he wanted to keep it that way until his came out.

The deputy leaned into the car and peered around. He said, "They's wooden crates in here."

Longarm said, "Strike a match and you can see better."

The deputy took a match out of his shirt pocket, scratched it on the floor of the boxcar, and then held it aloft as it lit. He said, " 'Pears to be 'bout nine er ten crates. Got some kind of markings on 'em. Says . . . U.—S.—ARM—ARMY."

Bird said, "U.S. Army?"

"Yeah."

Bird said, "Climb up in there and have a look."

Longarm suddenly reached out, took the man by the belt, and pulled him away from the car. He took a quick step backwards so he could have Bird and the deputy clear in his sights. He said, "Not so goddamn fast. We still got the question about the money. And the marshal. Where's the marshal?"

Bird said loudly, "Now!"

Longarm said, "What the hell you yelling at?"

Then he felt the unmistakable barrel of a gun pressed in his back. A voice behind him said, "He's yellin' for me to blow yore belly open."

Bird said, "Drop your gunbelt, Long."

The other deputy, the one standing by Bird, drew his revolver.

Longarm said, "This the way you do business, Sheriff?"

The man standing behind him prodded him with the barrel of his pistol. He said, "Din't you hear the shur'ff tell you to drop thet gunbelt?"

Very slowly Longarm began unbuckling the heavy gunbelt. He was doing most of it with his left hand while his right hand shielded the big, concave belt buckle that held the derringer. With his left thumb he pushed the derringer up out of its clip and into the palm of his right hand. The tongue came out of the belt hole at the same time his gun rig fell to the ground at his feet. He had his hands down at his side. The derringer was in the palm of his hand. But there was nothing he could do, not with the man behind him holding a gun in his back.

Bird said, "Aubrey, get around here and you and Sam keep this sonofabitch covered while I have a look in that car. See what's in them boxes."

Longarm felt the pressure of the gun barrel leave his back. The man came around, passing by his right side. Bird had not bothered to draw his pistol. The man Bird had called Aubrey passed between Longarm and the one the sheriff called Sam. The sheriff was taking a step forward. Longarm said, "I figured on something like this, Bird. That's why I got a man on the top of that boxcar right next door with a shotgun." As he said it he lifted his right arm as if to point. The three men did not actually turn their heads, but for an instant their attention was drawn away from Longarm. In that instant he leveled the derringer and fired. He shot Aubrey in the back. The deputy threw his hands in the air and yelled and pitched forward. But Longarm didn't see it. As soon as the shot was off he'd swung the derringer to the right and shot Sam directly in the chest. The deputy's eyes went wide open and he staggered backwards, the gun falling from his hand as he slowly fell over backwards.

Longarm was moving even before Sam could realize he was hit. Bird's mouth had fallen open at the sound of the gun-fire, but now recognition was setting in. He was three paces from Longarm and starting a fumbling motion for his revolver. He had it half drawn when Longarm, with the derringer still clutched in his fist, hit him with a looping, driving right hand. It was as if the sheriff had been hit in the face with a sledgehammer. He went straight backwards, falling so hard as Longarm followed through with the punch that he almost seemed to bounce as he hit the ground.

Still Longarm didn't pause. He grabbed the gun Sam had dropped and pried Aubrey's weapon from his fingers, and threw both revolvers as far as he could. Then deliberately and with as much force as he could muster, he kicked each man in the temple, in turn, with the toe of his boot. He didn't figure he had time to take their pulses and make sure they were dead. The kick to the temple was a lot simpler and a lot faster.

Finally he stopped and heaved a breath. He looked at Bird. The sheriff was lying as limp as the dead. Longarm walked over to where his gunbelt was and picked it up. Before he replaced the derringer in the belt buckle, he reached in his pocket and took out two .44-caliber cartridges. He broke the gun, expelling the empty hulls, and reloaded the little weapon. Then he slipped it back into its clip inside the concave buckle and buckled his gunbelt back around him. Before he moved he drew his revolver and cocked it several times to make sure it hadn't suffered any damage from being dropped on the rocks. Then he glanced over at Bob Bird again. The sheriff hadn't moved.

He went around to the end of the boxcar and up to his horse, and took his rope off the saddlehorn. He didn't carry a stiff lariat like a working cowboy who used it for roping. Instead it was a fairly soft cotton rope that he could catch a horse with or use to bind an ex-sheriff hand and foot. He came back to where Bob Bird was still lying unconscious. Without any preamble he rolled the sheriff over on his belly and dragged his hands together behind his back. Using the end of of rope he tied the sheriff's wrists tightly together, then moved down and jerked the sheriff's boots off. He pulled Bird's feet up until his knees were bent as far as they would go, and made three wraps around his ankles and tied the knot off tight. After that he got out his pocketknife and cut his rope just above the knot. He made a mental note to himself as he did it to remember to add a good cotton rope to his expense report. After that he rolled Bird back over on his back, and dragged him across to the side of the freight train that was warming up to leave. Bird was starting to come to and starting to be aware of the uncomfortable position he was bound up in. He said, in a bleary voice, "Huh? Wha . . . What tha . . . What tha hell goin' on . . ."

Longarm just said sharply, "Shut up, Bird. I'll get to you in a minute."

He went walking up and down the line of cars, looking at the bills of lading for one whose destination was Austin. He found one just two cars down from where he had Bird lying. He slid back the door and looked in. He couldn't tell what the cargo was. It was just all a jumble of burlap sacks. More than likely, judging from the smell, it was raw cattle hides, probably brought over from Mexico.

He crossed over to where the two deputies lay, and with some effort lifted and carried them to the car and slung them inside. When he was through, he hunted up the lock and key to his car and hung them on the unlocked hasp of the car that was bound for Austin carrying two dead deputies. Then he went back to Bird. The sheriff was staring at him. He said, "You'll hang for this, you sonofabitch!"

Longarm took his six-pointed badge out of his pocket and pinned it to his shirt. Bird gave a little start and said, "Whar'd you git that? You've killed Les Older!"

"Not yet," Longarm said. "And if he's lucky, I won't have to. No, this here star belongs to me. All along you've been doing business with two U.S. deputy marshals, except you didn't know it." He squatted down by Bird. "Now I've got a few questions I want to ask you and I want you to answer them damn quick. I recommend that you do because this here train is going to be pulling out at midnight and you are laying partway under it. At least your feet are. And when it rolls I reckon it ain't going to do you no good to get run over by a train." He got out his watch. "I got ten of midnight, and that freight agent tells me this is one train that leaves on the second. So I wouldn't count on too many of them few minutes to play around with."

Bird just stared at him. "I'll put you in jail. You've kilt two lawfully constituted deputies and you've hit and tied up the sheriff. You ain't ever gonna get out of prison. You probably will get hung. And will if I have anything to say about it."

For answer Longarm smiled and shoved the sheriff's legs a little farther onto the rails. "Just one main question. Was you running the gun-smuggling operation before Older came down or after? I know you were holding up the saloons and the card houses and the whorehouses. Did he take his cut of that too? Who was the boss? I figure it was him, but I want to hear it from you."

Bird gave him a snarl. At first Longarm thought he was going to spit in his face, but then he seemed to change his mind. He said, "You go to hell. I don't give a damn if you say you be a deputy marshal, which I don't think you are. You have shit an' fell back in it."

Longarm smiled. "So far as I can tell, Bird, you ain't done nothing to get hung for. And if you cooperate with me right now I'll shove you in that boxcar and you'll more than likely be alive when it gets to Austin. But you keep on fucking around, this here train is gonna run over you. Then you won't need to get hung."

Bird tried to wiggle around on the ground to get in a more comfortable position, but he was tied too tight. He said, in a whining voice, "Damn you, let me loose. Or at least slack off on these ropes. I tell you my shoulders is comin' plumb out of they sockets!"

Longarm looked at his watch. "I've already got Older. He's going to jail without a doubt. But I want some details from you. I know you offered him five thousand dollars. But I want to know if he made it clear he was looking for money or you just did it out of desperation. Now, my watch says five minutes to midnight. Of course I ain't on railroad time so I could be off two or three minutes. If I was you I wouldn't be betting my life on the accuracy of this old watch of mine. Was I you I'd start talking right this second if I wanted to be *inside* this train when it heads for Austin."

Bird looked at him. Even in the moonlight Longarm could see the pain in his face from the way he was tied. "What are you talking about? Sending me to Austin? What's Austin got to do with me?"

Patiently, like he was talking to a child, Longarm said, "Les Older was, is, a deputy out of the United States marshal's office in Austin. He was sent down here, as you very well know, to check up on you. They must of got a lot of complaints. Well, after a while, the chief marshal got the feeling that old Les had probably gone sour. So they sent me down here to catch him. And you. I'm out of the Denver, Colorado, office if it's of any concern to you. Which it ain't."

Bird said sullenly, "I ain't got nothing to say."

"That train is beginning to build up steam. I can hear that engine up there at the head of these cars. Listen."

In the far distance they could hear the slow chuffing sound as the engineer bled off the watery steam while his boiler heated. Longarm put his hand on the rail. He could feel it vibrating slightly. "It ain't gonna be long now."

"You ain't gonna let that train run over me. Not if you really are a U.S. deputy marshal."

Longarm laughed. He said in a delighted voice, "Why, you just go right ahead and believe that, Mister Bird. You see, you don't seem to understand that I think you're one of the sorriest sonofabitches I ever met. You tried to kill me. And would have if I hadn't expected it. And worse than that, you were rude to me in your office when you had me in for questioning. And I ain't even talking about the way you treat people in this town. And then there's that Mrs. Manly's husband. That is as low as a man can get. Hold her husband in jail while he tries to get in her underwear. And her a genteel young lady didn't know what to do. You are really a rare bastard, Bird. Not let that train run over you?" He reached to his holster and pulled out his revolver. With the end of the barrel he gave Bird a hard tap on the tooth. It split his lip and blood gushed out. Bird yelled. Longarm said, "Hell, if it wasn't for my oath as an officer, I'd sit here and knock out every tooth in your head, and *then* let the fucking train run over you."

Bird was now looking at him with real fear. "You're crazy. You can't stand there and watch a man get cut in half by no train!"

"You're right," Longarm said. He reholstered his gun, and then got out his pocketknife and cut a long, wide strip off the front of Bird's white shirt.

Bird had flinched back from the knife, but he watched as Longarm tore the strip loose. He said, "What's that for?"

"Gag you with. See, a big train like this will start off mighty slow. So it's gonna take a few seconds to cut you in half, and I reckon you're gonna let out some kind of squall. I'm already a little surprised we didn't draw no company when I fired those two shots, but a rail yard is a kind of noisy place. Besides, don't nobody pay much attention to gunshots around Laredo. Common as hot weather. But the yell you're gonna let out is another matter."

Bird was staring at him in horror. "You won't do it."

"Let me explain what'll happen. See, there is some slack in the couplings between these cars. So when the engine first takes off, it takes a while for all the couplings to let the slack out. Then, when the engineer has got the full strain of the string of cars on line, he'll push up that throttle and pour the power to her. Of course, with this many cars, it's hard to get going, and he'll spin his drive wheels a little. But he'll have a brakeman down there putting sand on the rails, and pretty soon, them drive wheels will catch hold and the train will start rolling." He looked toward the rear of the car. "I figure you're about eight feet from them back wheels. You'll have a good view of them as they start toward you."

Bird opened his mouth to say something, and Longarm whipped the gag between his teeth and tied it tight behind his head. Bird's eyes had gone wild. He jerked his head back and forth and made muffled sounds, but he couldn't speak. Longarm could see him trying to work at the gag with his tongue.

"The hell of it is that you're doing this for nothing. I already know from your wife, Shirley, how you and Older got together.

Had that first meeting right there in your parlor. She heard every word. Even the money you offered him."

Bird's eyes were wide and staring, and he was making strangling sounds as he tried to speak.

"That's another thing I got against you. Beating up Shirley. Ain't much of a man hits a woman, especially as fine a woman as Shirley."

Bird's eyes were about to bulge out of his head, and his face was turning a mottled red with the effort to get a word out.

"Did you want to say something? Did you want to talk?"

Bird was nodding his head up and down vigorously.

"You didn't want to talk before. How come now? I already know about the money you've got collected up in your safe from all them business establishments around the plaza. By the way, Shirley's brother, Mac, he don't like you one little bit. I mean I think he would like to see real bad things happen to you. You still want to talk?"

Bird nodded again, nodding so hard he bumped his head against the side of the car.

"Well, all right. But just for a minute." He reached behind Bird's head, pushed the gag up and over the crown of Bird's head, and pulled it away. He said, "There, that better?"

Bird's eyes were wide and staring. He said, "You talked to my *wife*?"

"Yeah."

"Where?"

"Why, in your house. In your bed, actually."

Bird's face swelled even more. "You're a liar!"

Longarm smiled. "Well then, I won't tell you that her bedroom is down the hall off the parlor. And I won't tell you that she's got a right pretty little nightgown with lace at the throat. Or that she's got this silk robe. And that's some mighty nice furniture you got in your parlor."

Bird's eyes were wild. "You could have peeked through a window and seen that."

Longarm leaned over and put his face close to Bird's. "How about that tiny little mole up at the top of where the curly hair stops on her belly. Or that she calls you a crook when she knows you're going to beat her anyway. Reckon I peeked and saw all that?"

"You screwed my wife!"

137

Longarm shook his head. "I hate to hear crude talk like that about a wonderful lady like Shirley. No, we took pleasure in each other. It was a nice, gentle time. And I'm going to do it again before I leave town. All the time you were trying to get that little Manly lady I was visiting your wife. And enjoying it plenty, I might add."

"You sonofabitch," Bird said. But there was no steam in it. He was sagged back like a deflated balloon. What manhood he'd pretended to had just been sucked out of him.

Longarm said, "So I don't really need your testimony."

At that instant, far up the line, came the sound of boxcar couplings clanging as they had the slack taken out of them. Longarm looked at Bird. "You got maybe less than a minute."

Bird said hurriedly, "I sounded him out first about taking five thousand dollars. He just laughed. Said he wanted half. After that it was more than half. He was the boss. He called all the shots. Even when I was negotiating with you he told me what I could pay."

"He tell you to kill me tonight?"

Bird hesitated.

"Did he?"

Bird said, "Yes. If we couldn't run you off. There's no money in that satchel, just some old torn-up paper. I was supposed to get a man in behind you and disarm you and kill you and put you on this very train that's leaving."

Down the line the sound of the couplings pulling taut was coming closer and closer.

Longarm said, "Where's all the money?"

Bird twisted his head as the sound of the cars came closer. "For God's sake, get me out of here!"

"Where's the money."

"Most of it's in my office safe! Hurry, please!"

"What's the combination?"

"I can't . . ."

"What's the combination?"

Bird almost shouted it. "Shirley's birth date! First number to the right."

Longarm shot out both hands and jerked Bird away from the tracks. Then, holding him by the belt, he dragged the smaller man back down the track toward the car that was bound for Austin. Even as he got to the open door the car jolted as the slack went out of the coupling. It was only about ten cars back to the caboose, and then the train would be moving. Dimly, through the openings between the cars, he could see flickers of red. He rightly guessed it was the conductor carrying a lantern to the end of the train to signal everything was in order. Longarm gave silent thanks that the man had chosen to walk on the opposite side of the train. Bending, he quickly slipped the gag back in Bird's mouth, and then got both arms under him and, with a shove, pushed him up and into the car. Bird was making sounds, but they were faint and hardly noticeable above the noise of the train. Longarm carefully slid the door of the car closed. Then he reached for the lock, joined the tongue and hasp, and snapped the lock in place and closed it, withdrawing the key as he did. Then he stepped back and looked at the number on the car. He didn't have pencil or paper to write with, so he had to commit it to memory. The train blew its whistle and slowly, very slowly, began to move. Longarm stood there looking at the car number of the now-sealed car, saying it over and over in his mind.

Finally the cars began to pass. The car carrying Bird and his two dead deputies moved away, and then another car and then another, slowly gaining speed. Finally the caboose passed. Longarm could see the conductor sitting inside. Little did he know he was carrying a bit more cargo than he'd been told about.

Finally Longarm turned away and started toward his horse. On the ground, near where he'd knocked Bird down, he saw the ivory-handled revolver. He bent and picked it up, and saw that the barrel and cylinder were gold-engraved. He wondered if Older's revolver was the same. Well, they certainly didn't mind treating themselves well. He stuck the revolver in his belt and started for his horse. He reckoned that Bob Bird, trussed up as he was, was going to have a mighty uncomfortable trip. He figured Mrs. Manly and her husband would enjoy hearing about it.

Now there was just Les Older to deal with.

Chapter 10

He mounted the dun, and then rode over to where Bird and his deputy had left their horses tied to a switch post. Leaning out of the saddle he got the reins untied, and then took the two horses on lead and rode slowly and carefully, mindful of all the iron that floored the switching yard, up to the telegrapher's shack at the end of the depot. He got down and tied all three horses and then went up the stairs of the depot. He opened the door, went up to the counter, and got one of the message blanks and a pencil stub. The car number was still in his head. He directed the message to the Chief Marshal, United States Marshal's Office, Austin, Texas. On the blank he wrote:

IN SEALED BOXCAR NUMBER LL5578P ARRIVING FROM LAREDO

He stopped and said to the telegrapher, who was sitting behind his little desk wearing a green eyeshade, "What time does that freight that left here at midnight get into Austin tomorrow?"

The telegrapher didn't look up. "This here is a telegraph office. We don't deal in train information."

Longarm was tired and ready to get to bed. He was also in a bad mood because of the trouble he'd had with Bird and his two deputies. He said in a flat voice, "I reckon I better not have to ask you that question again."

The telegrapher looked up, startled. Longarm was staring at him. The man said, even without consulting a timetable, "That's a express train. Gets into San Antone at six-forty-five on the dot and leaves for Austin at seven-thirty. Arrives at the depot in

Austin at nine-twenty-five A.M. Yessir. You kin set yore watch by that train."

Longarm stared at him for a moment and then took another blank. He began again. He wrote:

URGENT YOU MEET SEALED BOXCAR NUMBER LL5578P AR-RIVING AUSTIN FROM LAREDO AT NINE TWENTY FIVE AM STOP BOXCAR CONTAINS EX SHERIFF OF LAREDO BOB BIRD STOP I CHARGE BIRD WITH ATTEMPTED MURDER FEDERAL OFFICER AND OTHER CRIMES STOP TWO EX DEPUTIES ALSO IN CAR STOP BOTH KILLED RESISTING ARREST STOP WILL NOW DEAL WITH L O STOP BIRD READY TO TESTIFY ABOUT L O STOP WILL WIRE WHEN JOB IS COMPLETE STOP MORE LATER AS HAPPENS STOP

He signed it CUSTIS LONG, U.S. DEPUTY MARSHAL. When he was through he slid the blank across the counter and cleared his throat. The clerk got up quickly and came to the counter. He read the blank for a moment and then looked up at Longarm. Longarm pointed to the badge on his shirt. He said, "Send that urgent and send it quick. That gets charged to the United States government."

The clerk began to nod and bob his head. "Yessir, yessir, right away, sir."

Longarm reached out and got a handful of the man's shirt. "You send it while I'm here. One other thing. You even breathe a word about this telegram to anybody, you even think about it after you've sent it, and you're gonna spend a lot of years in a federal prison in Leavenworth, Kansas. You understand me?"

The clerk was getting pale. "Yes—yes—yessir. I—I un'nerstan'."

"You sure?"

The clerk licked his lips. "I jest come on duty. I don't leave till eight tomorrow mornin'. I won't remember nuthin' by that time."

Longarm said, "You don't remember nothing now."

The clerk nodded his head. "You're right, sir. Yessir, you're right. I have clean forgot everythang."

"Then send the wire."

The clerk hurried over and sat down behind his little desk. He put the message Longarm had written before him and started tapping out the words with the key. In less than two minutes he

142

was done. He looked up, sweating a little. "It's done, sir. An' not a word misspelt. Nosir, jest as you wanted. You get a reply, where you want it sent, Marshal?"

Longarm said, "The Hamilton. But I don't expect a reply."

He walked out of the office and got aboard his dun, and then reached down and took the other two horses on lead. It was awkward leading them by their bridles, but he didn't know what else to do. He couldn't just leave them out without food or water. It wasn't the horses' fault they'd belonged to crooks.

He made it out of the rail yard, and rode south toward town until he reached the fence at the end of the freight yard. He figured that the deputy that had snuck up behind him had left his horse there, and then climbed over the fence and come up on him and put the pistol in his back.

Yes, he could see the horse ahead in the moonlight. And just beyond the fence, as if in confirmation, stood the boxcar with the crates that hadn't contained guns for a long time. It wasn't sealed anymore, but then it didn't need to be.

He rode up to the horse, leading his burden, and dismounted, taking what was left of his rope with him. He untied the third horse, and then took the bridles of the other two horses, tied all three together, and then put a loop through the mass of reins with his rope. At least this way, he wouldn't have but one lead rope to hold on to, and the horses wouldn't be crowding up on him as they had been.

He took off his badge and rode through Laredo. It was still going strong. He'd seen all-night towns, but he believed Laredo had them all beat. He got to the hotel, and then rode around to the back and woke up the night stable man. Dismounting, he said, "Take care of my horse and see he gets grained, even as late as it is. Then tend to these other three horses. One belonged to the sheriff; the other two were ridden by his deputies. I don't know who owns them. But look out for them. The city will pay you for their upkeep until somebody claims them."

He left the stable man still half asleep and more than a little baffled, and walked around to the front entrance to the hotel. Longarm got his key from the sleepy desk clerk and started for his room. The clerk said, "That Meester Howard, he look for chou."

"When?"

"A leetle earlier. Maybe two hour ago. He look preddy bad."

Longarm said, "Well, if he comes looking for me again

143

you haven't seen me. I'm nearly dead for sleep, and if the sonofabitch wakes me up I'll shoot this hotel to pieces."

The clerk said, "I tell him you don't stay here no more."

"Good idea," Longarm said.

He climbed the stairs to his room, and started taking off his gunbelt and boots the minute he was in the room. He hung the gunbelt over the bedpost, and sat down on the side of the bed and poured himself out a large whiskey and lit a cigar. Between sips out of the glass and puffs of his cigar he finished undressing, leaving his hat, because it was the easiest to shed, for last. He looked at his watch. It said it was a quarter after one. He shook it and looked at it again. He could have sworn it was going to be dawn in an hour, tired as he was.

Still he sat there, thinking. His body was ready for sleep, but his mind was wide awake. He was trying to think of the best approach to Les Older. He already had enough on him to just simply walk up and arrest him, but he didn't want to do it that way. He wanted Older to expose himself to him, Longarm, so that he could have a personal hand in stripping the badge off the man's chest.

So he sat and thought. He was still tensed up, tired as he was. It was always like that after a fight. He'd get a big burst of energy to carry him throught the fight, but it always took time to wear off. He thought of Bob Bird, trussed up like a pig going to market, somewhere on the route to Austin. The next time he saw daylight he'd be in Austin being met by a small group of U.S. deputy marshals. He smiled at the thought. No doubt Bird would try to bluster his way through, but it wasn't going to do him much good.

Thinking of Bird made him think of Shirley. He realized he needed her birth date, the month, year, and day. Or whatever order she wrote them down in. He gave his own as month, day, and year. It would be good if he had the number right then at that moment, but he damn sure didn't feel like riding out to her ranch at that hour. And besides, he wanted an early morning conversation with Les Older. He wanted to catch him before he left the hotel, before he could go over to the jail, before he could begin to wonder where the sheriff was and why he hadn't reported in. He knew that Older was staying at the Hamilton. All he had to do was get his room number, which wasn't going to be hard. For a second he toyed with the idea of visiting Older right then and there, but he dismissed the idea. He knew he was too tired to be at his best, and you didn't go up against a man like Older when you weren't firing your best bullets.

After a few more minutes he finished the whiskey in his glass, stubbed out his cigar, and lay back gratefully on the bed. After another minute he made himself squirm around so that he was lying the length of the bed with his head on the pillow. He pulled a light sheet over him, reached out and trimmed down the lamp, and very shortly went to sleep.

He came awake with the sound of someone pounding on his door. He raised up groggily and made sure he was where he thought he was. The pounding went on. He fumbled around on the nightstand until he found a match, and then lit the lantern that sat on the table. With that light, for it was still dark outside, he was able to see by his watch that it was five minutes until six. Well, that part was all right. He'd meant to get up at six anyway. He yelled out at the door, "Goddammit, hold your horses! I'm coming!" He pulled on his jeans, took his revolver out of the holster, and stood up. The pounding had stopped. He walked over to the door, the revolver in his hand, his thumb on the hammer. He said, "Who is it?"

A thin voice said, "It's Willis, Willis Howard."

He said, "Oh, my Gawd!" But he unlocked the door, and then turned and walked back and sat down on the side of the bed. He heard the door open and saw Willis come in, shutting the door behind him. He found half a cigar and a match, struck the match, and got the slightly used cigar fired up and drawing. Willis had come into the middle of the room and stopped. Longarm shook out the match and pitched it at the tabletop. He said, "What the hell do you want?"

Willis looked like hell. Longarm didn't believe he'd ever seen a man look quite so haggard and desperate and whipped down in all his life. Willis said, "Long, I'm busted. Busted. Beaten."

He looked like he was about to cry. Longarm was in the process of licking a loose leaf on the chewing end of his cigar. He looked over at Willis. The gambler was unshaven, his white shirt was wrinkled and dirty, and his soft leather vest was gone. Longarm idly wondered if he'd lost it in a hand of poker. Then he said, in a not very kind voice, "That's why they call it gambling, Willis. You can win . . . or you can lose. You lost. You should have gone to bed last night. If you're here to get a stake to head back to the table, you've come to the wrong man."

Willis swayed slightly. He said, shaking his head, "No, I don't want to gamble no more. But they've locked me out of my room because I ain't paid the bill. And I ain't even got eating money. When I say I'm busted I ain't even got a nickel. I was wondering since I don't know nobody else—"

Longarm said, "You don't even know me, Willis. Not in the money-lending sense."

Willis looked down. "Yeah, you're right. I was—I was just desperate. I didn't know which way to turn. Last night I wouldn't eat, and it sitting right there in front of me. Now I'm so hungry I'd eat my shoes if I didn't need them to walk in. I mean, I ain't got a nickel."

Longarm studied him, an idea slowly beginning to form. Willis Howard hadn't struck him as the most reliable soul he'd ever met, but if he could follow a few simple instructions he could be of use to Longarm. "Can you ride a horse, Willis?"

The young man looked up. "What?"

"It's a goddamn simple question. Can you ride a horse?"

Willis said slowly, "Well, yeah, sure, if you're talking 'bout an ordinary riding horse and not some bronc. Hell, I grew up on a horse. Anybody can ride a horse."

Longarm was still thinking. If nothing else, Willis could save him some valuable time. "I'm not going to give you any money, but I'm going to give you a job. Pays fifty dollars all told and won't take but a day or two. You want it?"

Willis perked up. "Fifty dollars? Hell, yes!"

Longarm looked at him a moment, deciding. Maybe it was a good idea and maybe it wasn't. To his eye Willis looked like he needed a keeper, but Longarm felt terribly strapped for time— that is, if the plan he had decided on was to work. He just didn't have the time to do all that needed doing. "Willis, I want you to go downstairs to the desk and get a piece of paper I can write on and a pencil and an envelope. And bring them right back up here. Understand?"

Willis went back to looking downcast. "I don't know about that. I ain't exactly popular with the desk clerk. I owe the hotel eighteen dollars and they won't even give me my key, like I told you. Or let me get my stuff out of my room."

Longarm put his hand in his pocket and came out with two ten-dollar greenbacks. He handed them to Willis and said, "Pay your bill, but get back up here with that writing material right snappy. You understand?"

Willis looked at the twenty dollars in his hand. "When do I get the other thirty?"

Longarm sighed. "Willis, if you aggravate me any more I'm going to take that money back and give you a good whupping for your troubles. Now get!"

He closed the door on Willis's disappearing back, and turned to the task of shaving and getting dressed. He had one set of clean clothes left, and he decided the day deserved him looking his best.

He hadn't quite finished dressing when Willis came knocking at the door again. Longarm sang out for him to come in. The hotel boasted stationery, and Willis had a sheet of it and a pencil and an envelope. Longarm took the writing materials and then looked at Willis. He was a sight. It would probably be worth the time to have him clean up rather than scare Shirley Bird to death. He said, "Go get cleaned up and make it as fast as you can. Then get right back here. You've got an errand to run out in the country."

"Do I get my other money then?"

Longarm set his jaw. "Willis, you are leading a dangerous life right now."

Willis said, "I'm going, I'm going."

When he'd finished dressing, Longarm took pencil in hand and wrote a short note to Shirley Bird telling her that it was important and urgent that she should write down her date of birth giving the month and day and year. Then he instructed her to give the note to his messenger, a man whose name was Willis Howard, so that Longarm could have it in his hand as soon as possible. He ended by writing, "Shirley, I know this is a very strange-sounding request, but you must take me on trust on this. I am very close to ridding you of your brutal husband and this will be a big help. I assume he knows your true birth date. If not, give me the one he thinks is the real one. And please do not become coy on me by making yourself younger. Just the month, day, and year when Bob Bird thinks you were born. I will see you soon, perhaps this very night."

He signed it, "Custis Long."

After that he put the note in the envelope, sealed it, and wrote Shirley's name on the front. Finally, he was able to light a cigar and take a small drink of whiskey while he waited for Willis. By his watch it was half past six. He didn't know what time Older got up and got around, but he was praying the man was

147

still in his room. It didn't really matter if he confronted him this very morning, but he was anxious to get to the business and get it over with. He was tired of the job, tired of Laredo. In short, he was tired of the whole mess and all he wanted to see was a picture of himself heading for Colorado, with a short stop in Austin, on the fastest train available.

Willis came back looking considerably better. Longarm gave him the envelope, making sure he buttoned it into a shirt pocket so he couldn't lose it, and another ten dollars. He said, "Now you are to go down to the stable. No, I'll go with you. They might not give you my horse unless I'm along."

He put on his hat and strapped on his gunbelt and, with Willis following him, went down the stairs and out of the hotel and around to the stable. On the way he repeated, over and over, the directions to Bob Bird's ranch until he felt sure even Willis couldn't forget. In fact, after he'd made the young man repeat the directions back to him for the third time, Willis got an injured look on his face. He said, "What do you think I am, some kind of one-eyed ninny?"

Longarm said dryly, "I never said nothing about how many eyes you had, Willis."

The stable man brought the horse out and Longarm saddled and bridled the dun. Willis was near his height so there was no need to adjust the stirrups. Willis said, "Hell, it's just coming good light. What if that lady ain't up?"

"Then you wake her up," Longarm said. "You understand? You don't come back here without a note from her."

"Yes, sir!" Willis said. "My gosh. Think I was off on some gummit errand."

He was about to mount when Longarm put out a hand and stopped him. It was as good a time as any. "Willis, I'm fixing to tell you something and show you something. If you breathe a word about it to anyone before I'm ready to make it known, I'll do one of two things. I'll either shoot you or I'll put you in prison."

They were a little way from the stable. The town was waking up with the coming sun, but there was no one near to hear or see what Longarm was doing. Willis said, "Huh? Shoot me or put me in prison?"

"You said government work. That's right." He put his hand in his pocket and pulled out the six-pointed star. "I'm a United States deputy marshal. This is my badge."

Willis stared, first at the badge and then at Longarm. "But I thought that other feller was . . ."

Longarm nodded. "He is. Or was. He's what brought me down here. I came to catch him and Sheriff Bird."

Willis's eyes got big. He said, "Hot damn!"

Longarm said, "So you see why I want you to keep your mouth shut. To everyone. Including that lady you're going to see." He stopped and looked at Willis. He said, "I reckon I better deputize you. That way, if you open your mouth it's a federal offense. Raise your right hand."

Willis's eyes were still big and round. He said, "Damn! I knew from the first they was something different about you. I knew you weren't just some gambler. Hell!"

Longarm wasn't sure exactly how you went about deputizing someone. He said, "Raise your right hand, damnit."

Willis's face got solemn. He raised his right hand.

Longarm said, "All right, you're deputized."

Willis looked disappointed. "You ain't gonna say no words?"

Longarm said, "I said 'em. You're deputized. Now get on that horse and try not to ruin him. And hurry."

Willis mounted up, mumbling, "There ought to at least been a few words said."

Longarm said, "Get going. Look for me in the hotel restaurant when you get back. You better not take any longer than forty-five minutes."

He watched until he saw Willis round the south end of the plaza and head toward the river road. Then he headed back into the hotel and went over to the desk. Mac was just coming on duty. A man was checking out, and Longarm leaned on the counter until he'd finished his business and left. Mac turned to him and gave him good morning. Longarm said, "Say, wonder could you tell me what room the U.S. deputy marshal is staying in? I understand I'm privileged to be under the same roof with this Mister Older."

Mac gave him a cocked eye. "You do hobnob with the so-called law in this town, don't you?"

Longarm gave him a half smile. "More than you might think. Gonna tell me his room number?"

Mac said, "Well, the fact of the business is that Marshal Older ain't got a room, he's got rooms. Got one room for settin' an' one for sleepin'. What they call a sweet up in the big cities."

"Ah," Longarm said. "Which would be his parlor room?"

Mac said, "That would be One-oh-eight. Right down the hall off the dining room. One-oh-nine is where he rests his head at night. I wouldn't knock on that one."

Longarm said, "Reckon he's there?"

Mac shrugged. "I've been here since half past six getting ready to take over. Ain't seen him. He ain't exactly what you'd call a early riser. Times I've noticed, he usually saunters out of here about eight, eight-thirty. Say, was it you give that worthless kid the money to pay his bill? Goddammit, if you did, I ain't friends with you no more. He's got a soft-worked leather vest I had locked in his room, an' I was planning on making that my own."

Longarm said, "Wish I'd of knowed. Actually, I put the kid to work. I've just sent him out with a note for your sister. Something bad might have happened to her husband."

"What!"

But Longarm just pushed away from the desk and started toward the leg of the U of the hotel that led away from the dining room. He waved over his shoulder.

Mac said, "Hey, wait a minute! What are you talkin' about?"

But Longarm just kept walking. He said, "Tell you later. I got to hurry right now.

Older's sleeping room, 109, was about halfway down the hall. Longarm stopped in front of the door, loosened his revolver in its holster, and knocked.

There was no sound.

He knocked again, louder this time.

Faintly he heard stirring sounds and what sounded like a man swearing under his breath. A moment later the door was jerked open and Les Older stood there. He was dressed only in denim pants. His feet and head were bare, but the mate to Bob Bird's ivory-handled, gold-chased revolver was in his right hand. He had it up when he opened the door, but then, when he saw who it was, he lowered it to his side. He said, "What the hell do you want?"

Longarm said evenly, "Deputy Older, I think it's time we had a talk."

Older stared at him with his hard brown eyes. His hair was tousled, and it was obvious Longarm's knock had gotten him out of bed. Older said, "Why the hell should I want to talk to you? What the hell is your name?"

150

Longarm smiled. "I reckon you know my name is Long. And I reckon you know why you and I ought to have a talk."

"I do?" Older's face, even relaxed from just waking up, was still hard and harsh-looking. He was not a handsome man, but he would have been pleasant to look at except for the hard set of his mouth and the hard cast of his face and eyes.

"Yes," Longarm said. "And I wouldn't bother to go looking for the sheriff first. I hear he left town."

Older just stared at him.

Longarm said, "So, tell you what. I'm gonna go and eat breakfast. I'm going to take my time. My watch says it's a quarter past seven. I understand that's a little early for you. So I'll probably dawdle over my coffee. Then I'm going to saunter out of the hotel and straight out into the plaza to that first bench just opposite the hotel door. Then I'm going to sit down and smoke a cigar and wait on you."

Older stared at him for such a long time that Longarm wasn't sure he was going to speak. Then he said, "All right."

Longarm said, "No rush."

Older closed the door without another word, and Longarm turned and walked slowly back toward the dining room. He went inside, and got a table that gave him a commanding view of the hall that led to Older's room. He didn't know why he felt he needed to keep a watch on Older, but it seemed like a good idea.

And meanwhile, he was sweating out Willis's arrival. He needed to know the combination to Bob Bird's safe before he met with Older. If his thinking was right, Older got his money out of the same iron box that Bob Bird did. Or that Bob Bird used to get his money out of. Longarm didn't think Bird would need that combination for some few years to come.

He ordered his usual breakfast of ham and eggs and biscuits and gravy and coffee. When it came he set in to eat, but he did it slowly, glancing up every now and then to take a look down the hall, and to hope also to see Willis Howard suddenly coming through the door. He stopped eating once to look at his watch. It was twenty of eight. He figured he'd got Willis off by a quarter of seven. That was damn near an hour. What the hell was keeping the young fool?

He was on his second cup of coffee when Willis came bursting through the door. He hurried over to the table and sat down, looking sweaty and agitated and worried. He handed Longarm a little envelope, not unlike the one he'd received from Belinda Manly except this one was pink.

Longarm looked at him curiously. "What the hell's the matter with you? You look all hot and bothered."

Willis said, "She throwed down on me with a shotgun is what!"

"Shirley? I mean, Mrs. Bird?"

Willis said, "Naw. She was fine. But she's got some damn old fat Mexican woman works for her don't speak no English and kept threatening me with the biggest goddamn shotgun I ever saw. I thought she was gonna blow my head off. I like to have never got her to understand I needed to see Missus Bird. Say, did you notice that she's got the same last name as the sheriff?"

Longarm said dryly, "That ain't so odd, Willis. Especially when you consider the fact she's the sheriff's wife."

Willis opened his mouth and then shut it. He said, "My Gawd!"

Longarm looked at his watch. It was eight o'clock. He planned to be sitting on the plaza bench by eight-fifteen. He said to Willis, "Order yourself some breakfast."

When the waiter came to take Willis's order, Longarm asked for a large brandy and another cup of coffee. Then he waited until Willis was busy with his first cup of coffee before he opened the envelope. The writing was in a fine, feminine hand. It simply said, "August 15th, 1851. You had better have a good reason for such an indelicate question. Come to see me as soon as you can." It was simply signed "S."

He folded the note, put it in the envelope, and put it back in his pocket. Willis was watching him. He said, "Good news?"

Longarm said, "Drink your coffee, Willis."

But Willis said, "I got to tell you, that's a mighty handsome woman, Marshal."

Longarm shot his hand out and grabbed Willis by the throat. He said to the suddenly scared face, "You ever call me that again before it's time and I'll shove the words back in your mouth and cork it up with my fist. You understand?"

Willis gasped and rubbed his neck when Longarm let go. "I'm—I'm sorry. It just slipped out."

"Well, your slip could get me killed."

The waiter came over with his coffee and brandy. Longarm told him to put both meals on his bill. He said to Willis, "You are goddamn high-priced help, you know that?"

152

Willis said, "What do I do next?"

Longarm took his brandy down in two quick gulps, feeling its warming rays spreading throughout his stomach. He chased it with a sip of coffee and then stood up. He said, "Your job is to bird-dog me. I'm going out to sit on a bench in the plaza. I expect the U.S. deputy marshal to come and talk to me. You hang around the lobby and watch for him. If you see him go anywhere except over to me you come out and tell me."

Willis said, "Say, this is kind of dangerous work."

Longarm said, "Not as dangerous as you trying to cheat at poker in Laredo."

It was past nine o'clock before Longarm saw Older come out of the hotel and walk toward him. Older sat down at the far end of the bench. Longarm was about to light a cigar and he offered one to Older.

Older just gave the cigar a glance and said, "Not that cheap stuff." Then he reached inside his vest and came out with a long panatela. He bit off the end of it, struck a match, got it going, and then turned to Longarm. He said, "So you think me and you got something to talk about, do you?"

Longarm nodded slowly. "If I'm going to do any business I reckon it will have to be with you. The sheriff's dead."

Older raised his eyebrows slightly. "Yeah?"

Longarm nodded again. He was sitting in a relaxed position with his right leg thrust out and his right arm resting on the arm of the bench. His hand wasn't but a few inches from the butt of his revolver. He was holding the cigar with his left hand. He noticed Older was doing the same. He said, "Yeah, he's dead."

"Know how it happened?"

"Yeah. I killed him. Along with them two deputies you sent with him. That would include the one that tied his horse at the fence and was supposed to come up behind me. I think their names were Aubrey and Sam."

Older's face stayed the same. "I see."

Longarm said, "It's getting to be hell to find people you can trust to do a job. I understand your position, but I don't think none of it would have had to happen if you'd come along. Course I've got an idea you give the orders to kill me and take the rifles."

153

Older turned his head slightly so their eyes met. "That your idea, is it?"

Longarm nodded. "Yeah. Doesn't figure any other way."

Older said, "What makes you so sure I'm involved?"

Longarm said comfortably, "Well, I couldn't see a little frog like Bird being smart enough or tough enough to smuggle rifles right under the nose of a U.S. deputy marshal. I've known some sheriffs and I've known some federal officers, and by and large your federal men are two or three outs above a local sheriff."

"You've known some deputy marshals?"

Longarm nodded. "Done some business with a few."

"Care to give some names?"

Longarm shook his head. "No, I don't reckon. No more than you'd want me slinging your name around."

Older was quiet for a moment. "I could arrest you right now for the murder of those peace officers."

Longarm nodded. "Yes. You could try." He looked at Older and smiled. "And then you could take the rifles. Only problem with that is that I don't want to get arrested, and somebody might get hurt while you was trying. Hurt real bad. And what would be the point? There's profit enough in those five hundred rifles and the others I can get for both of us. If Bird or you had understood that, this business would have gone off without any trouble. Instead . . . Well, what can I say? I acted in self-defense."

Older said, a little edge in his voice, "You seem almighty sure of yourself."

Longarm said, "I got a right to be." He waved his arm around the square. "You and Bird been clipping every owner of every saloon and gambling joint for who knows how long. Comes a trial, you reckon they wouldn't come forward? And how many of them deputies you figure could keep their mouths shut through a long trial? You're not going to arrest me. You might try and kill me, but there are drawbacks to that too. I ain't all that easy to kill. So why don't we do some business?"

Older said, "Where's Bob Bird?"

Longarm drew on his cigar. "I don't know. I put him and them two deputies on that midnight freight last night. You'd have to ask the railroad where they've got by now."

Older was quiet again, staring off across the plaza. Finally he said, "So how do you want to do it?"

Longarm said, "The simple way. I figure twenty-five dollars a

154

rifle now, now that Bird's not involved anymore. That's twelve thousand, five hundred dollars. You go get the money, and I mean the money. Don't be coming out like Bird did with a carpetbag full of torn-up newspapers. You go get the money and I'll meet you on the road to the freight yard at about eleven o'clock this morning."

Older said, "I can't get the money that fast."

Longarm gave him a crooked smile. "You mean you can't think up a plan that fast. You could get the money in twenty minutes. Let's see . . ." He looked up at the sky. "I believe that combination starts off eight to the right and then fifteen to the left." He looked over at Older.

Chapter 11

Older was staring at him.

Longarm said, "Bob did quite a bit of talking before he choked on his own words. Man went out kind of hard. It was a sad thing to see."

Older said, "What if I just don't deal with you at all?"

Longarm shrugged. "Then I'll just ask you to look the other way while I run them rifles into Mexico myself. I know you wouldn't want me to open that safe in front of what deputies are left and let them have some idea of just how much money you and Bird have been cheating them out of."

Older stood up. "All right. I'll meet you on the road to the freight yard, just on the outside of town."

Longarm said, "Don't bring no deputies, will you, Marshal? I'll have some folks behind me. Just like I did last night. Let's just do the business and have done with it. I make ten dollars a rifle and you make fifteen. I'm happy with that. You ought to be too. Soon as I'm out of town you can get this mayor to appoint one of them deputies sheriff and go right on about business. I'd get him to appoint the dumbest of the bunch. I believe, though I haven't met them all, that that would be Billy Wayne."

Older just nodded. He dropped his half-smoked cigar, ground it out with his boot, and walked away.

Longarm called out, "Don't be late. I want to make the noon train."

Older glanced back, but didn't say anything.

Longarm sat a moment more, and then got up and went into the hotel. Willis was sitting in a big wooden chair where he could see through the large plate-glass window and look out onto the plaza. He got up when he saw Longarm. "Ya'll have a good talk?"

"Willis, when he left I think Older was heading for the jail. I want you to run right quick across the plaza after him. I don't think you can get there in time to see if he goes in the jail, but I want you to take up a position where you can see the jail door. Stay kind of far back so you won't be noticed. Have you got that?"

"You want me to watch the jail door. Watch for the deputy marshal."

"Yes. Where's my horse?"

"I put him in the barn, in the stable."

"You didn't lather him up, did you?"

"No, but I got to tell you that horse has got a mind of his own sometimes."

Longarm said, "Never mind about that right now." He gestured across the plaza. "Older ought to be coming out of the jail in a half hour or so. The second you see him come out, if he's headed this way—and I want you to make sure about that—the second he looks like he's coming this way I want you to tear out and come tell me. And I want you to notice if he's carrying a satchel of any kind. You understand?"

"Yes, sir. Am I still deputized?"

Longarm grimaced. "Yes, Willis, you're still deputized. You don't get deputized by the errand. Now go on, and hurry. But don't look like you're hurrying."

He stood in front of the plate-glass window and watched Willis cross the plaza half walking, half trotting. Finally Willis disappeared behind a clump of trees at the far end. Longarm sat down in the big wooden chair and prepared to wait. He didn't know how long it was going to be, but he had the feeling matters were about to get to the settlement point.

Mac came over and said, "Was you kidding about my sister?"

Longarm shook his head. "No."

"You mind telling me what's going on?"

"Your brother-in-law has been arrested. I'd imagine he's in jail in Austin by now."

Mac was standing to his side, just out of his vision. Longarm felt him jump more than saw him. Mac said, "You wouldn't kid a feller, would you?"

158

Longarm shook his head, his eyes steady on the plaza. "Nope."

Mac said, "Well, how did this come about?"

Longarm shrugged. "Sometimes things go right."

"You have anything to do with it?"

Longarm looked around at him. "What do you mean by that question?"

Mac said, "I mean that if you did, I'm going to buy you the best bottle of whiskey in town and tear up your bill."

Just then Longarm saw Willis emerge from the trees and come hurrying across the plaza toward the hotel. He got out his watch. It was ten after ten. Apparently U.S. Deputy Marshal Older was planning on being prompt.

Mac said, "Well?"

"Well what?"

"Did you have anythang to do with that bastard sonofabitch Bob Bird getting his?"

Longarm stood up. He looked around at Mac and smiled. "Why don't you stick around and find out."

He moved by Mac and went to the front door, which was slightly ajar. He pulled it open and stepped out onto the hotel porch. Willis was fifty yards away and coming fast.

Longarm stood, patiently watching him. He came hurrying up, slightly out of breath, and said, "He's coming. He came out the jail door and headed straight this way. I made sure of it and then I come on. What do I do now?"

Longarm shifted his gunbelt slightly and loosened his revolver in its holster. He said, "Stay out here. But stay off to one side. And listen. I want you to try and hear every word that gets said, but don't get in the way."

Willis said, his voice trembling a little, "You are fixing to face off with him, ain't you?"

"Probably. Why?"

Willis said, "Well, I was just thinking. I mean . . ." He cleared his throat.

Longarm looked at him in amazement. Then he laughed slightly. "Willis, you beat anything, you know that? What you want is your money now in case I don't come out on top. Don't you?"

Willis tried to look ashamed. "Well, I didn't exactly mean that."

Longarm dug in his pocket. He just did have a twenty left. He handed the bill to Willis. "The hell you didn't mean that. There's your money. You better do your job. Go ahead and wander off there to the side."

A moment later he saw the figure of Les Older coming across the plaza. There could be no mistaking the build and the erect carriage. Longarm thought, well, he sure looks like a marshal anyway. Even if he don't act like one.

Longarm passed down the steps and crossed the narrow boardwalk, and then walked across the dusty street and stepped up on the flagstone of the plaza. Older was still about thirty yards away. Longarm could see that he was carrying a bag of some kind in his right hand. As the distance between them closed Longarm could see that the small bag was the kind they used at banks, canvas with a leather closure flap and a leather carrying grip. Older had not as yet seen him. Older was walking steadily, but his eyes were cast downward as if he were doing some hard thinking. Longarm got to the bench where they'd talked just a little more than an hour past. At that instant Older looked up and recognized Longarm. For a second a look of surprise flickered across his face. Then it passed and the normal set, hard look returned to his eyes. He took a couple more paces and then stopped. No more than five yards separated them.

Older said, staring hard at Longarm, "I thought we were going to meet out on the road."

Longarm looked at the bank bag. "Well, I'll tell you . . . Last time I made that arrangement with a party he just brought me some old newspapers. I figured to make sure you had the money before I went to the trouble to get my horse out. You know how them stable hands are, how they hate to be woke up for no good reason."

Older said, "Is that the only reason?"

Longarm smiled. "What other could there be? You don't figure I'm here to rob you, do you? Hardly seems like the place. Is that the money?" He nodded his head toward the canvas sack.

Older said, "It will be when I see the guns."

Longarm was aware of Willis wandering off to his left some ten yards away. He really didn't need a witness, but he thought Willis ought to do something to earn his money. He said, "You're kind of early. I figure you know where that boxcar is. After all, you did go in my room to take a look at that one rifle I had to show."

Older just stared at him.

Longarm said, "I figured, you knowing where that car is—probably from the sheriff, who probably talked to the freight agent yesterday—that you might have sent a few deputies out there to kind of give me a welcoming party."

Older didn't say anything.

Willis by now had wandered on up the plaza to where Longarm could clearly see him without taking his eyes off Older. He was nodding his head vigorously as if to tell Longarm that he'd seen deputies leave the jail at the same time as Older.

Longarm said, "So, I thought I'd have me a look in that sack to make sure we was playing for actual money before the party got rough."

Older said, "You think I'm going to open this bag out here in the open, you're crazy."

Longarm said, "But the money's in there?"

Older's eyes were twin brown hard spots. He said, almost as if the word was being forced out of him, "Yes."

"How much?"

Older's face got colder. "You seem to make yourself mighty free with questions."

"I reckon I got a right to know if it's what we agreed on. Seems like I'm doing most of the trusting."

Older was silent for a moment, studying Longarm. "It's twelve thousand, five hundred."

"In that bag?"

"You kind of simple or something? Yes, damnit, in this bag."

Longarm had been holding his six-pointed badge palmed in his left hand. Now he raised his left hand, and seemed to be fumbling at his shirt on the left side of his chest. When he dropped his hand the badge was plainly visible. He said clearly, "Les Older, I'm U.S. Deputy Marshal Custis Long. You are under arrest. Surrender your weapons and your badge."

Older stared. Even as tan as he was, a little color seemed to go out of his face. He involuntarily took a half a step backwards. He said, "What the hell is this?"

Longarm took a step forward. "Exactly what I said it is. I was sent down here from the Colorado office by your chief marshal in Austin to investigate your activities. I will be charging you with any number of offenses, not the least of which, you low-down bastard, is bringing discredit on a law-and-order service

161

I'm proud to work for. Now you make us all look like we could be crooks."

Older said, "You can't prove nothin'."

Longarm said, "Oh, yes, I can. The sheriff ain't dead. Right now he's in Austin talking his head off to your boss. And like I said, there'll be plenty of people at this plaza be willing to give evidence. As will some of those deputies. And you just offered me a deal, so there's my own testimony. Oh, yes, make no mistake. I can prove plenty."

For the first time Older seemed to falter. His eyes darted back and forth as if looking for help from somewhere, and he ran his tongue out and licked his lips. He said, "I've had a hunch about you from the first. I smelled trouble, I just didn't know what it was. I should never have left it to that fool Bob Bird to take care of you."

"Keep on talking," Longarm said. "But I'm still going to have your weapons and badge."

Older cocked his head slightly. "You say your name is Custis Long and that you're from Colorado. Would you be the one they call Longarm?"

Longarm nodded, but he kept his eyes riveted on the bag in Older's right hand. "I've been called that."

Older swallowed and licked his lips again. "Longarm, I can't go to prison. I can't do it."

"That ain't my affair."

Older motioned with the bag. "Take this. All I ask for is fifteen minutes. I was heading for the stable to get my horse. Give me time to get my horse and get across the bridge. It's twelve thousand, five hundred dollars, man. And all I'm asking for is fifteen minutes."

Longarm shook his head. "No. If I did that it would make me the same as you and I don't want to be like that." Then he half smiled. "But it looks like the price is going up. I hear the sheriff only offered you five thousand dollars. Of course he didn't know you meant to take the whole thing."

Older took another half step backwards. "Long, I couldn't take prison. I couldn't take the disgrace."

Longarm could see what was in his mind. "Don't even think it, Older. First, you got that bag in your hand. You got to drop that before you can even start for your gun. And I'll be drawing as soon as I see that bag drop. So that's a big handicap right there. But even if you are that much faster than I am, and I don't

162

think you are, you'd be caught inside a month. You know you can't shoot a U.S. deputy marshal and get away with it. There's no place in the world you could hide."

A second passed. Older licked his lips. He looked beyond Longarm, and then his eyes settled on Longarm's chest. His right hand released the bag.

Longarm was drawing even before the money bag hit the flagstones of the plaza. He drew in one smooth, swift motion, cocking his revolver even before it cleared the holster. His arm was straight out and the sound of his own shot was loud in his ears even before Older got his ivory-handled, gold-chased revolver clear of its holster.

The bullet took Older in the chest, just to the left of center. The force of the slug knocked him backwards. He made one stumbling attempt to hold his feet, and then fell on his side and rolled over on his back. The revolver slipped from his fingers and lay on the hard stones.

Longarm went forward swiftly and knelt down where he could see into Older's face. The hardness was gone out of the brown eyes, replaced by pain and surprise. Older was gasping in ragged breaths. He tried to say something, but nothing came out of his mouth except a string of pink saliva. Longarm could tell the bullet had passed through his lungs. He could hear the whistle of the wind as it passed in and out of the sucking chest wound. He reached out and picked up Older's pistol and stuck it in his belt. Then he removed the badge from Older's chest. He said, "I told you not to try it." He sighed. "But maybe you are better off this way. It was your choice, and I reckon you made the one you wanted."

He stood up. A crowd was slowly inching forward. Willis had come to stare down at Older. Longarm snapped at him, "Willis, get your head out of your ass and get a doctor for this man. Wait to see how he's going to do and then come over to the jail. I'm going to need you." He bent and picked up the money bag and shoved it down his shirt.

He began elbowing his way through the crowd. It was vital that he get to the jail as quickly as he could and take the remaining deputies in hand. Without law Laredo was a powder keg, but the deputies were closer to *desperados* than lawmen. Right then he was the only peace officer in the town, and it was urgent that he take control of the situation.

He crossed the plaza as quickly as he could. He could see

163

men coming out of the different saloons and bars to stand on the boardwalk and look toward the plaza and speculate among themselves what all the ruckus was about. As he walked he reached into his pocket, found a .44-caliber cartridge, and reloaded the spent cylinder. A man never knew when he'd need that extra round. He replaced his revolver in its holster, and then worked the money bag around a little more comfortably under his shirt. It felt awkward and made him look potbellied, but he wanted both hands free.

Just before he went through the door of the jail he paused and reached into his pocket and pulled out Older's badge. It looked exactly the same as his, but it wasn't. Maybe there had been a time when Older wore it with pride, but now it was just a tarnished piece of metal.

He squared his shoulders and took hold of the doorknob of the jail. He didn't know how many deputies he'd find inside, but he didn't want to go in with a drawn revolver. Instead he just hooked the thumb of his right hand in his belt so that it was very near the hilt of his sidearm. He pushed the door open and stepped inside. It was slightly darker, even though there were plenty of open windows. As he came in he saw that there were three deputies in the big office. Bob Bird's separate office was empty. One deputy, and he recognized him as Billy Wayne, was sitting on a desk idly fiddling with his revolver. Two others were standing near a wooden water barrel. One had the tin dipper in his hand, and had been about to drink when Longarm entered. They all looked his way. He said, "My name is Custis Long. I'm a U.S. deputy marshal. You are all under arrest. Take off your stars and drop your gunbelts. Now!"

For a long second or two they just stared at him while what he'd said sunk in. He said, "Bob Bird is in jail in Austin. You are under arrest. Drop your gunbelts."

And then Billy Wayne erupted. He said, "Like hell!" He had the cylinder of his revolver snapped out in the loading position. He suddenly snapped it back into place and started to raise it, jumping off the desk as he did. Longarm's shot took him just below the throat, but still hit bone. The young deputy went backwards over the desk and lay there, sprawled, his arms and legs akimbo.

Longarm swung his revolver on the two men by the water barrel. The one holding the dipper dropped it. It hit the floor with a clang and a clatter. Without a word they both unbuckled

164

their gunbelts and let them drop on the floor.

Longarm said, "Now the stars. Pitch them on that desk right beside you."

Still holding his gun on the two, Longarm walked sideways over to where Billy Wayne lay. He felt the boy's chest. There was no heartbeat. Still watching the two by the water barrel, he took the star off Billy Wayne's shirt and dropped it on the floor. The deputy's gun was on the floor against the wall. Longarm said, "You got a jailer in this place?"

A deputy nodded. He said, "Yeah. Perez."

"Call him," Longarm said.

There was a barred door that led to the cells. The door was in the middle of the back wall, right next to the barrel where the two men were standing. The deputy moved over and put his face to the bars. He yelled, "Hey, Perez! Git up here. They's a deputy marshal out here wants you!"

Longarm said, "Does he have a gun?"

The other deputy shook his head. "Don't nobody go back there with a gun. Had a few git in the wrong hands."

After a moment Longarm could see a figure coming down the hall between the cells and toward the door, and walked over, motioning the two deputies to step back. The jailer stopped at the barred door and stared at Longarm. Longarm said, "Open that door and get out here."

The jailer said, "Wha' chou doin' weeth that *pistole*?"

Longarm said, "Fixing to use it on you if you don't hurry up and unlock that gate."

There was a rattling of keys, and then the jailer swung open the heavy door and stepped out. He was a fat Mexican, sweating profusely, with a large ring of keys worn on a belt around his waist. He eyed Longarm fearfully. "Ches, *señor*?"

Longarm said, "Take these two back there and lock them in cells." He motioned at the two deputies. "Then get back up here. And leave that door open while you're about your business."

The jailer looked over at where Billy Wayne lay. He rolled his eyes up but didn't say anything. Longarm motioned with his revolver. "You two get on back there. Don't make no trouble."

One of the deputies said, "Just what the hell are you arresting us for?"

Longarm said, "I got to get the bunch of you sorted out. And until I get that done I can't have you running around loose. Now go on, and if you've got nothing to worry about you'll be out pretty quick."

When the jailer came back, Longarm asked him if he had a prisoner named Manly.

Perez hesitated. "He es upstairs where we keep the bad ones. The cher'ff don' like him so berry mouch."

Longarm said, "Fetch him. Tell him to bring all his belongings."

While the jailer was gone Longarm went inside Bird's office and pulled the bank bag out of his pocket. It wasn't locked, just fastened with a buckle. He opened it and whistled softly to himself. The bag was just crammed with money, most of it in twenty- and fifty-dollar bills. He didn't reckon he'd ever seen so much money in his life. He reached in and got a handful and put it on the desk. First he took fifty dollars and put it in his pocket. That was to reimburse himself for what he'd paid Willis. He could just hear Billy Vail looking over his expense voucher and saying, "What's this here? Fifty bucks fer a part-time deputy?" Then he'd scratch it off and say, "First time I ever heard it called that. What'd she look like, anyway?"

After that he counted out two hundred and fifty dollars. He put that in a back pocket so he could keep it straight. He didn't know, rightfully, whose money it was, but he figured most of it was crooked and he didn't see any harm in using it for lawful purposes. He supposed, by law, it belonged to Bob Bird, but he doubted Bird was in a position to make a claim on it.

Finally he turned to the safe, squatting down in front of it so his eyes were on a level with the dial. It was of a size to do credit to a bank. Longarm figured it was four feet tall and nearly as wide. He spun the dial, then came back to zero, and went eight to the right because August was the eighth month. Then he turned the dial left to fifteen. Now came the hard part. The last number might be one, or it might be eighteen, or it might be five or one. It couldn't be be fifty-one because there was no such number on the dial. He decided on eighteen, and got it right on the first try. He pushed down the handle and pulled open the door. "My Gawd!" he said. The safe was just full of money. That and papers of all different kinds. It wasn't all big bills, however, so there was less than what he'd first thought, but he still reckoned it to be upwards of fifty or sixty thousand dollars. Shaking his head, he put the bank sack he'd taken from Older inside, and then closed and locked the door and spun the dial.

As he came out of the office Perez was bringing a young man through the cell block door. Longarm knew without asking that it was Lieutenant Manly. He was a medium-sized young man with a military bearing and a strong though fine-boned face. He was wearing whipcord breeches stuffed into calvary boots and a denim shirt. Though he was dirty and his clothes were rumpled and begrimed, he still carried himself with dignity. He had light brown hair, and looked as if he hadn't shaved for a week. He was looking around in confusion when Longarm walked up to him. Longarm said, "Lieutenant Manly?"

The young man turned toward him. He saw Longarm's badge, read what it said, and answered, "Yes, Marshal. I'm John Manly. I suppose I'm still a lieutenant, though I'm not on active service."

Longarm said, "Well, you are now. I'm cleaning up a mess and I need some help. I know you've had some shabby treatment, but that's getting straightened out. Will you help?"

The young man looked a little confused. "Of course, sir, I'll do whatever I can to help a federal officer."

"Fine," Longarm said. He took Older's pistol out of his waistband and handed it to Manly. "There's a weapon. I'm appointing you a temporary deputy sheriff of the county of Webb, Laredo being the county seat." He pointed toward the desk by the water barrel. "Get you one of those badges over there and put it on."

Manly took the gun, a little reluctantly. He said, "Marshal, I wonder—"

Longarm cut him off. "I know all about you. Take an hour and see your wife and calm her down. Also, get yourself cleaned up if you've got some other clothes."

Manly said, "You've seen my wife?" He looked anxious. "How is she?"

Longarm said, "She's quite a woman. And she's fine. I don't know how much torment the sheriff put you through, but I can assure you she maintained her honor."

Relief flooded the young man's face. "Thank you, sir." He looked at the revolver in his hand. "This has been a hellish time."

Longarm said, "I'm sure it has. But I have to ask you to hurry now. Get the badge."

While Manly was getting the badge and Perez was watching with wonder in his eyes, Longarm got out the money he'd put in his back pocket. When Manly came back, fumbling to pin on the badge, Longarm had one hundred fifty dollars waiting for him. He said, "Here's your pay. I don't know how long the job will last. Maybe just a couple of days. But I intend to see that you are reimbursed for your loss of time and false arrest."

Manly blinked at the money, but took it. He said, "This is a godsend. That renegade of a sheriff took every cent we had. Left my wife penniless." His face got hard. "I should like to see that gentleman."

Longarm put up his hand. "I know. Now get going. You'll find your wife at the Hamilton Hotel. It's straight across the plaza."

Before he turned to go, Manly looked at Longarm curiously. He said, "This is all very strange. I come out of a jail cell, and you appoint me a deputy sheriff and give me back most of the money the sheriff stole from me. Yet you've never seen me before and know nothing about me. Why?"

Longarm smiled slightly. "Well, you're an ex–cavalry officer, so I know you can handle yourself and know how to take orders. But mainly it's because of your wife. I have to believe that a fine, strong lady like her would be married to the same kind of man."

Manly thought a moment, nodded, and gave Longarm a brief salute. "Thank you," he said. "I plan to live up to your expectations."

Just before he could go through the door Longarm said, "Oh! Mac is the desk clerk at the hotel. Tell him to have me a lunch sent over here. Steak. And a bottle of whiskey. And tell him I need him over here himself as soon as possible."

Manly saluted again and then went out the door. It was only then that Longarm became aware of the crowd on the street in front of the jail. They weren't doing anything, just standing around and looking curious.

Longarm turned to the jailer. "Perez, do you know the mayor and county judge?"

The fat jailer said, "Chure. Know them long time."

"Well, you go find them and tell them I want to see them. Right now. And I mean in a hurry. And don't you forget to come back."

"Chou are not goin' to arrest me?"

"Not unless you give me reason. Leave those keys here. Oh,

and find an undertaker and tell him to come get that body." He gestured at Billy Wayne. "And if you see any of the sheriff's deputies, tell them to get in here. It won't do them no good to hide. And tell that crowd outside to move along."

Perez said, putting on his hat, "I am doing theeese thengs now, Boss. I am making a hurry."

A few minutes later Willis came in. He looked a little haggard. He said, "He's dead."

Longarm nodded. That was what he'd been waiting to hear. He went back into Bird's office and sat down at the desk with paper and pencil. Willis interrupted, wanting to talk about the shooting. But then he shut up as Longarm glanced up and gave him a very clear look. Sometime Longarm might want to think about what had happened that morning, but right then wasn't the time.

He addressed the telegram, again, to the chief marshal, Austin, Texas. He said:

LES OLDER KILLED RESISTING ARREST STOP AM ARRESTING ALL PREVIOUS SHERIFF'S DEPUTIES STOP STRONGLY URGE YOU TO DISPATCH IMMEDIATELY TWO FEDERAL DEPUTY MARSHALS TO STABILIZE LAW AND ORDER SITUATION THIS TOWN STOP I WILL AWAIT THEIR ARRIVAL STOP WILL REPORT TO YOU IN AUSTIN UPON ARRIVAL OF OFFICERS TO GIVE AN ACCOUNT OF WHAT OCCURRED HERE STOP AGAIN URGE OFFICERS LEAVE FIRST TRAIN STOP SITUATION COULD BECOME VOLATILE STOP

He handed the note to Willis. "Get that down to the telegraph office as fast as you can. I think you can make it on foot quicker than you can get my horse."

"I done got your horse. He's tied out front. Thought you might want him."

"Well, I'm surprised."

"This whole town is buzzing. Don't nobody know what to think. Mac caught me on the street and tried to ask me a hundred questions."

"What'd you tell him?"

Willis put his hand on his heart. "Not a thing. Not one blessed thing."

"I'll bet," Longarm said. But he got up and led Willis out of the office, and walked over to where the deputies' gunbelts

169

were lying on the floor. He picked up one and turned to hand it to Willis. The young man was staring round-eyed at the body lying over the desk. He said, "Lord A'mighty!"

Longarm handed him the gunbelt. "Put it on, damnit. Just me and you know you can't use it." He picked up a deputy's badge and pinned it on Willis's shirt. "Now get moving. I'm sick of this place. That telegram gets billed to the government, so don't give the telegrapher any money."

While Longarm waited for the mayor and the county judge, two deputies came in. They came in knowing something was going on, but not quite what. Longarm disarmed them immediately and took them back to separate cells. He locked the big barred door behind him, and then went back and sat in Bird's office. For the first time fatigue and a certain sadness were beginning to seep into his bones. It was sad about men like Older, sad for Older and sadder even for the public. When you couldn't depend on federal law enforcement it was a sorry day. But he couldn't give time to such thinking just yet; there was too much still to do.

Another deputy came in, all unawares, and was surprised to find himself suddenly in a cell. Longarm took a count. He'd killed four all told and arrested five. That left three, unless you counted the jailer, which he didn't. He didn't know how many deputies Older would have sent to wait for him at the boxcar in the freight yard, but if they'd heard what had happened he doubted they'd be showing up.

But then Perez returned with two more. They came in carrying their badges and their gunbelts and loudly proclaiming their innocence. Perez said, "I tell them chou es nobody to fool wiss. They theenk es smart they come en. But they es one not so smart. I tell him, but he don't theenk so berry good he see you. He say he go to Mexico. He say you can look heem down there."

Longarm sighed. "So, for all intents and purposes, that's all of them?"

"*Sí*," Perez said.

Longarm said, "Well, just have a seat somewhere. Where the hell are the mayor and the county judge?"

Perez said, pointing, "They es coming now."

The mayor was tall and lanky with muttonchop sideburns and a limp. The county judge looked a little like Perez, only he was dressed better and not sweating as bad.

They came in angry and furious, and demanding to know what the hell Longarm thought he was doing. He listened to them for half a minute and then said, "Gentlemen, I am tired. I'm tired of you, I'm tired of your goddamn crooked law enforcement, I'm tired of this town. You open your mouth again, either one of you, and I'll throw you both in jail. This town is under federal authority and I'm the federal authority. And I can bring army troops in to back me up if I want to. So sit down and shut up and I'll tell you what you're going to do."

He began by telling them the whole story, beginning with his assignment. He ended up telling them about Lieutenant John Manly. He said, "Now, I've appointed him an acting deputy sheriff. But two other federal officers should be arriving here tomorrow and I'll be leaving. I'm going to recommend to them that he be appointed acting sheriff until you can have an election. I recommend you go along with that idea or you are liable to get me angry. I'm pretty well convinced you've been a part of this corruption, but I'm not anxious to prove it unless you give me trouble. Now get the hell out of here and spread the word that I don't even want to hear anybody so much as making a loud noise. *Savvy?*"

They left very quietly, assuring him of their cooperation. He watched them go, shaking his head.

The undertaker came with a helper and took Billy Wayne's body away. And then Mac came in bringing Longarm some lunch by his own hand. He was easily persuaded to put on a badge and a sidearm and be an acting deputy sheriff. Longarm said, "My main interest is just keeping the lid on this town until the other officers arrive. Our biggest trouble is back there in those cells. So we're not going to go out and patrol the streets. I just want enough men in here that I can trust so we can all get a little sleep."

Mac had to go back to finish his shift, but John Manly came in shortly after. Longarm was just finishing his meal and relaxing with a drink of whiskey. Relaxing, he was just starting to realize how tired he was. It still wasn't very late in the day, but a hell of a lot had happened. The kind of work he'd done that morning was hard on a person, even if he'd done it many times before. It was, he thought, the kind of work a man never could really get comfortable with.

He told Manly of his plan to have him appointed acting sheriff. He said, "I don't know what the pay is, but I've got to tell you that I think you'd be walking into a prairie fire if you take that job down in Mexico as a military advisor to one of those leaders. Those ol' boys don't have a real permanent job, and neither do the folks that work for them."

Manly said that he'd be delighted to take the acting sheriff job if it was indeed offered, that he'd never much wanted to go to Mexico, but he hadn't been able to find another position that would pay enough for the care of a woman such as Belinda.

Longarm said, "I reckon Mrs. Manly will be happy with any kind of work you get just so you can come home to her at night."

Manly looked grateful. He also looked a good deal better cleaned up and shaved and in fresh clothes.

Willis came back looking a little awkward wearing a sidearm. For a few minutes they sat around looking at each other. Then Willis said, "What's next?"

Longarm leaned back in his chair and yawned. He said, "Nothing. It's over. All we do now is wait for whoever they send down from Austin."

Three days later he was on a train bound for Colorado, riding along in a stock car with just himself and the dun. He'd decided to keep the dun and add him to his personal string of trading horses. And since technically the dun was still on federal service, Longarm was shipping him back to Colorado at government expense. He and Billy Vail could discuss the ethics of that at some future date.

Two U.S. deputy marshals had arrived the day after he'd sent the telegram. Since it was their territory he'd officially turned the whole matter over to them. They'd agreed to keep Manly on as acting sheriff. But there were still a great many matters to be straightened out. Most of the deputies would be charged with varying degrees of corruption or extortion or malfeasance in office. Manly would have to bring in fresh men for his staff of deputies, though he wouldn't need a dozen as Bird had. But then he wasn't going to smuggle any guns.

While he'd still had the chance, Longarm had gone into the bank sack and taken out a sum of money. He'd given Manly two hundred dollars and the same to Willis. Willis had begged to come with him to Austin, where he hoped to become a U.S. deputy marshal, but Longarm had told him flatly that cheating at cards was a whole lot less dangerous where he was concerned.

He'd given the chief marshal in Austin a written report of all that had occurred. Bob Bird had talked his head off in hopes of making matters easier on himself, but it hadn't done him any good. After he was tried and sentenced, he'd be an old man before he got close enough to another woman to hit her.

Longarm had never taken Older's revolver back from Manly. By rights he supposed it belonged to Older's heirs, if he had any, but he had either forgotten to get it back or just hadn't given a damn. In his saddlebags was Bird's ivory-handled, gold-chased revolver. On his last night in Laredo Longarm had gone out to see Shirley. He'd taken twenty-five hundred dollars out of the bank bag to give to her. He didn't know if it was legal or not. He didn't even know if it was right or wrong. In fact he didn't know whose money it was, and he didn't think anybody else did either. But Shirley was now a woman on her own, and he figured she ought to have a little nest egg. He'd also brought her Bird's revolver. She'd insisted he keep it. He'd said no a hundred times, pointing out to her that such a pistol was worth a couple of hundred dollars. In the end he'd taken it as a memento.

Now, riding along in the coming twilight, he smiled at the memory of that last night. The only memento he needed of Shirley was just the remembrance of what they'd done that last night. When he'd regretfully left the next morning to catch the noon train for Austin, she'd wrung a promise from him that he'd come back. She'd said, "Don't write. It's not ink and paper I want. And if you don't come back, I'll come to Colorado and find you."

It had been a rough trip and now, using what daylight was left, he was laboriously trying to add up all the money he'd spent and what he could hope to get back from Billy Vail. He'd once asked Billy for a raise based purely on the grounds that he needed the extra money to be able to afford the job.

But this time he was pretty sure he hadn't gotten skinned. He had all his bills from the hotels and the stables. Of course he wasn't sure how Billy was going to feel about him having to pay for half the boxcar to ship the dun from San Antonio to Laredo, but he figured he'd be reasonable about that. What had hurt Longarm had been when he'd had to take his badge off and pay just like a regular customer. Like the telegrams he'd sent to Billy about the crates. But that didn't amount to much. He sat there in the open door of the car looking out at the passing scenery. He figured they were getting pretty close to where Texas joined New Mexico at the northern end.

All around, he decided, he'd done all right. This was going to be one time Billy Vail couldn't raise cain with him about spending too much money, mainly because it would be charged to the Austin office and wouldn't come out of Billy's budget.

And then Longarm remembered the twenty dollars he'd given Mac to pay Mrs. Manly's bill. He said aloud, "Well, I'll be damned! I'll just be damned!"

No, he'd never get that back. But he had seen her in that satin wrapper and that, he figured, was worth twenty dollars any day.

Howard said, "Son, I want you to get twenty-five thousand dollars in gold, get on your horse, and carry it up to a man in Oklahoma. I want you to give it to him and tell him who it's from, and tell him it's in repayment of the long-time debt I've had of him."

I didn't say anything for a moment. Instead I got up from the big double desk we were sitting at facing each other, and walked over to a little side table and poured us both out a little whiskey. I put water in Howard's. Out of the corner of my eye I could see him wince when I did it, but that was doctor's orders. I took the whiskey back over to the desk and handed Howard his tumbler. It was a little early in the afternoon for the drink but there wasn't much work to be done, it being the fall of the year.

Howard was father to me and my two brothers. Sometimes we called him Dad and sometimes Howard, and in years past quite a few other things. He liked for us to call him Howard because I think it made him feel younger and still a part of matters as pertained to our ranch and other businesses. Howard was in his mid-sixties, but it was a poor mid-sixties on account of a rifle bullet that had nicked his lungs some few years back and caused him breathing difficulties as well as some heart trouble. But even before that, some fifteen years previous, he had begun to go down after the death of our mother. It was not long after that that he'd begun to train me to take his place and to run the ranch.

I was Justa Williams and, at the age of thirty-two, I was the boss of the Half-Moon ranch, the biggest along the Gulf Coast of Texas, and all its possessions. For all practical purposes I had been boss when Howard called me in one day and told me that he was turning the reins over to me, and that though he'd be on hand for advice should I want it, I was then and there the boss.

And now here he was asking me to take a large sum of money, company money, up to some party in Oklahoma. He could no more ask that of me than either of my two brothers or anybody else for that matter. Oh, he could ask, but he couldn't order. I held my whiskey glass out to his and we clinked rims, said "Luck," and then knocked them back as befits the toast. I wiped off my mouth and said, "Howard, I think you better tell me a little more about this. Twenty-five thousand dollars is a lot of money."

He looked down at his old gnarled hands for a moment and didn't say anything. I could tell it was one of his bad days and he was having trouble breathing. The whiskey had helped a little, but he still looked like he ought to be in bed. He had a little bedroom right off the big office and sitting room we were in. There were plenty of big bedrooms in the big old rambling house that was the headquarters for the ranch, but he liked the little day room next to the office. He could lie in there when he didn't feel well enough to sit up and listen to me and my brothers talking about the ranch and such other business as came under discussion.

It hurt me to see him slumped down in his chair looking so old and frail and sunk into himself. I could remember him clearly when he was strong and hard-muscled and tall and straight. At six-foot I was a little taller than he'd been, but my 190 pounds were about the equal of his size when he'd been in health. It was from him that I'd inherited my big hands and arms and shoulders. My younger brother Ben, who was twenty-eight, was just about a copy of me except that he was a size smaller. Our middle brother, Norris, was the odd man out in the family. He was two years younger than me, but he was years and miles different from me and Ben and Howard in looks and build and general disposition toward life. Where we were dark he was fair; where we were hard he had a kind of soft look about him. Not that he was; to the contrary. Wasn't anything weak about Norris. He'd fight you at the tick of a clock. But he just didn't look that way. We all figured he'd taken after our mother, who was fair and yellow-haired and sort of delicate. And Norris was bookish like she had been. He'd gone through all the school that was available in our neck of the woods, and then he'd been sent up to the University at Austin. He handled all of our affairs outside of the ranch itself—but with my okay.

I said, "Dad, you are going to have to tell me what this money is to be used for. I've been running this ranch for a good many years and this is the first I've heard about any such debt. It seems to me you'd of mentioned a sum of that size before today."

He straightened up in his chair, and then heaved himself to his feet and walked the few steps to where his rocking chair was set near to the door of his bedroom. When he was settled he breathed heavy for a moment or two and then said, "Son, ain't there some way you can do this without me explaining? Just take my word for it that it needs doing and get it tended to?"

I got out a cigarillo, lit it, and studied Howard for a moment. He was dressed in an old shirt and a vest and a pair of jeans, but he had on his house slippers. That he'd gotten dressed up to talk to me was a sign that what he was talking about was important. When he was feeling fairly good he put on his boots, even though he wasn't going to take a step outside. Besides, he'd called me in in the middle of a workday, sent one of the hired hands out to fetch me in off the range. Usually, if he had something he wanted to talk about, he brought it up at the nightly meetings we always had after supper. I said, "Yes, Dad, if you want me to handle this matter without asking you any questions I can do that. But Ben and Norris are going to want to know why, especially Norris."

He put up a quick hand. "Oh, no, no. No. You can't tell them a thing about this. Don't even mention it to either one of them! God forbid."

I had to give a little laugh at that. Dad knew how our operation was run. I said, "Well, that might not be so easy, seeing as how Norris keeps the books. He might notice a sum like twenty-five thousand dollars just gone without any explanation."

He looked uncomfortable and fidgeted around in his rocking chair for a moment. "Son, you'll have to make up some story. I don't care what you do, but I don't want Ben or Norris knowing aught about this matter."

Well, he was starting to get my curiosity up. "Hell, Howard, what are you trying to hide? What's the big mystery here? How come *I* can know about the money but not my brothers?"

He looked down at his hands again, and I could see he felt miserable. "If I was up to it, *you* wouldn't even know." He kind of swept a hand over himself. "But you can see the shape I've come to. Pretty soon won't be enough left to bury the way I'm wasting away." He hesitated and looked away. It was clear he didn't want to talk about it. But finally he said, "Son, this is just something I got to get off my conscience before it comes my time. And I been feeling here lately that that time ain't far off. I done something pretty awful back a good number of years ago, and I just got to set it straight while I still got the time." He looked at me. "And you're my oldest son. You're the strong one in the family, the best of the litter. I ain't got nobody else I can trust to do this for me."

Well, there wasn't an awful lot I could say to that. Hell, if you came right down to it, it was still all Howard's money. Some years back he'd willed the three of us the ranch and all the Half-Moon holdings in a life will that gave us the property and its income even while he was still alive. But it was Howard who, forty years before, had come to the country as a young man and fought weather and bad luck and *bandidos* and Comanches and scalawags and carpetbaggers, and built this cattle and business empire that me and my brothers had been the beneficiaries of. True, we had each contributed our part to making the business better but it had been Howard who had made it possible. So, it was still his money and he could do anything he wanted to with it. I told him as much.

He nodded. "I'm grateful to you, Justa. I know I'm asking considerable of you to ask you to undertake this errand for me without telling you the why and the whereofs of the matter, but it just ain't something I want you or yore brothers to know about."

I shrugged. I got a pencil and a piece of paper off my desk. "Who is this party you want the money to go to? And what's his address?"

"Stevens. Charlie Stevens. And Justa, it ain't money, it's got to be gold."

I put down my pencil and stared at him. "What's the difference? Money is gold, gold is money. What the hell does it matter?"

"It matters," he said. He looked at the empty glass in his hand and then across at the whiskey. But he knew it was wishful thinking. Medically speaking, he wasn't supposed to have but one watered whiskey a day. Of course we all knew he snuck more than that when there was nobody around, but

180

drinking alone gave him no pleasure. He said, "This is a matter that's got to be done a certain way. It's just the way and the rightness of the matter in my mind. I got to give the man back the money the same way I took it."

"But hell, Howard, gold is heavy. I bet twenty-five thousand dollars would weigh over fifty pounds. We'll have to ship it on the railroad, have it insured. Hell, we can just wire a bank draft."

He shook his head slowly. "Justa, you still don't understand the bones of the matter. You got to take the gold to Charlie on horseback. Just like I would if I could. You understand? I'm askin' you to stand in for me on this matter."

I threw my pencil down and stared at him. I nodded at the empty glass in his hand. "How many of them you snuck before you sent for me? You expect me to get on a horse and ride clear to Oklahoma carrying twenty-five thousand dollars in gold? And that without telling Norris or Ben a thing about it? Howard, are you getting senile? It's either that or you're drunk, and I'd rather you was drunk."

He nodded. "I don't blame you. It's just you don't understand the bones of this business. Justa, this is a weight I been carrying a good many years. I done a man wrong some time back, but it took a while for me to realize just how wrong I done him. When I could of set matters straight I was too young and too smug to think they needed setting a-right. Now that I can look back and be properly ashamed of what I done it's too late for all of it. But I got to make what amends I can. If you knew the total of the whole business you'd agree with me that the matter has to be handled in just such a way."